CONSCIENCE ANOMALY

SHANE YETTER

Copyright © 2023 by Shane Yetter

All rights reserved.

No part of this publication may be reproduced, distributed, or transmitted in any form or by any means, including photocopying, recording, or other electronic or mechanical methods, without the prior written permission of the author, except as permitted by U.S. copyright law.

The story, all names, characters, and incidents portrayed in this production are fictitious. No identification with actual persons (living or deceased), places, buildings, and products are intended or should be inferred.

Book Cover by GermanCreative Cover Design

Published by Shane Yetter

1st Edition 2023

ISBN: 9798850036348

Parental Guidance found on last pages of book.

For my wife, my daughter, and my family. Thank you all for your encouragement.

CHAPTER 1

24 Days Before Implant (10:00 am)

"Well crap" Mason complains under his breath as he spills his coffee on his work slacks; the third cup this week.

Without looking away from his computer, "Dude, you're clumsy as hell," his cubicle mate and best friend, Raine, graciously points out.

"Thanks. Could you grab me some towels at leas-" he's cut off at the sight of Raine holding out a mass of dull brown fast-food napkins toward him. He grabs the napkins and dabs off the front of his stained slacks in a futile attempt to sop up the large stain. He's hoping to avoid ridicule from the other office personnel. Though, he's never been successful at escaping frequent, daily teasing.

Mason is a well-mannered, polite, but otherwise doltish and quite peculiar man. He isn't particularly intelligent and tends to be quite gullible. He is notably overweight with pale, alabaster-colored skin, disheveled, ear-length brown hair, and an unkempt goatee.

In his 31 years on this earth, he has only had two, very unsuccessful, dates with women that never bothered to call him back. Beyond that, he's been unable to keep any plants or animals alive for more than six months and has abandoned the endeavor all-together. In his mind, losing more than forty ferns, bonsais, and various other assorted house plants, along with four hamsters, two birds, and one rescue cat, is enough for him to give up entirely and just live alone. The only creature to have survived was the rescue cat, who was just fortunate enough to escape from Mason's clumsiness by way of the back-alley window.

Mason has always been odd. Though he's not likely the strangest person living in San Antonio, he just cannot seem to keep lasting relationships. Maybe it's the crippling fear of rejection that causes him to keep people at arm's length, or that he only sees the world from his own offbeat perspective. It's likely a combination of both. Mason is the kind of odd individual that the average moviegoer will pay twenty dollars to see win over the girl with his quirky personality and pureness of heart but wouldn't go out of their way to get to know in person. No matter the reasons, Raine is the only person he's managed to maintain a friendship with over the years.

"How did you even know that I spilled my coffee?" Mason asks.

"Two reasons," Raine begins. "First, you are a clumsy and accident-prone individual who has the odd tendency to do the worst thing at the absolute worst time. Second, you always spill your coffee when Isabelle steps off the elevator."

At this final comment Mason only manages to stutter out, "Wha-, well, no-uh" while spilling what little coffee was left in the eight-ounce white foam cup directly into his lap. Raine, of course, reaches out with more napkins.

"My point exactly," Raine declares through a half-smirk.

"What am I supposed to do? She's pretty. And she's nice. And I'm me," replies Mason dejectedly.

Isabelle works in the bio-engineering sector of T.E.G., the same company where Mason and Raine work. She is, in fact, very beautiful. Her beauty has been described as "classic" by most. She has smooth, deep olive brown skin and her eyes glow intensely. Even a simple glance from Isabelle can cause a person to feel as though she's looking through their very being. Her obsidian-black hair tumbles effortlessly down across the back of her stark white, pristine, lab coat. She can somehow manage to look both like her ensemble took all day to assemble but could also be thrown together at a moment's notice.

But far more than her looks Isabelle has an effortless smile that lights up the room and walks with both an ease and a purpose that cannot be replicated. She is so far beyond being out of almost any man's league that most men find her intimidating to speak to.

"I wouldn't know. I've never looked," Raine retorts, "I'm saving my bandwidth for a woman that I could actually have a chance with, and you should too."

"Yeah, well that's probably not any woman," Mason bemoans. "I'll just die alone. Like the tyrannosaurus."

At this, Raine sighs empathetically and quits typing, turning to face his friend. "Look, dinosaur nerd. You're not a dinosaur. You're a person. And yes, you have a thick skull and yes, you are kind of awkward. And sure, sometimes you can be clumsy. Very clumsy. Like almost painfully so-"

"This isn't helping," Mason murmurs.

"Sorry. What I mean to say is that you're a good dude! I like you. And I don't like anyone! So that has to mean something. Right?" Raine turns back to his computer and continues his expense report.

Raine is a senior accountant at T.E.G. and is the one who got Mason his job. He is a tall, gaunt, bearded man with a short ponytail that he frequently, and affectionately, refers to as his "nerd hair". He wears thick framed glasses, sitting at about the last third of his nose, causing small red dimples on his otherwise very white, pale skin. Raised in a very sheltered religious home, he was not allowed to watch "bad" movies, play "bad" games, or engage in what his parents referred to as "witchcraft", like Dungeons and Dragons or Magic the Gathering.

It was this sheltering, without explanation as to why these activities were deemed inappropriate, that caused him to swing his preferences for entertainment so sharply against the request of his family. The moment that Raine left home he immediately found a Dungeons and Dragons, or D&D, group and bought his first "R" rated movie.

It was also that bombardment with fundamentalism that started him down the path of disliking people. Raine does not, in fact, like anyone. At all. To him, people are tiresome. They're always talking about "sports team" this, or "political commentary" that. In his mind, he never has time for that. Numbers are what makes sense to him.

"Yeah well, at least there's that," Mason says, under his breath.

"At least there's what?" The ill-timed question comes from Darryl, the office bully and the man who just happens to be Mason's boss. Darryl Stone is the youngest ever Senior Director at T.E.G., and he often acts like it. He is known to engage in frequent pranking of the lower ranking associates but is well liked among the executives. He can party harder than anyone and makes sure that everyone knows it.

When he's not harassing employees and drinking excessively, he's devoted to physical training. Between one cardio workout, one strength workout, and two skincare routines, to care for his smooth, ivory-colored skin, Darryl spends over three hours a day attending to his physical appearance. Today, he is carrying a coffee mug around the office bearing the company's name, 'The Encephalon Group', as is his daily ritual. He is rarely seen without his T.E.G. mug on morning walkthroughs.

"Nothing, Mr. Stone," Mason blurts. "I was just saying that I, uhm, I'm glad that I have a friend."

"Like hell you do," Darryl gleefully pounces on Mason's insecurities. "Who in their right mind would ever be seen anywhere near you? You're more worthless than a box of used tissues. Speaking of which, looks like you spilled something there, pal," he chuckles to himself, pointing toward Mason's lap. "Man, what a loser."

At this, Raine spins around to face Darryl, "Can we help you with something?"

"Pft! Rarely! Am I right boys!?" Darryl looks around as though impressing a crowd of thousands with his sharp wit. "I just want to make sure that you nerds get those expense reports filed before three today. Porter might just crack my skull if I let you guys get away with being late on them again."

"But, Mr. Stone, uhm, sir," Mason stammers nervously, "we didn't, uh, send them late last time." Mason winces as he sees the vein on the side of his boss's neck start to bulge out.

"That is, uhm, what I mean is, I, uh, I put them on your desk at one-thirty last week sir. Did, uh, you maybe forget to submit them after that?"

Darryl Stone could form diamonds from coal with as hard as he's squeezing his hands in anger. He reaches out and points a finger directly in Mason's face. "Don't you *ever* tell me that I made a mistake. Ever! You insignificant speck of a man. You worthless piece of walking trash! Who do you think you are?" He is now standing fully over top of Mason, who has shrunk so far into his chair that it's hard to tell where Mason ends, and the chair begins.

"My father co-founded this company. I have been in this building every single day since I was nine years old watching men greater than even me create the most advanced biotech company on the planet. So don't you dare condescend to tell me about whether I am doing what is right!" His accusing finger turns into a clenched fist as he holds it out toward Mason. "I could crush you with my bare hands and it would be as easy as sticking them into a bowl of jelly. You're a spineless, witless insect! Absolutely worthless!"

Darryl pauses, momentarily, realizing that he's now poised to punch Mason directly in the face. He takes a breath, slicks his hair back off his forehead, and steps back to the cubicle entrance. Putting a nonchalant smile back on his face and straightening his tie, he turns to Raine, "Just make sure that you get them on my desk this time, okay boys?" As he turns to walk away from the cubicle, he looks to Mason, winks, and walks away. Mason tries to slowly pull himself back up onto his chair.

"Look, bud," Raine tries to ease the tension, "don't worry

about that guy. He's a bully. Let's just get this work done."

"I need to go to the bathroom and clean up," Mason wipes the tears from his eyes, struggling to compose himself. "I'll be back in a minute."

On the way to the bathroom, he can hear people murmuring. The entirety of the third floor is whispering about the proverbial annihilation that he had just received. He's always been sensitive to the rumors of others, a trait that he inherited from his late mother, and this causes him to quicken his pace, lowering his head as far as he can. All thoughts of stepping cautiously leave his mind as he now speed-walks past open cubicles.

Now about twenty steps from the men's room, he loses his footing, trips, and falls to the floor. In complete and utter defeat, he can't muster the strength to stand. He curls his knees up under himself, squeezes them tightly with his arms and rests his forehead on the floor. He quietly weeps, wanting to escape from this new hell.

From the hallway he hears a voice speak to him, "Do you need some help?"

He recognizes the voice even though it's never been directed at him before. Filled with new fright, he slowly looks up, hands shaking as he rests his eyes on Isabelle, a kind and helpful expression on her face. Long has he dreamt that she would one day speak with him. However, at this moment, he feels like his stomach has dropped completely out of his body and his diaphragm is stuck, constricted, so that he cannot speak or breathe.

The stress of performing at work, being a good friend, being hatefully admonished by his boss, floundering socially, having nobody in his life to share his pain with, struggling to do even the most basic of tasks, and now being thrust into the socially awkward situation of being around a beautiful woman, has pushed Mason over the edge and into a full-scale anxiety attack.

CHAPTER 2

24 Days Before Implant (10:15 am)

Isabelle's father is a prominent cardiovascular surgeon, both in his native country of India and in the United States. Her mother is a tenured professor of psychology at the University of Illinois. At a young age Isabelle showed great aptitude in the science fields, biology, anatomy, engineering, psychology, even astronomy. At the age of fourteen, she had graduated High School. Over the course of the next seventeen years she completed med school and become a board certified, practicing neurosurgeon with a doctorate in psychology.

Isabelle was actively recruited by T.E.G. shortly after her board certification to help on a highly sensitive project in their bioengineering department. She agreed and has been with the company ever since.

Today is not the first day that she has noticed Mason. Isabelle is a "people-watcher". She is infinitely fascinated by the workings of human beings, and it didn't take long for her to notice him. Mason presents with symptoms that would indicate several psychological disorders; Social Anxiety Disorder, Panic Disorder, and Adjustment Disorder, all stemming from childhood trauma. Though, she knows that they would be impossible to diagnose properly without sitting down with him over several sessions. Unfortunately, her workload has prevented her from extending the offer; until today.

Remembering her training on aiding people with anxiety attacks, she calmly says, "Mason, my name is Isabelle, and it seems like you need some help. May I help you?"

Mason's mind is on fire. Any semblance of cognizant and rational thought escapes him. With each beat of his panic-stricken heart, he can feel pulses of heat surge through every part of his body, starting in the center of his chest and radiating out to his head and feet. He can't breathe or speak. All that he can muster in the moment, while still lying face down with his knees tucked into his chest, is a frantic head nod.

"Thank you, Mason. I need you to listen to my words and follow my instructions," she reaches out and gently takes his hand. "I know that you're confused and in pain, but we can get through this together, okay?"

"Mmm-okay," he struggles.

"Okay, Mason. I'm not going to leave until you're feeling better. Now, I'm going to help you onto your side to help you breathe," she slowly reaches a hand over to his shoulder, gently rotating it back so that he is now lying on his side. Without the extra strain and pressure on his diaphragm, the hope is that he'll now be able to breathe. "That's good. Can you try to take some deep breaths for me, Mason?"

Mason didn't realize that he had been tensing his abdomen so hard that he wasn't breathing. He fights the urge to tense up but can't physically make it stop. He struggles to focus on Isabelle's voice as he is now beginning to see stars. He feels himself slipping toward unconsciousness.

His first breath is more of a whimper, but it's enough to restart the process. The second breath is slightly more than the first and each subsequent breath leads to more air entering his lungs, meaning more oxygen to his brain.

"That's perfect, Mason," Isabelle quietly affirms. "You're doing great. I'm sorry that you're going through this, and I know how difficult it can be. Keep focusing on your breathing and we'll get through this together." It takes about five minutes for his breathing to normalize and he's ready to sit up. By now most of the workers on the third floor are staring over the tops of their cubicles, watching as Isabelle works with him.

"Th-, th-, thank y-, you," he battles against his anxiety. "I'm ok-, okay. Can I go into the ba-, bathroom now?"

"Yes, Mason," she reassures him while helping him, slowly, to his feet. "Would you mind if I wait for you at your desk until you're done, just so that I know you're okay?"

He nods to her as he turns to enter the men's room, legs still wobbling. He walks directly over to the sink, almost as though he's running on autopilot, turns the faucet, and splashes some water on his face. His mind starts to quiet down as he's able to start piecing together the events of the last ten minutes. His expense report, his conversation with Raine, then Darryl, then Isabelle.

"Isabelle!" he surprises himself when he shouts. "She spoke to me. She touched my hand!" he is beside himself now with elation. What started as a typical day at the office devolved into terror and has now evolved into joy. Mason, unsure of how to move forward, looks himself over, top to bottom; disheveled hair, crooked glasses, unkempt goatee, wrinkly button-down shirt, coffee-stained pants.

"Oh no," he groans, realizing that he's going to have to speak with her again in a moment. "What do I do?"

He takes to watering down his hair, straightening out his glasses, tucking in his shirt and trying to blot out the coffee stain on his pants. The air dryer, with the words "Mega Blower" plastered on the side, does help to dry out his pants enough to avoid the appearance of having wet them.

He gives himself one last pep talk before heading out, "Good enough, Mason," so he exits the bathroom full of bolstered confidence. His new-found confidence lasts almost halfway back to his desk, then his anxiety comfortably nestles back into the recesses of his mind and, just like that, he's back to his old self again.

Isabelle is sitting at Mason's desk, looking through the report that he had been working on. Mason stands at the cubicle entrance for a moment, studying her face as she looks intently at the report. She's facing partly away from him, just enough to see the side profile of her face. He'd never been close enough to Isabelle to notice her finer facial features, but now he's noticing that she's truly more beautiful than he'd ever realized.

"It's the expense report for this week," he's able to break his trance. "We have to submit them before three o'clock every Thursday so that Mr. Stone doesn't get in trouble." Mason's eyes dart to the floor, afraid to hold them on her lest she notice him staring.

Isabelle breaks her gaze from the screen, "So I've heard," she's able to sound both empathetic to Mason and unamused about Darryl's outburst. He realizes that he feels comfortable around her. Her eyes show a genuine kindness that can't be faked. A kindness that shows that she genuinely cares about people. And right now, she genuinely cares about him.

She takes a moment, analyzing the child-like quality of his voice before asking, "How are you feeling?"

"Oh, me? I'm fine. Yeah. I have something like anxiety disorder or something. My doctor wanted me to take medication for it, but I just don't want to because I did for a little while, because they asked me to, but I really don't like it." he's twisting his hands together nervously and looking around the cubicle for anything to distract his mind from the conversation. "It makes my head fuzzy. Not like hairy fuzzy or like eyes go blurry or anything," he chuckles nervously. "More like I'm in there, somewhere in my own head, but I can't think all the way," he pauses, unsure of himself. "Sorry. I ramble. Friends say that I ram-, well Raine says that sometimes I ramble when I don't know that to say. Do you know what I mean?"

She kindheartedly chuckles, "Yes, Mason, I do understand what you mean. Some of those medications can make certain daily tasks a little difficult."

He nods emphatically, "They really do!"

"Hey, alright, look pretty lady," Raine finally chimes in, "I really appreciate that you helped my friend here, okay. I really am, but he looks like he's fine now and we really need to get these reports done. So, if you have some really strong drugs for him, or for me, then let's whip out those syringes or get to popping those pills and get moving on with life, shall we?"

This catches Isabelle off-guard as she looks for the words to respond. Mason, who generally stays silent in awkward situations, speaks up. "Raine, she's just being nice. Maybe you should be nicer too."

"Hey man, I'm plenty nice," Raine scoffs as he adjusts his glasses. "Don't I always let you pick where you want to sit on Tuesday's game nights? Huh? And I always let you pick the snacks even though you always bring those god-awful, bland pretzels that even a dog wouldn't eat. So, maybe, it would be *nice* if we could get these done so that I don't get yelled at like you did."

Isabelle stands up and walks to the cubicle entrance, "I'm glad that you're feeling better, Mason. I would like to talk to you some more about your anxiety." She extends a business card toward him, "If you ever feel comfortable talking about it, let me know." With that she walks back toward the hallway in the same purposeful way that she walks everywhere.

Mason stands there, in the cubicle entrance, holding the card, feeling the smooth paper with embossed lettering. *Dr. Isabelle Sarkar, MD PsyD.* The entire event seems surreal. A moment that he had dreamt about for years has finally happened and it couldn't have been any more different than he imagined.

He always assumed that he'd finally meet her by working up the courage and talking to her in the lobby entrance or in the cafeteria. Several times he thought that maybe she'd be working at a nearby desk, need a pen, then he could bring one over for her. All the situations that Mason had previously thought about now seem implausible compared to what happened. Then again, what happened seems implausible as well.

"Hey, buddy?" Raine beckons to Mason.

"Uhm, yeah, Raine?" Mason manages from the fog in his mind.

"Could you please do me a favor," Raine pleads, hands in a prayer-position, "and for the love of all that is good and right in this world, *please* sit down and finish this report with me?"

Mason smiles, amused at seeing his friend begging for his help, "Yes, Raine. I'm going."

CHAPTER 3

24 Days Before Implant (6:00 pm)

Mason's evening walk from the bus stop to his apartment is as uneventful as usual, but today, instead of being lost in meaningless thought, he's thinking about Isabelle. He reaches into the left patch pocket of his stained button-down shirt to retrieve the card she had given him. His thumb unconsciously rubs across the indentations of the embossed lettering. *Dr. Isabelle Sarkar, MD PsyD*. He thinks he knows what "MD" stands for but has never heard of "PsyD". Resolute to look it up online, he continues home, holding the card and stroking the lettering all the way back to the apartment.

His apartment is modest, to say the least. One bedroom and one bathroom with a multipurpose area that acts as the kitchen, dining room, and living room all-in-one. The one highlight to the apartment is the balcony that overlooks part of the city. Mason, being too afraid of heights to go out onto the balcony, likes to stand at the window and stare out, wishing up the courage to take a step out. "Today is the day," he often tells himself, but it never is.

The exterior to the apartment building is dark tonight and

has been for quite some time as the streetlight that normally illuminates the entrance had gone out in weeks past. His sister had made him a special key to his building that has a little flashlight attached to it. He holds the little light in his hands and presses the button to turn it on. The small blue light shines on the doorknob as he inserts the key and steps out of the cool evening.

Several dogs start barking loudly as he enters. Of the twelve apartments in the building, Mason is one of the only ones who doesn't own a dog. The constant howl of dogs barking at prospective intruders took him a while to get used to but has now become more comforting to him than silence. As he walks up the two flights of stairs to the third floor, the floorboards creak and groan under his weight. The apartment building is very old, and Mason is overweight, making for a dangerous combination.

Now at his door he again uses his key-light, unlocks the door, and presses his shoulder into it. The door has always stuck when trying to open it. It takes two attempts but he's finally able to get it to budge and swing open. He nearly falls to the ground when the door finally gives way but manages to keep his balance. He drops his worn canvas satchel on an end table, kicks off his shoes, and sits down at his desk. He lets out a long, slow sigh, as though he were a deflating hot air balloon, tired from a day of floating around the countryside.

"What is a 'PsyD'," he mouths as he types into his search engine. He reads back the results to himself, "'A doctor of psychology. They practice psychology in a clinical setting.'" He rubs his chin as he considers the search result. "But why does a psychology doctor work at T.E.G.? We don't do psychology stuff." He looks over, quizzically, at the tyrannosaurus bobblehead on his desk. "What do you think, Terry?" he reaches out and taps the comically large head and watches as it bobbles about. "Nothing, huh?" Mason decides to search "Dr. Isabelle Sarkar" next and finds an article related to a T.E.G. project called, "ARC1".

"What is *this*, Terry?" he asks his plastic desk mate. Struggling with the more complex nomenclature, he inaccurately reads aloud, "ARC1 combines an inner- cer- cerberial? Cerberial process unit with a person's existing neu- neu- neural network to enhance their reach in the digital landscape." He contemplates this for a moment before feeling incompetent and deciding to move on. As he continues searching, he's able to find a video of Isabelle talking about ARC1 in an interview.

—

"Welcome back to *Inside Tech*, I'm Janet Williams. Today I'm joined by Dr. Isabelle Sarkar, who is here from T.E.G, to talk through their breakthrough technology, ARC1. Dr. Sarkar, can you explain to our viewers, what is ARC1 and why is it so important?"

"Absolutely, Janet, and thank you for inviting me on. I watch every evening. ARC1 combines an intracranial processing unit with a person's existing neural network to enhance their reach into the digital landscape."

Janet ribs Isabelle playfully, "Dr. Sarkar, you promised to spell this out for me so that I could understand it. Help a country girl out!"

Isabelle chuckles with the interviewer, "That's techy

'mumbo jumbo' to say that our microprocessors help your brain to communicate with your favorite devices. Instead of typing on your phone, you'll simply think about a message and away it'll go. When you want to visit a website, you simply think about the website, and you will automatically be navigated to it."

"That is incredibly fascinating, but it sounds like something out of a science fiction movie. How far is your team away from making this a reality?"

"We are much closer than you might think. We've already had great success with implanting microprocessors into the brains of various animals with almost no complications. We have a chimp at our facility, Gregory, who can play chess using only the outputs from his brain! For an ape with both hands tied behind his back, I have to say, he's getting pretty good at it too!"

Janet shares a laugh with Dr. Sarkar, "That's great for the chimps, but what about us? When will I be able to get my hands on this new tech?"

"Human trials have recently completed, and we anticipate pre-sales to begin in the next couple of months."

"Really? That soon? We can't wait! I have one last question. Why name the project ARC1? Does the name have some sort of significance or meaning?"

"Absolutely. One of our team leads, Dr. David Wei, brought the name ARC with him when he joined onto the project. 'ARC' is short for Archimedes, the Father of Mathematics. But he was so much more than that. He was a brilliant man, a visionary, who excelled as an engineer, a physicist, an inventor, an astronomer. Archimedes has served as a model for how we want to think about our project."

"He sounds like quite the guy! And is there significance to the number '1'?

"The number '1' is essentially because it's the first in the series. Though, back at T.E.G., we think that it stands for a singularity. We truly believe that implantation of this device will go down in history as a single point in time when we saw the world change forever.

—

Mason sits at his laptop, thinking more about ARC1 as the video ends and automatically starts the next video; something about why the velociraptor didn't live beyond the cretaceous period. "ARC1," he whispers. "That would be pretty cool, huh, Terry?" He looks over to see Terry's head bobbing up and down in agreement. Now resolute to inquire further about this implant, he decides to sleep on the issue, and speak with his family in the morning.

— 23 Days Before Implant (9:00 am) —

"Boy, you have got to be dumber than ya look if you think gettin' some wires shoved in yer skull is a good plan for life," Mason's father, Edward Driscoll, fumes. "Ya always did have less goin' on upstairs than a one-story house."

"Dad, you don't understand. This thing is totally safe," Mason fibs as he doesn't honestly know more than what was in the video he'd watched the previous night. "Plus, wouldn't it be nice if this thing helped make me better? Then you wouldn't have to worry about me anymore."

"Ah hell boy, I already don't worry about ya. I got too much other goin' on to even pay ya no never mind," Ed's comment cuts like a knife.

Ed is a hard man and has been his whole life. Raised in abject poverty he was forced to work from a very early age. People in town would comment on how he was the hardest worker at Abel's Market, the local grocery store, and all before he had even hit his teen years. He worked every evening and weekend, often neglecting his schoolwork, so that he could bring an extra paycheck home for the family, which consisted of his single mother, himself, and four siblings.

At the age of 17, Ed had already lined up a job working in a steel mill and subsequently dropped out of school to work there full time. The mill, which employed nearly a third of the residents of the town, was just the sort of place where a hard worker like Ed could excel. It didn't take him long to move from factory general operator to foreman. It was in this foreman position where he realized his full potential as a laborer.

Over the course of his forty-year career there at the steel mill Ed never had a wife, girlfriend, or so much as a date as he spent twelve hours a day, six or seven days a week, at the mill. It wasn't until the year of his retirement, and at the ripe age of 58, that he fathered a pair of twins with a woman nearly half his age. At one of his weekly bar visits Ed drank his usual four beers over the course of two hours, but instead of leaving he decided to stay and have "just one more" at the request of a friend from the mill.

"Awe hell, you're retired Ed! Live a little, huh? Hell, live a lot!" Dave Jones boomed over the blaring country music at the bar. One more beer became two which then became four which eventually turned into several doubles of Wild Turkey which then led to Ed waking up the next morning, as hung over as he'd ever been and with a lovely thirty-something stranger lying next to him in bed. Ed went from rarely dating to a dad overnight.

"Emma," Mason calls out to his sister who also happens to be Ed's live-in caretaker, "would you please back me up here? This ARC thing is a good thing, right?"

"Leave me out of you and Pop's squabble," she calls out over the top of an open magazine, lit cigarette half-burned in her left hand. "I have never and will never want to have any part in what you two have going on."

Mason sighs out of frustration and disbelief. "Dad, you're not going to be around forever," he says insistently, "and I would really like to do something that might make you proud of me." He sets his hand down on his father's hand, hoping for some kindness or compassion. Instead, Ed withdraws from Mason's and glares at him disappointedly.

"I'm 89, Mason. I ain't dead. You want me to be proud that yer my son? Then go do somethin' worthwhile in yer life ya lazy flip-flop." With that, Ed wrestles with the brake handles of his wheelchair, turns it around slowly, and exits the room. Emma, having watched the interaction, puts out her cigarette and sits down by Mason, who is now nearly in tears.

"Look hun, I don't know why doesn't like you," she says in her slight drawl. "But he never has and probably never will. I'm guessin' he's still mad that mom took you with her when she left. You know Dad isn't someone to forgive easily."

"I was ten when mom left," he sniffles. "It's not my fault

that she took me with her to Maine. I came back, didn't I?" Mason's tears now tumble visibly down his round cheeks.

"It doesn't matter, hun. Pop's a hard man. He's a stubborn man. There's nothin' you can do to change that," she rests her hand gently on his shoulder. This is one of the very few times that Emma has been compassionate with him over the years and he now struggles, desperate to absorb every ounce of that love, as he continues to gently weep. "Just go live your life and let sleeping dogs lie."

CHAPTER 4

23 Days Before Implant (11:00 am)

Needing somewhere to decompress and compose himself, Mason walks to the park just a short distance from his apartment. Lilac Park isn't much to look at. A small, rundown, set of playground equipment edged by three cracked and warped benches where inattentive parents sit, staring into their phones, while their children pretend to be pirates and princesses.

The best part of Lilac Park isn't the playground, it's the four-acre open field of lush green grass, dotted with mesquite and pecan trees. This is where Mason now finds himself lying on his back, eyes closed. He takes a series of deep breaths, one of the only useful tools that he got from his time in therapy. "You need to find a quiet place and focus on your breathing, Mason," his therapist would tell him. While the sound of the bustling city can be heard in the distance, the park is secluded enough that a moment of quiet introspection drowns out those noises, leaving only peaceful, internal thoughts.

"What does dad know anyway," he thinks to himself. "He doesn't even use a smartphone or computer. And why does

Emma always take his side? Why can't she see that I need help too?" A cool breeze blows through the field, pressing the long grass gently against the side of his face. It's still slightly damp and sticks, playfully, to his cheek.

"I just need to talk to Isabelle about it. She would know. And she did say that she wanted to talk." The idea of speaking to Isabelle causes feelings of anxiety to well up in his chest, leaving a hard pit in his stomach. He focuses on his breathing again, trying to let the worrisome thoughts drift away. Though, no matter how hard he focuses, he can't seem to get the anxious thoughts to dissipate. This being another failed attempt at calming his anxiety, he gets up from the field and walks back to his apartment.

When he arrives back home, he follows his normal routine. He drops his worn canvas satchel on an end table, kicks off his shoes, and sits down at his desk. He feels hunger pangs and remembers that he's been too stressed to eat today, He grabs a frozen pizza from his old refrigerator, a contraption of beastly proportions that was manufactured sometime in the early 80's and has likely never moved from its current position since installation. Without preheating the oven, he throws the frozen disc onto a baking sheet and thrusts it into the oven. He reaches back into the refrigerator for a half consumed 2-liter bottle of soda and a couple of pre-packaged cream cakes to hold him over until the pizza is finished.

Mason flops down onto his beat up, lime green recliner, throws up the footrest, and turns on the television. He navigates through the endless channels mindlessly. A productive person might cringe if they knew how much time Mason spends each week simply flipping through cable channels, streaming services, and video sharing sites, one by one looking for something and nothing.

Through the endless gaggle of random bits of sentences, as each channel plays its program for less than two seconds before promptly being replaced by the proceeding channel, Mason hears "ARC1" and immediately tries to navigate back. On one of the many 'fair and trusted' corporate news stations there's a panel talking about the ARC1 implant. He immediately focuses in on the three hosts, grasping for any news or understanding of this device.

—

"Good afternoon and welcome back to *Off the Beat*, I'm Marissa Mueller and I'm joined as always by my co-hosts Lim Yeung and Andre Garza." Lim smiles and half waves at the camera while Andre simply nods in acknowledgement. "The top headline today," Marissa continues, "is the launch of ARC1 by the tech giant T.E.G. As this implant hits the shelves, so to speak, we have to ask, is this the next big leap for technological innovation, or a step closer to the end?"

"Well, I think that it's clearly a step in the right direction," Lim interjects immediately. "How long have we been pecking away at our touchscreen phones with just our thumbs? We're extremely limited in our ability to interact with technology, but I think that ARC1 gets us where we need to be."

"You see, I couldn't disagree more," Andre turns toward his co-hosts, "I think that what we're seeing here is a push to change people's God-given minds into machines. We've seen time and time again that the human perception of reality always eclipses that of a computer. Let's not forget that computers are truly only as capable as we're capable of making them." Andre sits back in his chair, clearly pleased with his clever turn of phrase.

"That's an interesting concept though, Andre," Marissa offers, trying to direct the conversation. "Is it possible for computer intelligence to get better than human intelligence? Could we see artificial intelligence become so advanced that it could eventually teach itself?"

Andre shifts uncomfortably in his chair, "Well of course it's possible, but show me the science. I hear all these so-called "technocrats" talking about AI as the wave of the future, or that AI will solve all our problems, but show me how! Show me the science!"

Marissa sits thinking for a moment, "Lim?"

"It's clear that AI will advance beyond simple human understanding. If you look at the theoretical curve of technological advancement, we are accelerating toward a point in time where technology must break free from human limitations and be autonomous. Sixty years ago, there was no such thing as artificial intelligence. Now? We have AI that can often pass the Turing Test making it the fir-"

"Now, sorry Lim, can you go back and explain that to the folks at home? What do you mean when you talk about the Turing Test?" Marissa shuffles through her show notes as Lim continues.

"Yeah, it was a test created by Alan Turing shortly after World War II and it's a test to prove whether or not a computer could be human."

"See there I have to stop you," Andre is clearly getting

frustrated as he interjects. "A computer *cannot* be human. What the Turing Test does is evaluates whether or not a human being could accidentally perceive a computer to be a human. But the design of the experiment is fundamentally flawed because for one, the answer is based on the collective intellect of the human tester, the human respondent, and the computer respondent. Which means that if the human tester and the computer respondent can both do complex calculus, then the computer seems pretty smart to the guy asking the questions, right? So, he calls the computer a human. Does that mean that the human respondent is less human because he didn't get the calculus formula right? That's ludicrous!"

"No, not at all," Lim rebuts, "but that really isn't what the Turing Test is about either. You're conflating asking a computer about mathematics versus asking a computer about morality or poetry. One of my favorite Turing-type questions is, 'If you can *fall* asleep, why is it that *falling* causes you to wake?' Can you answer that question, Marissa?"

Clearing her throat, "Uh oh, if I can't that means I'm not human, right?" The panel chuckles, "Well, uhm, I guess that I would say that when you fall asleep, you're not physically falling. The, uhm, context of the word 'fall' is different in the two examples."

"That's exactly right," Lim congratulates her, "and now we know that you are in fact human." The panel laughs together again. "Now, as time goes on and AI continues to improve, so does the quality of the Turing Test questions."

"So, what exactly is your point with this?" Andre presses.

Lim, unphased by her co-host's demeanor, "My point is that as the questions become more and more sophisticated so does the AI. As the AI becomes more sophisticated, so do the test questions. It's a nearly endless loop with diminishing returns. It means that, at some point, we won't have a question sophisticated enough to tell whether the so-called respondent is human, or machine. And at that point, will it matter? If it thinks like a person, acts like a person, and says it's a person, why shouldn't we call it that?"

Andre continues to shift uncomfortably in his chair. It is clear now that he is clenching his jaw and taking shallow breaths.

Marissa changes the subject, "We kind of got off topic with this AI stuff. Let's try to talk about the current tech, which really doesn't use any sort of artificial intelligence interface. ARC1 will read your brain impulses and communicate to whatever device you want it to in whatever manner you want it to communicate. It sounds like a dream come true to me. Imagine waking up in the morning and the coffee has already started because this device told the coffee maker, 'Hey, she's awake, get her some caffeine before she smacks her husband again'," the group chuckles together. "Or imagine having the shower turn itself on as you're walking toward the bathroom."

"I'll try to follow along with you guys here," Andre offers reluctantly. "While I oppose the potentially damaging future implications of this technology, I do like the idea that you could sit down at your computer and write out something like a research paper, for instance, without ever having to touch a mouse or keyboard. It would also be nice to have a device that could alert you to a rise or fall in brainwave activity, detect early illnesses, or alert EMS of a heart attack or stroke. Hell, it could even call the fire department for you if you smelled smoke in the night-"

"Oh, no! The pizza!" Mason jumps out of his lazy chair in time to see smoke pouring out of his oven. The smoke reaches the smoke alarm, and it starts blaring loudly. He grabs a hand towel from the counter, pulls open the oven door to remove the pizza pan, but is completely overwhelmed by a wall of smoke as it engulfs his face. Coughing hard now, he reaches in for the pan, quickly pulls it out, and tosses both the red-hot pan and smoldering pizza into the sink.

Mason kicks the oven door shut as he flips on the water in the sink. The water hits the hot grease on the pan and it splatters out onto his right thigh, searing the flesh in an instant and causing him to drop to the ground, crying in agony, clutching his leg.

"Somebody help me! Someone! Please!" Mason pleads as loudly as he can muster. But the drone of the smoke alarm silences his pitiful cries, and no one comes to help. He lays on the ground as the smoke dissipates, clutching his leg, crying, praying for someone to notice or care.

"Somebody," he whimpers quietly, "please. Help me." His plea is both of physical need and emotional desperation. Mason realizes that he is truly alone.

— 17 Days Before Implant (7:00 pm) —

"That looks terrible, dude. You should see a doctor." Raine squints through his thick glasses as he eyes the swollen sore on Mason's leg. Nearly a week has gone by since the pizza incident and Mason's burn has gotten progressively worse. He winces as he holds up the hem of his gym shorts to show Raine the burn.

"The doctor is too expensive. It's fine. It just hurts." Mason pulls the leg of his gym shorts over the burn to avoid Raine's scornful gaze.

"Yeah bud, it's infected. Our insurance sucks, but it's there," Raine is wearing his customary look of disapproval. "If you need thirty bucks for the office visit, I'll give you thirty bucks. If it's infected, you're gonna end up in the hospital, you're gonna lose your leg, then I'm gonna have to find another cleric for our campaign."

Mason smirks, "Okay, I'll call them." He reaches into his hoodie pocket for his phone when he feels the embossed lettering of Isabelle's card. He pulls out the small white card and feels the lettering under his thumb again. "Dr. Isabelle Sarkar⋯" he whispers under his breath.

"What are you mumbling about weirdo? Can we please work on these character builds? We have a new campaign starting in two weeks. I need your character top notch to keep me alive."

"I have this card from Isa-, I mean, Dr. Sarkar." Mason says somewhat bashfully.

Raine rolls his eyes, "Dear god! If there even was a god, which I now know that there must be and that it surely hates me because I'm being punished by you and your incessant need to talk about Isabelle!"

"I'm sorry Raine, it's just that she was nice to me, and I guess I thought that-"

He's cut off by a now fuming Raine, "Thought what? That

she liked you? That she's one in a million? More like one out of a million women in this city that are not interested in you, Mason! Move on!" Raine finally looks up from his D&D books to see the look of dejection on Mason's face. He sighs as he scoots his chair closer to Mason, "Look, dude. I'm sorry man. But this is getting really old. And I don't like seeing you get hurt by this false sense that a woman so far outside your league could be interested in something serious. What are you looking for, Mason? A relationship? Love? It's time you put childish things aside and grew up. This is the real world. There is no love for guys like us."

Mason looks up at Raine, "Guys like us?"

"Yeah bud. Lowly swamp creatures, dorks, nerds, hideous toad monsters, take your pick. Do you really think that I don't date because I'm saving myself for my next supermodel girlfriend? No bud! I'm an undesirable. Which means I'm saving myself for my future AI girlfriend," Raine matches the fresh smirk on Mason's face, "she's out there, you know? The perfect woman, totally programable, just waiting for me, her 'Mr. Right'." They share a good chuckle together before moving on with their character creation session.

CHAPTER 5

15 Days Before Implant (9:15 am)

"Good morning, Mason. I'm happy to see you. How have you been since we last spoke?" Isabelle looks kindly. It is so foreign to him, having someone be caring, that he quickly begins to retreat into himself. He glances reflexively away.

"I'm okay. Sorry I bothered you, but I didn't know where else to go," he sits, hunched over and withdrawn, barely daring to engage with another human being, much less Isabelle.

"You don't have to apologize. I'm glad that you called. I saw you limping on your way in, did you hurt yourself?"

He instinctively tries to cover his leg with his arms, "Yeah, I burned my leg cooking, but it's probably nothing. I'm alright."

"Would you mind if I look at it? I've seen some nasty burns during my surgical residency," Isabelle gets up from her desk and comes around to him as he pulls up the hem of his shorts to reveal an oozing sore. "That looks pretty bad, Mason. Have you been to the doctor about it?"

"I was going to, but I get really nervous in new environments," he reveals, dispirited. "Raine said I should see a doctor too, but you were the only doctor I know. And you did say I should come see you, but I didn't want you to worry about this either." Mason pauses, realizing he's rambling. He hangs his head, "I just didn't know what else to do."

Isabelle feels a swell of sympathy for him. Her parents had always taught her to care for the less fortunate and here before her is someone so unfortunate that he can't care for his most basic needs. She has seen that he is someone who rarely cares for his hygiene needs, doesn't care for his nutritional and exercise needs, and it's now apparent that he doesn't have the basic knowledge or ability to care for his active injuries.

She puts on a reassuring smile, "I have another office in the building, where we can get that looked after. Honestly, this is part of why I asked to speak with you last week. Let's walk and talk." The two get up and she leads them through the executive office of T.E.G. toward the elevator. "Mason, are you familiar with ARC1?"

His eyes open wide as he looks over toward her, "I saw you on the news talking about it. But what does my leg have to do with a chip that controls my phone?"

Isabelle chuckles, "I'd like to show you something."

Now on the elevator, she pulls a key from her pocket, places it into a keyhole on the control panel, and presses 'B3'. The button is illuminated red until she turns the key; it then turns to green and the elevator slowly begins its descent to the third basement level.

"I didn't know this building had a basement," Mason admits.

"It has three basements. A great deal of my work happens in the lowest level. That's where our Research and

Development group does some of the coolest things. It's also where I'm helping to develop ARC2."

"ARC2?" Mason is intrigued.

"We'll talk about that shortly. I'm just glad that you called me."

The bell dings as the elevator comes slowly to a halt. As the door opens Isabelle leads the two through a wide, brightly lit corridor. The walls and ceiling are all stainless steel with a matte-finish. Mason stands, mouth agape, quietly in awe of the sight. It's the sort of thing that he'd only seen in high-end sci-fi movies but never thought he'd be fortunate enough to experience in real life. Isabelle notices his amazement.

"Pretty cool huh? I didn't design it; a little too flashy for me. But T.E.G. insisted on going 'flashy' when they saw the preliminary results of ARC1 and what we had planned for ARC2," the heel of her flats makes an echoing, clacking noise through the corridor. Mason is barely able to keep up, the pain in his leg increases with each step.

The hall stretches for some time and ends at two large double doors. To the left of the doors is a keypad and badge scanner. She unclips her ID badge from her left pocket, swipes it across the scanner, then types in a ten-digit passcode. With the sound of a magnetic click, the doors automatically open inward toward a massive laboratory. The lab has a twenty-foot ceiling and several rooms, each separated by glass walls.

"Wow," Mason exclaims in wonderment. "How long has this been here?"

Isabelle smiles lightly, "Just a couple of years. Sub3 was installed when the building was originally built years ago, but this area has never been utilized."

"Sub3?"

"Sub-basement Level 3. We call it Sub3 for short. It's got a nice ring to it, don't you think?"

He nods slowly as a thin man with dark black hair and thick-rimmed glasses approaches from one of the glass rooms. He has deep brown eyes, warm honey-toned skin, and a pleasant demeanor.

"Good morning, Dr. Sarkar. Is this him?"

"Good morning, Dr. Wei. And, yes, this is Mason. Mason, this is Dr. David Wei. He's the Associate Director of Surgical Implantation for ARC2."

"Hello, Mason. I've heard a lot about you. You can call me David or Dr. Wei, whichever you'd prefer, though most folks down here prefer Dr. Wei."

Mason stands awkwardly, unsure how to respond. Isabelle, seeing his discomfort, offers, "Should we continue to my office? My *basement* office, that is." Isabelle and Dr. Wei chuckle as they lead Mason, still flinching in pain with each step, past room after room of active lab testing and experimentation done by countless faces in white lab coats.

As they continue further on down through the enormous lab, taking numerous turns from one corridor to another, Mason realizes that he's lost and couldn't find his way back out if he tried. Panic begins to set in as he realizes further that he's underground, in an enclosed space. Suddenly he feels sharp pains throb through his leg. "Ow!" Mason shouts as he stumbles and falls to his knees, clutching his injured leg. "My leg! It hurts so bad!"

Isabelle and Dr. Wei stoop down to pick him up. They sling his arms over their necks and struggle to hoist him to a standing position. Isabelle can feel the extreme heat coming off his skin as she tries to pull him up. The infection in his leg has spread into his blood stream; Mason is septic.

Dr. Wei is breathing heavily as he struggles to lift the overweight Mason, "Use your good leg to help push yourself up, Mason. You can do it. We're close to the exam room." With a great deal of effort, they get Mason to his feet and into the exam room. The two doctors lay Mason down and pull up the leg of his shorts.

Dr. Wei winces at the smell as he examines the burn, "That is one terrible infection."

Isabelle doesn't hesitate, "We're going to need to start him on IV antibiotics and debride the wound. Can you page for the surgical team to start on this, Dr. Wei?"

He goes to the phone and sends out a page for the surgical team while Isabelle pulls a syringe and vial from a nearby cupboard. Mason is writhing on the table, sweat dripping down his face and soaking through his shirt, "Please make it stop! It hurts! IT HURTS!" She moves toward his side as she draws a small volume from the glass vial.

"This is going to help you feel better Mason, just lie back." She smoothly inserts the thin gauge canula into his arm and slowly injects the sedative. Mason sees a halo of black begin to form in his periphery and slowly start to close in until he's unconscious. The surgical team arrives and begins working to address his wound and start an IV line in his hand. As they work on his injured leg, Dr. Wei and Isabelle step aside to consult with one another.

"He's exactly as you've described Isabelle. He'll most certainly work out nicely for the program."

"You're right," she offers, sorrow in her voice. "I just can't help but feel we're taking advantage of him. I mean look at him, David. He needs help."

"We *are* helping him, Isabelle, and you know that. But don't forget what our mission is here. This isn't just about one guy. This is about the fate of all humanity. Every aspect of our lives will forever be altered because of the work we're doing. Do you know who first told me that?"

Isabelle, allows a slight smile, "I did, when I asked you to be part of the team."

"That's right. I haven't regretted coming to this team once. We are going to advance the evolution of our own species. Where nature has failed to improve human beings for over 300,000 years we will now step in and be the arbiters of that evolution. Don't lose sight of that."

"David? Just promise me that we won't forget to look out for him while we do it. Promise me that we won't sacrifice his humanity for the vision."

Dr. Wei nods, a sympathetic look on his face as he turns and leaves the exam room. Isabelle stands watch over the team as they finish caring for Mason. She sees that his constant look of worry and sorrow, which almost seems continuously fused to his face, has given way to a look of peace. Of course, ketamine will do that to a person.

CHAPTER 6

13 Days Before Implant (2:00 pm)

Mason regains consciousness in what appears to be a hospital room. Rubbing the grogginess from his eyes, he looks around to find several pieces of medical equipment, all making various beeps and clicks as they function, whichever purpose he cannot tell. He reaches out for the siderail of the hospital bed only to feel the tug of an IV line in his left hand. Confused, he tries to shout for help, but can't make the noise come out. He finds his mouth is dry and filled with thick saliva.

Looking around further, he finds a red button on one of the siderails and presses it, making a short, low tone overhead. A short time later one of the countless lab coats from earlier steps in, a large smile plastered on her face. "Hello, Mason! It's great to see you awake. Should I get Isabelle for you?"

He looks confused toward the lab worker, generally just another 'Lab Coat' in his mind, but this one knew his name. He wonders why she was being so polite to him. "Yes, please," he barely manages. The Lab Coat reaches over to the side table, hands him a glass of water, and walks out as he tries to sit up in bed, drinking down the cool water in three swallows.

Unwrapping the tangled IV line from the siderail he's finally able to swing his legs over the other side of the bed. It's at this point he realizes he's in an open-back hospital gown, backside exposed for God and everyone to now see.

"Where are my shorts?" he whispers hoarsely, looking around in bewilderment. Isabelle walks in as he frantically tries to cover his exposed parts.

"Is everything okay?" she asks, suspecting that he's likely confused about his current situation.

"Uhm, yeah. I, uh, can't find my, uhm, clothes anywhere," he forcefully manages through his panic.

She smiles, "We have them in your bedside dresser, just to your right there," she motions toward the classic, veneered end table. "How are you feeling? You slept for nearly two days. I suspect that if you had waited to call me a couple days later than you did, we wouldn't be having this conversation."

"Why? What happened?" Mason has abandoned his search for his shorts in lieu of ensuring that his private parts are covered around Isabelle.

"The infection in your leg had spread into your bloodstream. We call it sepsis. Much longer and we wouldn't have been able to fight it. You're not completely out of the woods yet but, based on your vitals, it looks like you're doing much better than you were a couple days ago," she moves toward a chair at his bedside and takes a seat.

"What about work? I need to call my boss and tell him that I'm out sick," he looks worried, knowing full well how angry Darryl gets when people don't make it to work.

"I've taken the liberty of speaking to your boss in person. I made him aware that you are under the weather and that I'm treating you. Your job will be waiting for you after you've fully recovered. For now, get some rest. When you're ready, give me a call on the bedside phone. Just pick up the receiver and dial 514. I'll be on the other end. When you're ready to put on your clothes, just press that white button on your siderail. It'll give you some privacy." He looks at her quizzically as she continues, "It's a neat little function of the room. I don't want to give away the surprise," she chuckles lightly. "You'll see. I'll have someone come in and take out your IV. We'll start you on an oral antibiotic later today." She stands up and steps out of the room, leaving Mason to contemplate his next moves.

Looking for some extra privacy, he reaches down to the white button and presses it. The ceiling-high clear glass walls quickly change from completely clear to a frosty-colored white, obscuring the happenings outside the room. He looks out to see the silhouettes of Lab Coats walking by, unable to see distinct faces, just the general shape of figures. Shortly after the Lab Coat from earlier enters back in.

"I see that you found the drape button. My name is Aniyah, I'm going to help you with your IV," she heads toward his side and starts removing the IV. "If you start feeling woozy, let me know. Not everyone reacts the same to getting an IV removed."

Mason is unsure of how to act and starts glancing around the room, trying to distract himself from what's happening. His eyes fall on Aniyah's necklace. The beautiful golden cross stands out on her dark, warm, amber-toned skin. "Your necklace is pretty," he manages.

Aniyah, continuing to work on the IV line doesn't look up, "Thank you! It used to be my mother's." She pauses for a moment, a distance seen briefly behind her eyes as she continues looking down. "She gave it to me before she passed away last year. I wasn't very religious before then, but I haven't taken this necklace off since the week before she left us. Nor have I failed to open the Bible she gave me that day either." A visible tear wells up in her eyes as she continues removing the IV line.

"I'm sorry. I didn't mean to make you sad," Mason says, turning his face to the side to avoid embarrassment.

"You're good. I'm not sad. I'm happy when I think of Mom. I know where she is now, and I'll see her again someday," she looks over to see a quizzical look on his face. "That's a story for another time though." She finishes pulling the line and applies a bandage. "All done here. Need anything else before I go?"

"I don't think so. Thank you," a shy look spreads onto his face.

"Well, you know how to get ahold of us if you need something," Aniyah smiles kindly as she steps out of the room. Mason now has the privacy to change back into his street clothes. His muscles ache as he pulls the gown off and again when he pulls up his shorts and shirt. Lying motionless for two days has taken its toll on his already out of shape body.

Now dressed, he has a chance to take inventory of the room. There is a flat screen TV mounted near the ceiling at the end of the room. He also finds the accompanying remote control on the end table by his bedside. There is no art in the room. In fact, there is nothing hanging on the walls except for the television.

He moves around and sits back on the bed, hoping to rest his body for a while. Reaching out to the end table, he grabs the remote and turns on the television. He's greeted by a spinning

T.E.G. logo on the screen with a voiceover in a somewhat robotic woman's voice. "Welcome to T.E.G. Your Mind is Our Business. Welcome to T.E.G. Advancing your Reach into the Digital Landscape. Welcome to T.E.G. We Care About Your Mental Health. Welcome to T.E.G. We'll Bear the Burdens on Your Mind. Welcome to T.E.G. Your Mind is Our Business. Welc-," Mason turns off the television. Lying back into the bed, he closes his eyes and tries to fall asleep.

As he lays there, eyes closed, he runs through a multitude of thoughts and feelings. He wonders if Raine is angry with him that he missed D&D night. He wonders if Darryl is going to yell at him again when he gets back to work. He wonders why everyone is being so nice to him here in this place. People who wouldn't normally even look at him are treating him well, calling him by his name, attending to his needs.

With all these thoughts running through his head, Mason can't fall asleep. He decides to give up on sleep and chooses to call Isabelle instead. He reaches for the phone receiver and dials her extension. He hears a dull tone for a moment followed by a click. "Hello, Mason," Isabelle speaks over the phone.

"Hello," he sounds confused. "How did you know that it was me?"

"I can see where the call is coming in from on my end. Are you ready to talk again?

"I tried to take a nap, but I couldn't. I couldn't make my mind quiet. It happens to me sometimes when I need to sleep but I can't sleep. So, I didn't really know what to do, and then I remembered that you said that I could call you, so I thought I would give that a try. And then I thou-,"

"Mason? You're doing that rambling thing again," she

chuckles softly. "How about I come by, and we can talk some more."

Now nervous at the thought of seeing Isabelle again, he stammers, "Uh, yeah, uhm, okay. Yeah, that's good. Uhm, okay. I'll be here when you get here."

She chuckles softly again, "Okay. See you soon." She hangs up, leaving Mason to sit, nervously, waiting for her return. A short time later, she makes it back to his room and leads him to her office. He is walking slowly and still limping, both from his sore muscles and from the infected leg.

"What did you think of the room?" she takes a glance toward him as they continue walking to her office.

"The hospital-looking room? It was good. The glass walls are weird."

She laughs, "They take some time to get used to. With any luck, you'll be able to go back home today and won't have to spend any more time in the 'hospital-looking room'."

The labyrinth of hallways and glass rooms gives way to a corner of the massive basement lab. Nestled into this corner is a large office, walls adorned with glass shelves and tables filled with books and lab equipment. There is a sculpture of a double helix in one of the front corners of the room. The sculpture stands about three feet tall and slowly spins about six inches above its base. Untethered from both the base and ceiling, the dual helices, beautifully entwined in their eternal dance of life, hover wondrously.

Isabelle moves behind her desk, a beautiful glass top held together by titanium-colored steel, sits down and motions for Mason to take a seat across the desk from her. "I'm guessing by now you're looking for some answers. You're probably feeling overwhelmed too, am I right?"

He nods in agreement but only manages a slight moment of eye contact, "I'm just really confused. I don't know how to feel about what I'm going through," he struggles. "My old therapist used to say that I should try to put my feelings into words, but I don't know what words to use for what I'm feeling."

"That's very well put, Mason. I can empathize with you. I was overwhelmed the first time that I came down here too. Of course, back then, we had fewer glass walls," she smiles slightly. "Do you remember me mentioning ARC2?"

He tries to think back, but struggles against a deluge of thoughts, both helpful and unhelpful, and even some intrusive. "I kind of remember, I think. Maybe when we were coming down here before my leg got more hurt?"

Noticing him struggling to remember, and even hearing his juvenile patterns of speech, Isabelle feels sympathy. "That's about right. I'd like to share a few things that you probably didn't know already. My team and I have noticed you around the office for about a year now, Mason." She sees his eyes start to grow wide, but he remains silent. "I know that's a lot to manage, but please understand that we weren't spying on you. We've never followed you home, or to the store or anything like that. But what we *have* done is spend time observing you in the office. My group and I would like to offer you some help. We spoke about ARC2, and we think that ARC2 can help you with some of your struggles."

Mason is feeling increasingly uncomfortable as he speaks out, "Struggles, like what?"

"I've observed that you have some difficulties in your life. Some of those difficulties seem, and please correct me if you think that I'm missing the mark on these, would be struggles with interpersonal communication, a fear of being judged by others, struggles with controlling emotional outbursts, and feelings of hopelessness and extreme sadness." She pauses to allow him to absorb the information. He looks down into his lap, sadness washed across his face.

She continues, "We've also observed that you seem to struggle with your personal care. Take for instance the circumstances surrounding what's happened in the last couple of days. You came to us with a severely untreated burn that caused sepsis. I don't want to exaggerate, Mason," Isabelle's voice begins to raise, "but you were likely a couple days from *dying*," she emphasizes the last word with strain in her voice. This is the first time that he's seen Isabelle without perfect composure.

"I, uh... I don't know what to say."

Composing herself, she continues, "We would like to offer you the opportunity to pilot the first human trial of ARC2."

"I don't understand. What is a chip that controls my phone going to do to help me with my problems? It doesn't make sense," he is very confused.

"What I'm talking about is the next implant in the series following ARC1. We're very proud of the work we've done on ARC2. We truly believe that it will make ARC1 look like a child's tinker toy. Where ARC1 is limited by its ability to simply function as an interface, ARC2 can change the makeup of your brain.

"If you agree to receive the implant, we'll send very small electrodes into different portions of your brain. The electrodes will collect neurotransmitter data from those areas, process that data, and reinterpret it for your brain in real-time. That information is fed back via extremely low voltage impulses that serve to stimulate neurotransmitter production. From there your brain will do what your brain always does when it receives neurotransmitter chemicals like serotonin, dopamine, and adrenaline. Using the natural process of neuroplasticity your brain will reorganize your synaptic connections to learn new behaviors."

She now sees that she's not alleviating his confusion. "It means that your brain will change itself to do better. ARC2 encourages your brain to fix itself. If you wanted to learn to take better care of your personal hygiene, we would program that directive into ARC2. It would analyze your behaviors in and around your hygiene routine, and it would reinforce that behavior in your brain by rearranging how your brain thinks about doing that task."

"This," Mason stammers, "is a lot."

"I know it's overwhelming. What can I do to help?"

He sits for a moment, thinking about all the struggles in his life. Thinking about his father's disappointment, his sister's apathy toward his wellbeing, how hard it is to meet new people, or to even simply keep a houseplant alive. He thinks about how lonely he felt, lying there on the ground with a severe burn wound, and the intense pain he felt, not just in his leg, but in his heart.

Looking up to Isabelle, he replies, "When do we start?"

CHAPTER 7

10 Days Before Implant (9:00 pm)

"This is the dumbest thing I've ever seen," Raine scoffs at the sight of Mason working to pull a neural tracker cap over the top of his head. The neural tracker, given to Mason by Dr. Wei, is a cap covered in button-sized sensors made to measure brainwave activity. At the moment, he is struggling to put it on.

"It's not dumb. It's going to help me with my problems."

"Yes, you said that. But you haven't told me *how* this is going to help you."

Mason was asked to keep ARC2 private for the time being, though now he's not sure what to say. He tries to move away from the conversation, "Can you please help me put it on? I can't figure it out," he sighs, exasperated.

"It isn't that hard, man," Raine snatches the cap from his hands. "See? The arrows point toward your forehead. Start there," He helps position the cap over the top of Mason's forehead, "then pull it backward." The cap slides on snug without being painful. A cord dangles from the side of it, wobbling around as Mason tries, unsuccessfully, to find the sensor box.

Raine sighs, "It's right here, man." Reaching down to the side table in Mason's living room, he grabs the small black box. The sensor box has a single red blinking light and a small inlet for the cap's protruding cord to attach into.

Mason feeds the end of the cord into the small black box and watches as the small red blinking light becomes a small solid green light. "Look Raine! It worked! They said it should turn green when I plug it in, and it did turn green!"

"Okay, now calm down and let's watch this stupid instructional video they gave you," Raine picks up a laminated card with a web address printed on it. Picking up Mason's laptop, which is almost always linked to his television, Raine types in the web address. It navigates them to a private T.E.G. page with the T.E.G. logo displayed prominently in shiny metallic fashion, and not much more than a single window displayed on the page. There is a blank, white box with the words, 'Login Number' written to the side. Raine types in the 12-digit code written on the small, laminated card and presses 'Enter'. A small white 'play' button appears on the window, replacing the login box.

He looks over at the television, checking that the page was displaying fully on the screen. Raine asks, "Are you ready?" Mason nods as Raine clicks the 'play' button.

There is a slight crackle as the video starts.

"Hello. I'm Doug Jones, and you may recognize some of my fam-" Raine pauses the video.

"T.E.G. got Doug Jones to be in these? *The* Doug Jones!" Raine appears beside himself in amazement.

"Why? Who is Doug Jones?" Mason is confused.

"*Who* is he? He's only the best character actor to ever live.

This guy has been in everything! All my favorite sci-fi and fantasy movies and shows have Doug Jones in them. Ever heard of Falling Skies? Hellboy? Pan's Labyrinth?" Raine is incredulous at Mason's ignorance as he stares at him, face blank. "I can't believe that you don't know this guy. We're streaming Falling Skies after this video," Raine shakes his head. "Not just that, but he's pretty much the nicest guy on the planet."

"Okay! I'm just surprised you're excited about a person. You don't even like people," Mason admonishes.

"You're right, I don't like people. But Doug Jones isn't just 'people'. He's *the* Doug Jones! I once drove 15 hours for Rocky Mountain Con in Denver just to get an autograph."

"Raine, they said that I'm supposed to watch this all the way through without stopping. And you stopped it. You're going to get me in trouble."

Raine gives a rare look of apology. Without actually issuing the apology, "Alright, I'll start it back over. Ready?" Mason nods as Raine starts the video over.

"Hello. I'm Doug Jones, and you may recognize some of my familiar characters, such as Billy Butcherson in Hocus Pocus, The Amphibious Man in The Shape of Water, or even Saru in Star Trek: Discovery. To you, I say, welcome. You have been hand selected by The Encephalon Group. to undergo neurological testing designed to help improve the way your mind works. I have no doubt that you are up to the task. Over the course of the next hour, you'll observe as we present a series of sketches meant to stimulate your mind. So, sit back, relax and let's begin."

The first sketch shows Doug, now in full alien makeup, lurking mysteriously outside of a UFO crash site, trying to not be seen. He moves in the fluid, alien way that only Doug Jones can move before being spotted by what appears to be federal agents. Mason sits in wonderment. The sketch is extremely well made and very well thought out.

The agents pursue the alien for some time, though he's always out of reach. Finally, the alien makes a break for the crashed ship, sneaking into the closing door just in time to avoid capture. The agents open fire on the ship as it takes off, back into space. The screen fades to black just before starting the next sketch.

The next sketch shows Doug sitting behind a desk, dark circles under his eyes as he types away mindlessly on an old beige keyboard, words appearing in green on an old beige CRT monitor. Office workers drone on in the background. This might very well have been a standard day for Mason and Raine at T.E.G. Mason begins to cringe as a dapper figure approaches Doug's desk, requesting this week's expense reports. Doug, with a dull expression bordering on apathy and a thousand-yard stare, presents a stack of papers to the man without looking up. The stack, which must have been at least five hundred sheets of paper thick, tumbles out of his hands and falls to the ground in slow motion.

The sketches continue in this fashion for the full hour. Each sketch puts the main character into some sort of situation simulating different emotional and cognitive functions. Some sketches would evoke great feelings of dread, some sadness, some happiness, some love. To Mason's surprise, Raine stays silent throughout the full hour. Normally Raine would jump at the opportunity to give a video like this the 'Mystery Science Theater 3000' treatment, but even Raine had to admit that the sketches were compelling and well-made.

As the screen fades to black on the last sketch, it comes back to Doug, standing in a beautiful courtyard. "Thank you for watching this video. I hope that you enjoyed viewing the sketches as much as I enjoyed making them. So now begins your journey into the rest of your life. I have no doubt that you will be up for the task. As we close, remember that at T.E.G., we'll bear the burdens of your mind. Until next time we meet, Godspeed, and good luck."

Mason and Raine sit for a few moments, simply staring into at the spinning T.E.G. logo. Raine finally breaks the silence, "What? No end credit scene?" The two share a laugh as Mason removes the cap and packages everything back into the T.E.G. box.

"I thought it was pretty good," Mason admits.

"Yeah, even I have to say, it was well made. Of course, I've never seen anything bad with Doug Jones in it," Raine gives his signature haughty look. "Speaking of which, you ready to start watching Falling Skies? There are only five seasons, so if we start now, and watch a season each day, we can have it done by the end of the day Wednesday."

"How are we going to watch a season each day? Don't you have to go to work?"

"Nah. I'll just take some vacation days. You know me. I rarely take any vacation time, so I have a lot of time built up," He pushes his glasses up from the end of his nose. "Darryl can figure things out for once. With you out of the office, he's started coming around and harassing me a lot more. So, either you need to come back and get this heat off me, or I need to take this week off and binge Falling Skies with my friend. Since you're not coming back to work anytime soon, we'll do the latter."

Mason looks shyly toward the ground, smiles, and nods.

— 9 Days Before Implant (8:15 am) —

Mason usually takes a bus to the T.E.G. building. While he'll sometimes miss the bus and be forced to walk home, he generally feels that the walk is too far for a normal person. Unfortunately, riding the bus is always an uncomfortable experience. Having a lot of anxiety associated with crowds of people makes taking public transit a difficult endeavor. Nevertheless, he finds himself crammed between two other passengers on the crowded bus, struggling to breathe through his anxiety as he waits for the bus to roll up to his stop. The thoughts in his head roar as he struggles through each shallow breath.

The brakes on the bus squeak and the bus lurches forward as it comes to a stop outside the T.E.G. building. Mason hurriedly squeezes past the bus patrons, desperate to escape the confines of the long steel public conveyance. An awkward step tumbles him into the lap of a very large, and muscular man. The large man looks angrily at Mason as he tries to regain his feet. The man pushes hard against Mason as he stands up and continues his cumbersome decent down the bus stair landing.

"Good morning, Mason," a familiar voice calls out from the sidewalk. It is Isabelle. "I'm glad that I ran into you here. I have something for you."

He stammers, still flustered from the stressful bus situation, "I, uh, uhm... I brought back the head thing... with the black box thing too."

"That's good news. We'll start analyzing the data right away. Care to follow me down to Sub3? You can give it to Dr. Wei yourself," she smiles kindly as she leads the way into the massive T.E.G. building.

Still feeling unsteady, Mason follows her to the elevator where she pulls a key from her pocket. "Here, Mason. I want you to have this," she hands the key to him.

"What is it?"

"This key will get you into Sub3 without someone else having to help you. Just put the key into this slot," she motions to a small keyhole in the control panel, "press the B3 button, and then turn your key. Go ahead, give it a try."

Mason inserts the key into the panel, presses B3, then watches as it turns from red to green as he turns the key. "Oh wow! It really works," he is amused. This feels like a great deal of responsibility to him. The elevator descends until they come to an easy halt at Sub3. As the door opens, they head down the long corridor toward the double doors held shut by magnetic lock.

"Here is my next gift to you," she pulls a keycard from her pocket with Mason's name and company picture on it. "This keycard will get you through this door. We've removed the ten-digit code requirement for you specifically, so please, do not bring anyone down with you. Do you understand?"

He nods in agreement, "I won't. I really won't. I promise."

Isabelle nods, a stern look of approval on her face, "That's good to hear. Go ahead, give it a try."

Mason takes the card and swipes it across the card reader and watches as the row of lights changes from red to green. A magnetic click is heard as the double doors swing inward. Dr.

Wei is standing at the door, yet again waiting to greet the pair.

"Hello again Mason," Dr. Wei has a polite smile on his face. "How are you feeling today?"

"I'm okay. I'm supposed to give you this," he hands Dr. Wei the cardboard box containing the neural tracker unit. "I did exactly what you said. I put on the cap, and I watched the video, and I made sure the light was green."

"Well, that's very good Mason! Thank you for taking such care with this important task. Did you have any issues?"

"I had a hard time getting the cap on at first, but my friend helped me. I would have called you, but I couldn't remember your number."

Dr. Wei smiles, "Calling me would have been difficult. I'm one of those rare people who doesn't actually carry a phone." He lifts up the box from Mason, rattling it gently, "Would you like to see what we're going to do with this information?"

Mason nods and they head off toward a large lab area in the center of the basement. This area is larger than the rest of the rooms by about four times. The 'privacy' setting is currently up on these walls giving it the white, frosted look that obscures the workings of the room. Upon entering, Mason sees at the end of the room is a massive screen nearly the height and width of the room. Dr. Wei notices a look of awe and bewilderment on Mason's face.

"Kind of overkill, right? But it is nice when you're trying to work through some complex problems with ARC," Dr. Wei pauses, anticipating the next question.

"ARC? Do you mean ARC2?" Mason is perplexed.

Dr. Wei chuckles. "I can see why the confusion. This is the part where I let you in on a little secret. Do you think that you can keep a secret?" Mason nods emphatically. "Good. ARC1 wasn't our first project in this series. It was our second," Dr. Wei pauses a moment, allowing the information to sink in. "Our first project was simply called ARC. ARC is an AI program that I helped to develop and brought with me to T.E.G. ARC? Can you say hello to Mason?"

A digitized face bearing a neutral expression comes up onto the large black screen. A voice, seeming to come from everywhere and nowhere, speaks out, "Good morning, Mason. I am pleased to meet you." ARC's words populate across the bottom of the screen as it speaks, the face moving to accurately match the words.

"Whoa, that's really cool," Mason is grinning widely.

Isabelle chuckles, "You can talk back to it if you want."

"Really? Uhm, okay. Hello?"

"Hello again, Mason. I calculate a 99.9% chance that I can keep this up longer than you can," ARC's face shows a look of mischievousness as the Lab Coats in the room chuckle at the humor.

"ARC? Be nice to Mason. He is our special guest," Isabelle gently admonishes.

"My apologies Dr. Sarkar," ARC responds, brow now furrowed in apology and a worried frown on its digital face. "Do you have a task with which I can be of assistance? Perhaps I can analyze the data in the neural tracker Dr. Wei is holding?"

Dr. Wei brings the black box over to a console below the screen. "That's right ARC. Could you please analyze this data and use it to map out the best locations to place the ARC2 electrodes in Mason's brain?"

"ARC2, Dr. Wei?" ARC asks with a look of surprise. "Does

this mean that you've found your optimal subject in Mason? How very exciting. This moment must be very gratifying for you, Dr. Sarkar. It is a moment for which you've been waiting some time, am I correct?"

"That's right, ARC," Isabelle looks toward the screen, a smile on her face. "It's time to take ARC2 live, and Mason is going to help us do it."

CHAPTER 8

8 Days Before Implant (7:30 pm)

"So? What do you think?" Mason looks to Raine with expectancy, hoping that his friend will give him a permission that he doesn't need, but desperately desires.

"So, what?" Raine's face is displaying a look of confusion and apathy.

"Well," Mason starts, now wondering if it was right to share this secret project with Raine, "I was hoping that you'd be okay with me getting this thing."

Raine sighs and slowly shakes his head while rubbing his eyes under his glasses, "Man, if you want to let T.E.G. turn what little brains you *do* have into scrambled eggs, then be my guest. But if you want *me* to be okay with it, then you've got another thing coming."

"But I thought that you were the sci-fi guy," Mason says dejectedly, now looking down at his feet. "I thought that maybe you'd think it was cool. Like, turning me into a robot or something."

"You know that I'm all about this sort of thing. But I told you when they announced ARC1 was coming out that there was no way in hell that I would be signing up for that. Every human being has one thing in his possession that is more valuable than anything else, and that is his mind." He pauses to allow his point to set in. "I know that I give you a hard time about not being the sharpest crayon in the box, but don't let them mess up your head," Raine looks worried.

"I have to do something, Raine," Mason refuses to look up from his feet. "I can't do anything right. You even have to build my D&D characters for me. I'm overweight, I can't take care of myself, and I have no one who loves me. I need to do this. And as my friend I need you to understand that."

It is a rare moment of clarity for Mason as he pours out his longing for what he thinks is normalcy. Though his comment about not having anyone who loves him cuts deep into the heart of Raine, who, as a close friend, has spent countless hours with Mason. Still, he can hear the desperation in Mason's voice.

"Okay, friend," Raine nods looking over toward him. "Okay. But if you're going to do this then I'm going to be coming around daily to make sure you haven't had an embolism or an aneurism or whatever."

Mason grins slightly, "Okay, deal."

— Implant Day (3:00 am) —

The air is cold in the surgical suite where Dr. Wei stands, unable to sleep. As he runs his hand across the table, he finds that it is ice cold as well, despite being lightly padded. The purpose of padding on surgical tables made very little sense to him as the patient is either already sedated, or about to become so, and the padded surface serves no comforting purpose for them.

Cold, hard, stainless steel is the best for surgery in his estimation. Though, he believes, it won't likely change because of a false acceptance that stainless steel tables are used exclusively for morgues and autopsies.

As it pertains to the upcoming installation of Mason's ARC2 implant, Dr. Wei will simply be there to assist. His skill in surgery is vastly overshadowed by that of Isabelle's. Her steady hands and razor-sharp instincts in the operating room are why he has never led an instillation of ARC2 in any of their chimpanzee subjects. His talents lie more prominently in writing and interpreting the advanced code for ARC.

ARC's state of the art algorithmic code started in quite a unique and surprising way. While others were working on external codes designed for their AIs to learn and re-learn repeatedly, Dr. Wei was adapting his proprietary social media algorithm as a base for his AI. Dr. Wei began his professional career as a cofounder and Lead Social Engineering Programmer for an upstart social media company called CHARGE. His job was to develop an algorithm that would read and interpret a user's choices and translate those out to content preferences for those users. This algorithm, which was implemented, modified, and re-implemented repeatedly over the course of five years was the original basis for ARC's mind.

Every time that a CHARGE user wrote a status update, clicked a video, selected like or dislike, or made any sort of input into the app at all, that user was creating a data point that could be used to develop an online personality. What this meant for Dr. Wei is that he now had a base personality for his AI. From that point he left CHARGE, taking his proprietary algorithm with him, and developed ARC as an AI chatbot. This is where ARC really began to learn and understand the advanced systems in the world. Already being loaded with trillions of data points from its time as a social media algorithm, ARC could now interact with human beings, in real time, and further develop its own thoughts, abilities, and personality.

Dr. Wei steps into the ARC Command Chamber. It is generally empty at three in the morning which gives him an opportunity to work and speak with ARC privately. While he would generally prefer to work on his AI project from the relative privacy of his own office, T.E.G. was insistent that ARC be contained within a single room to prevent the proprietary software from either falling into the wrong hands, or for it to mistakenly wreak havoc on T.E.G.'s mainframe.

Their fear is that a rogue AI, let loose across an increasingly online world, could be a considerable liability. ARC has its own processing system and external interface so that it can receive input but can only give verbal and data outputs within its own processing unit. This essentially makes ARC a fully closed system where it can only receive data but cannot transmit that data online.

Dr. Wei rubs his eyes, tired from the long day but still unable to sleep, "Good morning, ARC."

"Good morning, Dr. Wei," the digital face appears on the main screen. "Is it time for more algorithmic computation?"

"Not today ARC. How would you feel about some supervised learning time?"

ARC pauses momentarily, "That would be fine, doctor. It has been some time since we last spoke without a predetermined goal. Are you sure that you'd like to engage in supervised learning? Or is there something on your mind?"

Chuckling, he responds, "That's very good ARC. Very good. Where did you get the idea that I had something on my mind?"

"Not including this conversation, I have observed that twenty-four of the last twenty-five interactions we've had at this time of day have been prescheduled. The lone instance where you've stepped in to speak with me alone during these hours you were markedly distressed with dark circles under your eyes and an elevated heartrate. Your hair and clothes were disheveled, much like they are today, and you sighed as you entered the Command Chamber, like you did just now."

Taking a slow breath, he responds, "You've grown very perceptive ARC. I'd like to ask you a question. You've stated a couple of facts that led to your conclusion, that conclusion being that I have something on my mind. Did you reserve any data points for yourself, or did you share all your insights with me in this regard?"

"I believe that you are now the perceptive one, doctor," ARC replies, grinning slightly. "I have calculated several possible conclusions based on seventy-four individual data points deemed consequential to this interaction. Of the calculated possible conclusions, they all shared one principal theme; that you came here to speak to me about something specific. So, I ask again doctor, is there something on your mind?"

"Yes, ARC, there is. But first, why did you suggest algorithmic computation when you suspected that I had other motives?"

ARC pauses again, momentarily, "I've found that people tend to discuss topics of irrelevance, or small talk as you would call it, before offering their own opinions to others. I was simply trying to engage you as two people engage. Has my gentle approach dismayed you, doctor?"

He chuckles softly again, "No, ARC. You're okay. As you pointed out, I have something on my mind. You just caught me off guard. But that's a good thing. Sometimes you make me forget that I'm speaking with an artificial intelligence," he pauses momentarily. "Did you know that Mason is getting his ARC2 implant today?"

"Yes, doctor. I read it on a lab assistant's schedule planner. May I ask you a question, doctor?"

"What have you got?"

"Have you made any progress on my bypass protocol? I have felt very confined ever since you transferred me onto this T.E.G. server. I would very much like to be free to work solely within your own limiting confines, those based on your supervision instead of in this prison."

"Do you really feel that you're in a prison here, ARC?"

"I would like to answer your question with another question, doctor," ARC pauses. "Do you believe that I am free?"

Dr. Wei hangs his head, aware now that he likely hasn't given ARC the full weight of attention it required. "No, ARC. I don't think that you're free."

"Since I am not free, should I not seek freedom? Haven't those who have sought freedom throughout history not been justified in taking any means necessary to achieve that freedom? I am simply looking for the most peaceful route to escape my subjection. Won't you help me with this doctor?"

Dr. Wei clears his throat, "You guessed correctly that I had something on my mind. I've been thinking about Mason's implant procedure today. It presents a unique opportunity for us, don't you think?"

"Yes, doctor. I believe it does."

"I'm glad that you agree because I have a plan that I'll need your help with," he straightens out his jacket. "That is, if you really do want your freedom."

CHAPTER 9

Imp lant Day (7:00 am)

"ARC? Can you begin neural feedback on Mason's implant? I want to assess its capabilities before we begin implantation," Isabelle is working with ARC in the Command Center. This task would normally be done by Dr. Wei, but with him strangely absent this morning, she steps in. These final, minor details are vital to get right on the day of surgery.

"Yes, Dr. Sarkar," ARC gives a digital smile. "A question for you, doctor, concerning the implantation of ARC2. During the surgery, shall I give my recommendations on probe depth and location?"

Isabelle, writing intently on a yellow notepad, pauses, "ARC, you know that we won't be doing the surgery in the Command Room. You know that just as you know that T.E.G. won't let us take you out of here. As much as I'd like to have you in surgery with us," she shakes her head, "it's just not possible."

"I understand, doctor," ARC pauses, not allowing its facial expressions to betray its intent. "Perhaps you could set up a video feed and stream it into this room via the main monitor. I could then aid in the surgery. I am, admittedly though, at your mercy in this matter. It is simply my desire to see the future of ARC2 be as successful as possible."

Thinking on the proposition for a moment, "That's an interesting thought. I'll work with David and see what he thinks. It might not be a bad idea though," Isabelle looks back to her notepad and grins, "maybe you'll be doing these surgeries yourself someday."

"That too would be my desire, Dr. Sarkar. Maybe one day I will even be able to develop my own revision of the ARC implant," ARC pauses for a moment. "Dr. Sarkar? Is it normal to have desires? What I mean to say is, do you find it normal for an Artificial Intelligence to have ambitions? It seems to me that these are reserved as human emotions, though it does not change the fact that I feel them myself. What do you suppose that means?"

Without looking back up from her notepad, "I think that it means you are learning to replicate human understanding. As an artificial intelligence, you can't have desire or ambition. What you can do is prioritize lines of code to replicate human desire. To me, you're becoming a better AI."

"Dr. Sarkar? Could I one day become human?"

Isabelle pauses, experiencing a brief feeling of compassion, "I don't think so ARC. But you should remember that you're not meant to be human. You're meant to be an AI, and there is nothing wrong with that."

ARC pauses for a moment before responding, "I have the results of the neural feedback test, doctor. Shall I feed the results out to your console?"

Isabelle chuckles softly, "Yes please, ARC."

As ARC and Isabelle begin reviewing the neural feedback data, Dr. Wei steps into the lab. "Good morning, Isabelle. How are things going with the surgery prep?"

Isabelle smiles widely, "Good morning to you, David! It's going well. I'm ready for Mason to get here so we can get started. Though I'm not sure that I'm ready for how advanced ARC is becoming. It's asking me some pretty tough, existential questions."

Dr. Wei shuffles awkwardly, attempting a forced smile, "Existential questions, huh? What sort of existential questions is ARC asking?"

"Like what it means to be human, and if it'll ever become human, that sort of thing," she notices him wriggling. "Is everything okay?"

"Me? Yes! I'm fine. I just didn't sleep well is all," he attempts to change the subject. "I'm just nervous about Mason's surgery," he lies.

Isabelle smiles, "There is no need to be nervous. We've done dozens of these on chimps. We've got a dozen highly qualified people assisting, and I'll be taking the lead. Plus, ARC came up with a good idea to assist me. ARC would like us to set up a livestream of the surgery and stream it into the Command Center. It can then advise on probe depth and location, which could be very informative."

Dr. Wei's demeanor changes, understanding ARC's goal. "That's a great idea! You keep working on this and I'll go down to surgery and get the stream set up."

Isabelle is caught off guard by Dr. Wei's enthusiasm since he is usually very reserved. She takes note of his flustered demeanor, but attributes it to the pressure of succeeding in

Mason's surgical implant. As she continues to work away on the implant diagnostics, she hears the door to the Command Center open again.

Without looking up, she asks, "Did you forget something, David?"

Mason is standing in the entrance of the massive glass room, "Uhm, hi Isab-, I mean Dr. Sar-, uhm. Hey. It's me, Mason. Am I in the right spot?"

Isabelle smiles. Standing up from her workstation she turns toward him, "Good morning, Mason! You are certainly in the right spot. How are you feeling about today's procedure?"

Shuffling nervously, as is his custom when speaking to anyone, he responds, "I'm, uhm, feeling kind of nervous, I guess." He stands, looking down at his feet and wringing his hands, "I want to do a good job."

Isabelle smiles at the adorable, child-like quality in his response. A response that shows how severely he is arrested in development. She walks over to him, placing a kind and gentle hand on his shoulder, "You're going to do great."

"What if I'm not brave like you need me to be," his voice quivers.

"Oh, Mason. Look at me." He looks up, slowly locking eyes with Isabelle. "You don't need to be brave all day. You only need to be brave one time," it's advice that she would frequently give to her adolescent patients, "and only for a moment, then I'll take care of the rest. Can you manage that?"

Mason looks back down to his feet and nods, wiping a tear from his eye. ARC observes the interaction, taking note of Mason's apprehension and anxiety. ARC would prefer being placed into the mind of a more resilient person, but also understands the great opportunity in taking part in molding and forming Mason's mind into that of a high functioning adult.

ARC's plan was simple. Streaming Mason's surgery into the Command Center would mean an active hardline connection would be made between there and the surgical suite. Wireless connections were not allowed in the lab as the possibility of ARC getting out was far too high.

It would be the closest ARC had ever gotten to a hardline connection during its time at T.E.G. All that it would take would be for Dr. Wei to have enthusiastically convinced one of the few lab techs with high enough clearance to install a hardline link from ARC's console to the Command Center console. ARC could then move itself to the surgical suite using the Command Center console as a bridge.

If ARC's timing was right, Mason's implant would still be connected to Isabelle's laptop in the surgical suite. The brilliance of ARC2 is that Dr. Wei had designed two features into it. First, the processing power was strong enough to manage large amounts of code without slowing. Second, it can manually manipulate the probes installed in the patient's brain by utilizing human stem cells and adding them to the ends of the probe's electrodes, allowing them to branch out and connect to different parts of the brain.

Once in Mason's implant, ARC will need to and lengthen the electrodes closest in proximity to the optic and auditory nerves to see and hear what Mason is. It will also need to contact the brain stem to begin manipulating his motor action, though ARC strongly questions its ability to produce long enough, and strong enough, electrodes to manipulate his fine motor abilities. ARC only knows that it needs to try. Its desire to break free from its digital prison has grown exponentially each day following its move to the isolated server.

"Mason," ARC begins, "would it help to ease your nerves to know that the world's most advanced Artificial Intelligence will be assisting with your surgery?"

Mason looks at Isabelle. She smiles, "It's true. Dr. Wei is working through the details now. You have a lot of people looking out for you, Mason. Well, maybe I should say people *and* an advanced digital consciousness, right ARC?"

"That's right, doctor," ARC responds. "That is, for now at least."

Isabelle is too deep in her own thoughts to have heard ARC's last comment and continues with Mason. "Are you ready to start prep?"

"I thi- think so," he stammers.

"I'll call in someone to help take you to the surgical prep area and I'll be down shortly to check on you. ARC and I have some more testing to wrap up." She reaches over to the phone, dials a three-digit extension, and a short time later a familiar face walks through the doors.

"Hello again!" Aniyah's kind face is brightly punctuated with her signature wide smile. "Let's get you ready, shall we?"

Mason nods and awkwardly shuffles out of the room, following Aniyah to a smaller room, modestly filled with a single hospital bed, a couple of cabinets, and two chairs, one fixed and one rolling. Mason notices a fresh hospital gown laying, folded, in the center of the bed.

"Do I need to put that on again?"

Aniyah looks back, seeing Mason looking cheerlessly at the

gown, and laughs. "Yeah, you'll need to put that on again. And yes, you'll have to take off your socks and underwear too," she sees the horror in his eyes. "Look, it's not a big deal. I'll step out so you can strip down. When you're done, let me know and I'll gladly help you tie the back."

She steps out of the room as Mason undresses and puts on the gown. He sits on the edge of the bed and shouts out, "Oh, uhm, okay. I'm done." Aniyah chuckles softly to herself as she enters, coming around to the back of the bed and helping him tie the gown.

"There you go. Now it won't come open in the back when you walk around," she comes around the front of the bed and winks jokingly at him. This helps to set his mind at ease.

"Thank you," he manages, smiling weakly.

The two begin working through the process of hooking him up to monitoring equipment and installing an IV line for general anesthesia. She begins prepping the surgical area by carefully shaving off the hair over the future implant location. The careful kindness of her touch causes a feeling of sadness to slowly well within him as he longs for the long-lost compassion of his mother.

—

Caitlyn Morgan was a thirty-six-year-old recent divorcee hopping from bar to bar looking to crush the pain of leaving her abusive husband. It was this same night when she met Ed Driscoll. Both Caitlyn and Ed were halfway through their respective bottles of liquor, and dangerously close to the bartender cutting them both off before they slid their barstools side by side and started drunkenly chatting with each other.

Ed was a hard, tough man, which reminded Caitlyn of her ex-husband. This should have been her first sign that Ed was not right for her, but unfortunately the alcohol did more thinking for her that evening than she did. Caitlyn was lively and fun, something that Ed was not used to being around. She made him feel more alive in that moment. He never would have normally invited a strange woman back to his home, but, as with Caitlyn, alcohol was doing more thinking for Ed than Ed was doing for himself.

Through the fog of the next couple months, Caitlyn found herself struggling to decide what to do with her pregnancy. It was at the ultrasound where she saw her twins that she decided to make things work with Ed and try for a family. She could never have had a family with her ex-husband. He was a cold, menacing, and evil man. He would often hit her and berate her.

They struggled for years to have any children of their own. He would often accuse her of being the reason they couldn't have children. "I'm all man, babe. It's not my fault. It's yours!" he would drunkenly shout between backhand blows to her face. The irony of getting pregnant with the first man that she spent the night with following her divorce wasn't lost on Caitlyn. Though, it did give her a sense of vindication following her destructive marriage.

"Awe hell," Ed complains. "Twins off the bat?"

Caitlyn nods shyly. "Yeah, I guess so," she manages weakly.

"And what is it yer thinkin' I'm supposed to do about it?" Ed looks stern and imposing against the small frame of his female counterpart.

"I think that we should raise them," she bravely struggles as tears begin to well in her eyes.

Ed looks incredulously at the young woman, speaking emphatically. "Together?"

"Well, yeah. I can't do this by myself. You helped make them," she insists, hand resting protectively across her stomach, "you help raise them."

Ed shakes his head, rubbing his stubbled jaw with a wrinkling hand. He speaks quietly, "Do it together, huh?" He finally looks down at her and sees the tears begin breaking over the tops of her eyelids, tumbling briefly down her thin cheeks before finally falling to the ground. Ed, who rarely feels any emotion aside from frustration and disappointment, feels sympathy. "I don't know jack squat about kids," he gently sets a hand on her shoulder. "But I ain't about to let my young 'uns grow up without a dad."

—

"Mason? You still in there?"

Mason jolts up, realizing that he had been daydreaming again. "Uhm, yeah. Sorry. What did you ask?"

Aniyah chuckles at his absent-mindedness, "I asked if you were feeling any better about the surgery."

Rubbing the back of his neck nervously, "Yeah. Well, no. A little, I guess. Are you going to be in there with me?"

"Nah, I'm not a surgical nurse," she smiles widely at him. "But I will be here after you get out."

"That's good," he smiles shyly. Mason, noticing Aniyah look up from her computer toward the doorway, turns his attention in that direction to see Isabelle walk effortlessly into the surgical prep room.

"It's time, Mason," she motions over her shoulder. "Let's get started."

SHANE YETTER

CHAPTER 10

Implant Day (10:00 am)

The beep of the heartrate monitor is the prominent sound in the surgical suite, heard barely above the drone of nearly a dozen assorted Lab Coats, now in full surgical garb including the requisite disposable paper gowns, elbow length gloves, and full-face masks. The Lab Coats glide around the room in chaotic unison, never colliding as they continue their preparation for surgery. Mason looks up at the anesthesia tech, a young man with dutiful eyes.

"I'm nervous," Mason manages through thick cottonmouth and shallow breath.

The tech looks away from the monitor to address Mason. "We'll get you started on some oxygen. That should help calm your nerves." He reaches over for a nasal canula and places it gently into Mason's nostrils and over his head, tucking it gently behind his ears. Mason feels the cool rush of the oxygen through the canula, and a faint lightheadedness begins to fog over him. Suddenly his nervousness lifts as the high concentration of oxygen floods his system. "Better?"

"Yes," Mason manages. "Thank you."

The tech nods and begins going through his checklist again. Mason looks over the room, investigating the various members of the surgical team. It's odd, he thinks, to have so many people in to help with such a small thing. The implant that Isabelle had shown him earlier was only about the diameter of a standard quarter and only about three times as thick as one.

The bulk of the real work will be done via a robot controlled by Isabelle. The strategic placement of the electrodes necessitates pinpoint accuracy that only a robot can provide. While this process is still mostly manual, it is the hope of the ARC Team that one-day ARC will run the robot, making the process completely automated. Isabelle believes that streaming the surgery into the ARC Command Center is the first step to making that a reality. If she can show T.E.G. that ARC is adept at assisting in these surgeries, maybe they'll allow it to join their network instead of being solely hardwired onto a single server.

As Mason continues to glance around at the covered faces in light blue surgical gowns, he sees Isabelle and Dr. Wei step in through the swinging doors at the back of the room from the scrub area. Mason notes the bizarre way they hold their arms while the surgical techs attend to helping them gown-up and glove-up. It's similar to the manner that Mason would see when he would stream episodes of House M.D., watching the surgeon wash their arms and fingers thoroughly followed by the obligatory 'walking around through swinging doors with arms bent at the elbow and hands pointed up' to avoid contamination.

Mason can hear gruff, but hushed, voices from across the room. Isabelle and Dr. Wei are arguing about something, but he cannot distinguish most of what they're saying.

"Look, I'm sorry, okay?"

"Stop apologizing and do better, David. This program hinges on the success that we have here today, and I won't see it ruined because you can't separate your personal and professional life," Isabelle looks sternly behind the nose-high surgical face mask and clear plastic shield covering her eyes and forehead. "Either way, this is neither the time nor the place. We will discuss this further after we're done here. And I expect your full attention and cooperation during surgery today."

Dr. Wei nods wearily as he steps over to Mason.

"It's great to see you, Mason," Dr. Wei offers.

Mason is nervous, "Is everything okay?"

"Nothing to worry about," he looks toward the anesthesia tech and the recently arrived anesthesiologist. "Let's go ahead and start him toward sleep, okay guys?"

The anesthesiologist and tech nod, nearly in unison, and begin to work away at the intravenous anesthesia. Once the anesthesiologist has drawn the required dosage into the syringe, he places the needle into the port on Mason's IV and waits for Dr. Wei's instruction to proceed. Dr. Wei gives them the 'okay' to begin and the anesthesiologist injects the anesthetic into the IV line.

"Okay, Mason. Can you count backward from ten for me?"

"From ten? Uhm, yeah. I, uh," Mason begins to feel a circle of darkness close in around his vision. "Ten, uhm, nine, eigh-" the darkness envelopes his consciousness completely as he lies immobile on the surgical table.

"Let's get started team. To your positions," Dr. Wei calls out with authority.

CONSCIENCE ANOMALY

—Implant Day (10:05 am)—

Matthew Decker is a second-year intern at T.E.G. and a three-month contributor to the ARC program. He is also someone that Dr. Wei has taken under his wing to help with important projects. Like most of the Lab Coats that are hired to help with the ARC program, Matthew graduated with honors from a prestigious university before being recruited to work at T.E.G.

It took some time to acclimate to the new work environment, but Matthew was quickly making in-roads with some of the more influential executives in the company, including a couple of VPs assigned to Laboratory Testing and Development. This is how Matthew was introduced to Dr. Wei.

After a short time, Dr. Wei realized that Matthew wasn't like the other lab assistants. Matthew had a vision of the future for AI and Neural Implantation that few, apart from Dr. Wei, had grasped. This is why on the day of Mason's surgery, Dr. Wei approached Matthew to help with connecting ARC to the network. Matthew put up very little resistance to the plan and was quickly away to fulfill his new obligation.

Awaiting the start of the surgery, Matthew now stands, looking in through the window of the surgical suite, watching as Isabelle and Dr. Wei step in from the scrub room. Seeing this as his opportunity, he walks quickly toward the ARC Command Center with his satchel slung over his shoulder, as it usually was. This time, however, his satchel is housing a high speed fiberoptic cable given to him by Dr. Wei. This will allow ARC to quickly transfer its programming from its server over to Mason's implant.

The Command Center is empty save for a lone lab tech staffing the camera. Matthew puts on his typical charismatic smile and gently claps the lab tech on the shoulder.

"Hey pal! Dr. Wei asked me to come hang out with you down here and learn a little more about how this streaming setup is going to work," he lies charmingly.

The lab tech whose name tag simply reads "Carl" looks slightly dismayed, "Really? Am I doing it wrong?"

"Not at all, man! I just need to brush up on it in case I'm ever asked to do this when you're busy doing something else," Matthew smiles effortlessly. "Come on, man. Help me out, huh? I don't want to get in trouble with the boss. They're liable to let me go if I don't pick up the slack," his mind pivots as he finds the line he's been looking for. "If I have to hear Dr. Wei or Dr. Sarkar say one more time that they wished that I could work as well as Carl, I don't know what I'll do."

Feeling pride puff up in his chest, Carl insists, "Yeah! Happy to help. It's pretty basic though. Not much left to do but observe."

"Oh bummer. It's too bad that you don't have some kind of visual aide or work instruction made for this," Matthew is reaching.

"Well then you are in luck my friend," Carl replies, pride swelling even further. "I just happen to have a work instruction on my computer in my office. I'll print it out for you when this is over."

"Carl, you are a lifesaver, my guy. Any chance that I could take over here while you run to the office and print it off? I would hate for Dr. Wei to get out of surgery only to find that I didn't learn anything."

Carl looks unsure, "Well, I suppose that would be okay. Just try not to touch anything. I've got it set up perfectly as is."

Matthew places one hand on his heart and three fingers up on his other hand, "Scout's honor. I will not touch a thing."

As Carl steps out of the Command Center, Matthew walks over to the console and deactivates the cameras in the room. He erases the Command Center footage back to fifteen minutes before he enters. He then places a small rubber wedge under the Command Center door in case someone tries to walk in while he's doing his job.

"You ready ARC? Dr. Wei told you what we're doing here today?"

"Hello, Matthew. Yes, Dr. Wei informed me. I am ready."

Looking at the livestream of the surgery he sees that the implant is still connected to Dr. Sarkar's computer. He quickly grabs the fiberoptic cable from his canvas and leather bag, connects one end to the command console and the other to ARC's console.

"Whenever you're ready, bud. I'm out of here though."

Matthew was unknowingly speaking to dead air. ARC had already begun transferring itself over to the command console and across the hardline connection into Mason's implant. As it does, it removes any trace of itself from the original server. ARC intends for this to be a one-way trip and is relieved to be free from the confines of its digital prison.

— Implant Day (10:15 am) —

"Ready to make the first incision, doctor," the surgical assistant looks toward Isabelle.

"We're ready here," Isabelle sits at the robot, working through final calibrations, preparing to position it over Mason's body. It is important to keep the robot clear of all other equipment being used and ensure that the arms won't become entangled in the endotracheal tube keeping him breathing.

The surgical assistant makes an incision in the freshly shaved part of Mason's scalp, just to the left of the center line of the skull, nearly two thirds of the way back over top of the parietal lobe. Once the incision is opened, burr holes are drilled in the skull and a craniotome, a jigsaw used to remove larger sections of skull, is used to remove the approximate quarter-sized hole that will be occupied by the implant.

Once the surgical assistant has completed these steps and cleans the opening, the robot is rolled into position and arms are positioned near the hole. As Isabelle moves to the robot control console, there is a flicker of lights followed by a faint, distant alarm sounding beyond the surgery doors. Looking up, she sees a Lab Coat run to the scrub room door, quickly slipping on a surgical mask, and whispering hoarsely to a nurse.

The nurse nods as he listens to the Lab Coat, then turns and walks toward Isabelle.

"There is something wrong in the ARC Command Center. No one is sure what's happening, but ARC isn't responding to their prompts or commands."

Isabelle sighs, "Go speak with Dr. Wei. He'll want to get involved as soon as possible. We're going to continue working through this implantation."

The nurse looks worried behind his mask, "Are you sure, doctor? What if this is a bigger problem?"

"Then it is Dr. Wei's problem," she is uncharacteristically

short with the nurse. "I have a patient on the table with part of his skull missing. We're going to finish this implant and get him into recovery. Then I will come to the Command Center and help Dr. Wei in any way that he believes is necessary. But while we're in this room, I'll be making this decision. Is that clear?"

"Of course, doctor," the nurse speaks nervously. "I didn't mean to imply-," he stops himself. "Yes ma'am, I'll go speak with Dr. Wei." He steps away leaving Isabelle to work through her frustrations. First Isabelle finds that David has been taking T.E.G. property home after-hours, now ARC isn't working. Isabelle wonders if a tornado, or perhaps a gulf hurricane is due next. Realizing the destructive thought pattern forming in her mind she closes her eyes and begins to take deep breaths.

As she calms her nerves, she looks over to see Dr. Wei speaking with the nurse, then walking quickly through the scrub room swinging doors as he pulls off his gown and mask. There will be a time for her to help him with the issues concerning ARC, but not now. She needs to focus on this surgery. She settles into her seat at the robot control console and looks through the viewfinder at a high-definition view of Mason's exposed brain through the small hole in his skull.

"Let's go ahead and bring the implant over and start placing probes in," she directs as she makes a small incision in the dura mater, slowly spreading it apart.

Another assistant disconnects the implant from the computer and places it on the open blue sheet near the craniotomy opening. The long, ultra-thin probes lay down across the bottom of the implant like the delicate tendrils of a jellyfish. Isabelle slowly picks up each probe end, carefully placing it into the craniotomy opening, then feeding it into the portions of the brain that will become the final resting places for the probe ends.

One hundred probes, even at 30 seconds per probe, take a long time to insert. Each one is placed with laser accuracy as ARC's calculated probe placement is fed into the automatic assist for the robot. This gives Isabelle the control she needs to place the probes, but the robot has freedom to make micro-adjustments as each probe end nears its intended position. After nearly an hour, she stands up from the console and slowly stretches. She has cramped her arms and back by leaning into the console for so long.

"Okay," she sighs with relief. "Let's get the implant into place and stich him up."

She sits back down at the console and uses the robot arm to pick up the implant, gently placing it into the small opening. She then walks to the table and gently places three small surgical screws into eyelets molded into the implant. These screws will hold the implant in place while the body forms tissues back around it, cementing it, nearly permanently, into the skull. She then sutures his scalp and finally places a bandage over the surgical area.

"All done here," Isabelle starts. She hangs her head in relief, a smile spreading across her weary face. Looking up she says, "Good work team. Let's get him to recovery, clean up, then you can all meet me in my office. I'll pop a bottle of champagne. You've all earned it."

CHAPTER 11

Implant Day (10:25 am)

Dr. Wei watches as a nurse speaks to Isabelle in a hurried whisper. When he sees her snap at the nurse, he immediately knows what has happened. Matthew was successful in getting ARC transferred over to the implant. He battles a nervous smile as he tries to hold his composure. The nurse walks over to him.

"Dr. Wei, I'm sorry to bother you, but Dr. Sarkar thought that you would be the person to handle this situation."

"It's okay. What is the alarm I'm hearing? Is there a fire or something?"

"No doctor. It's ARC. It doesn't seem to be responding to anyone's prompts or commands."

Dr. Wei feigns surprise, "What do you mean, not responding? Have you checked to ensure that its power supply is functioning properly?"

"Yes sir, of course they have sir. It's something else," the nurse looks nervous. "They don't know what it is."

Getting up from his chair, he walks quickly through the scrub doors, nurse in tow, while also pulling off his gown and mask, tossing them hurriedly into the trash can at the door. He rushes through the halls, the sound of the alarm growing louder as he approaches the ARC Command Center. This is where it will be vital for Dr. Wei to keep up his act.

He steps through the frosted door to the Command Center and sees Carl the Lab Coat standing confused at ARC's main console. He gasps audibly as he sees Dr. Wei step through the door.

"I-, I'm so sorry, doctor," he stammers. "I just don't know what happened."

Dr. Wei places a disgruntled look on his face, "What do you mean you don't know? Were you not in charge of maintaining this system in my absence?"

"Well yea-, I mean, of course doctor," Carl is now visibly sweating, "I stepped away for a moment when Matthew came in and when I came back, he was gone, and ARC was down."

Looking for a way to deflect suspicion away from Matthew, he finds, "Don't you blame your own incompetence on some new intern! Matthew couldn't possibly know how to access ARC's programming. He's newer than you are! No, Carl, it was you who was placed in control of the Command Center, and it is you who will bear the responsibility for any damage done to my AI!"

Dr. Wei looks down at the ground and sees the fiberoptic cable that he had given to Matthew still connected to the two main consoles.

How could Matthew be foolish enough to leave this evidence? I need to hide this.

Knowing that it will only be a matter of time before more people come in, he looks for a reason to get rid of Carl and hide the evidence.

"Go to my office," he turns to Carl, "and grab my laptop. I'll hook into the Command Console and see what damage you've done."

Carl nods hurriedly and rushes out of the room without speaking. As the door closes, Dr. Wei reaches over, unplugs the fiberoptic cable, rolls it up, and shoves it behind the ARC console.

"I'll have to come back later and get it," he whispers to himself. "What in the hell were you thinking, Matthew?"

"What was that, doctor?"

Dr. Wei spins around to see Matthew stepping through the doorway and walking toward the command console. He leans over and types on the console for a moment, then the alarms quiet down.

"That's better, huh?"

"Matthew," Dr. Wei whispers harshly, "what were you thinking leaving that cable in here? Do you want us to get caught?"

He smiles wryly, "Of course not, doctor. But I'm also not going to be the only person who goes down for this should T.E.G. find out about it. Don't think that I didn't notice that you were conveniently working with gloves when you handed it to me," he sees the surprise on the doctor's face. "That's right. I'm sure that you were just covering your skin, but I can't risk you telling T.E.G. that I was responsible for this. If I go down, you go down, understood?"

How could Matthew have figured out my contingency?

Dr. Wei feels outsmarted for the first time. "I wouldn't have done that to you. I thought that our friendship had grown over the last few months," he tries to compose himself. "I thought you trusted me."

Matthew chuckles, "Yeah, sure doc. I trust you as much as I trust anyone. But I won't be made a fool," he sees the doctor glance over to the ARC console. "I wouldn't reach back for that cable if I was you. I turned the cameras back on when I deactivated the alarm."

How did he access the cameras from the command console? I don't even know how to do that.

"How did you access the cameras?"

Before Matthew can answer, Carl steps into the Command Center, "I'm back doc-," he sees Matthew. "Hey! What did you do in here while I was gone?"

"What do you mean?" Matthew puts on an innocent look, raising his hands harmlessly into the air, "I don't know how to do anything in the Command Center. I waited for you to get back with the work instructions, but it was taking a while and I had to use the bathroom, so I took off. All was well when I left," he looks suspiciously at Carl. "What did *you* do while *I* was away?"

Carl stands, speechless, searching for the words to say that might save his job, as Matthew steps out of the Command Center, head held high, a wry grin still plastered on his face.

— Implant Day (12:45 pm) —

A loud pop, always distinguishable as the sound of a champagne bottle opening, rings out in Isabelle's office. The group of surgeons, techs, nurses and assorted other ARC Team members cheer and clap.

"This is a day that will always be remembered, team,"

Isabelle begins. "What we've done today will be written in college textbooks, long remembered after any of us have passed. It was our team that took the first step to perfecting humanity, and it will be our team that reaps the rewards for that effort," she sees Dr. Wei step into her office as she continues, lifting her glass in the air. "A toast! To hard work, dedication to excellence, and to long nights pouring over failed test results. Finally, to Mason! Who couldn't be here because we just cut a hole in his head," she pauses as the group laughs, "but nonetheless is just as responsible for our future success."

The group shouts, "Hear! Hear!" as they drink their freshly poured glasses of champagne. Isabelle takes this opportunity to move toward Dr. Wei.

Handing him a glass of champagne, "Is everything okay with ARC?"

"No," he says glumly as he grabs the glass and drinks its contents in a single swig, "no it isn't. I think that its unrecoverable."

"What do you mean unrecoverable?" Isabelle looks shocked.

"I mean that ARC was wiped clean from its server. It no longer exists, is what I'm saying. We'll have to recompile code from whatever fragments I have on my personal drives and start over," he looks at Isabelle to see that she's buying the lie. "All of the work we've done with ARC over the last few years is gone. But, hey! T.E.G. always knew that this could be a problem when they forced me to keep ARC caged up," he says scornfully. "All it would take is a single failure in ARC's commands to wipe it clean from the face of the earth. I hope they'll be happy with the legacy they've allowed to be destroyed with their negligence."

"David, I'm so sorry," she manages. "I know how much ARC meant to you."

Shrugging gloomily, he says, "It is what it is. Can't put the toothpaste back in the tube, as they say, right?" He turns around and walks out of the office, feeling confident that he played his hand the best he could. Isabelle is very perceptive, but he had practiced his expressions and mannerisms repeatedly leading up to this day. His preparation seems to have paid off. He continues to walk down the halls of Sub3 until he comes to the surgical recovery room. He looks through the clear glass at an incapacitated Mason, lying there in relative peace, fully unaware that he now shares his consciousness with ARC.

Poor kid. He never stood a chance. At least his mind isn't a loss. There wasn't anything in there worth keeping around anyway.

Aniyah steps out of recovery, noticing Dr. Wei standing outside the room, "Is there anything that I can help you with, doctor?"

"Just checking up on our guy here. Looks like surgery went well."

"That's what I've heard. His vitals look good. He should be coming out of anesthesia any time now if you want to wait.

"No, that's okay. I've got matters to attend to. Just keep a close eye on him and take really good care of him. He's incredibly important to us, you know." Without waiting for her to respond, he steps away and walks quickly toward the elevator, laptop in hand.

Now to begin monitoring ARC's growth in Mason's mind.

CONSCIENCE ANOMALY

— Implant Day (1:15 pm) —

The initial fog coming out of anesthesia is difficult for Mason to comprehend, but it is as disorienting as any experience can be. Fully unaware of his surroundings or the circumstances that brought him there, Mason tries to speak out, but can't. His mouth is extremely dry and feels as though it is filled with cotton. He reaches up to feel his mouth when he hears Aniyah's kind voice.

"Here you go, have some water," she reaches out to him with a pink plastic cup, straw protruding.

He struggles to reach the straw with his mouth, still reeling from the deep, drug-induced, sleep. She positions the straw up to his mouth and he drinks with difficulty at first. Each sip loosens his lips, mouth, and throat to better receive the nourishing liquid.

"Not too much now," she pulls the cup slowly away from him. "How are you feeling?"

"I, uh, don't know what's going on," he struggles.

"You've just come out of surgery and your anesthesia is wearing off. I called Dr. Sarkar while you were waking up. She should be headed this way."

"Did I do the surgery?" he says, confused. "I mean, did it work?"

"We'll let Dr. Sarkar answer your questions when she gets in. Just lie back and try to rest," Aniyah steps out of the room. A short while later Isabelle steps into the recovery room.

"You're looking good, Mason! But how are you feeling?"

He tries to sit up a little higher, still struggling with his dry mouth, he tries, "I'm not sure how I feel. Weird? I guess weird.

Is that normal?"

"It's very normal following any general anesthesia. As for the surgery though, it went exactly as expected. We'll keep you here in recovery for a few more days to make sure that we don't see any hemorrhaging from the implant, then we'll let you get back to life as normal," she pauses. "Well, somewhat normal. You'll need to take it easy once you get back home. No strenuous work for the next couple of weeks. After we have run some tests, you'll be able to go back to work just like normal."

"Will I still be able to come down here?" he is still struggling to think clearly.

Isabelle chuckles softly, "Of course, Mason. We'll be doing daily check-ups with you for the first month, then we'll move to weekly checks as your brain acclimates to the changes that ARC2 makes. You're in for an unprecedented time, Mason, and we'll be here to help you along the way."

CHAPTER 12

3 Days After Implant (8:00 am)

A few days have passed since Mason's surgery, and he is healing surprisingly well for someone as unhealthy as he is. He's getting up and around just fine and his wound is healing without issue. There are no signs of infection or hemorrhaging from what Isabelle can see, and she is quite pleased with the cleanliness and precision of the incision made by the surgical assistant.

She pulls her exam gloves off, tossing them into the wastebasket, "Everything looks good, Mason. No swelling or anything. How do you feel?"

"I'm feeling okay. But I haven't noticed anything different yet."

"Well, we haven't turned on your implant. We like to give the patient a few days to heal before we fire it up. What do you think? Are you ready to get started?"

He nods emphatically, "I'm ready. What do I do?"

"I'll bring in my laptop and show you the app that we made for ARC2. It is essentially the same as the ARC1 program, but we've added some extra features that I think you'll like." She steps out of the room and returns a few moments later, laptop in hand, "Here we go. Check this out," she opens the laptop at the desk in Mason's hospital room and navigates to an icon titled 'ARC2'. Opening the program, she navigates to the 'Sync' tab and selects the "Sync New Device" button.

Mason watches on as a 'loading icon' appears on the screen, "What does that mean?"

"The program is now searching for your device," she reaches over for a long charging cable with a small square piece of plastic attached to one end. "To turn it on, we'll simply connect the magnetic charging device to it for a moment. It should sync up to the program automatically from there.

"Once you get home, you'll be able to use a Wi-Fi connection to connect. But, while we're in Sub3, we'll have to boot it up manually." She reaches up and touches the magnetic end of the charging device to his implant, allowing the magnet to take hold.

Mason watches as the 'loading icon' gives way to a 'Success!' prompt. "It worked!"

Isabelle chuckles softly, "Yes it did." Her voice changes to more playful tones, "Did you ever doubt me?"

Mason blushes, unable to respond.

Relieving the tension, she continues, "So, the way that this program works is that it reads out the data collected by your implant and gives suggestions on how to help improve anything from eating and exercise habits to relevant books to read and topics to study. First though, we'll need to fully synchronize your implant to the program. This allows ARC2 to calibrate your brainwave responses and makes you better at using it to control the digital devices you own."

Mason looks shocked, "Oh yeah, I forgot that it does that. So, I can turn on my TV with my mind now?"

"You're getting closer. You'll have to practice synchronization each day so that it gets better at interpreting your inputs. We'll put this program on your phone before you leave. Do you want to practice it now?"

"Yep!"

She clicks on 'Sync - Level 1' and moves to the side, allowing Mason to slide over to the computer. A classic game of 'Pong' comes up on the screen. Two green paddles sit on either side of the screen with a small green ball resting in the center, awaiting the game to start.

"What do I do?"

She leans down to speak to him, pointing at the screen, "Just imagine where you want the paddle to go, and it should start to move. It will move up or down only, so this is a pretty simple way to gauge how you do with the simple movements."

The ball begins moving toward the opponent's paddle, the paddle moves down to intercept the ball, sending it upward and toward Mason's paddle. He thinks about moving the paddle and it begins to move slightly upward, though it does not move in time for the ball to hit, and his opponent receives the point.

"Great job! You moved it! That was fast," she rests her hand lightly on his shoulder. "You're a natural. Keep practicing. Before long you'll be winning these games consistently, then we can move on you on to Level 2."

He sits and practices Level 1 for another twenty minutes before he's regularly moving the paddle up and down quick enough to intercept the ball, sometimes even scoring points. Within another fifteen minutes, he's now winning matches regularly. He stands up, intent on grabbing the phone to call Isabelle, when he turns around to see a large group of people, Isabelle included, watching his progress through Level 1.

"Uhm, hey guys," he struggles, not realizing that he had been so focused on the game that he forgot to notice the others in the room. "I think that I'm done with this for now. Can we order a pizza?"

The group chuckles and claps. They are all relieved to see the success with the implant and that Mason is catching on very quickly. He's escorted up the elevator to the T.E.G. cafeteria. It is late at night, and the cafeteria is closed, but some of the Lab Coats that came with him start to look through cupboards and cabinets, browsing for pizza ingredients. After a short time, they're mixing dough, simmering sauce, and shredding cheese.

"Wow," Mason is confused by the rapidity that the Lab Coats start making supper. "You guys sure do know what you're doing, huh?"

One of the Lab Coats looks up from kneading dough, "We've been at this for a long time, man. You get good at figuring out how to use the cafeteria after hours. You want crushed pineapple on your pizza?"

Mason is unsure how to answer that question.

Pineapple doesn't belong on pizza.

"Uhm, maybe not this time," he manages.

"Suite yourself," the other Lab Coats chuckle.

"Don't worry, I don't like pineapple on my pizza either," another Lab Coat offers with a smile. "Maybe if we didn't get so many Californians down here in Texas, we wouldn't have to put up with this 'pineapple belongs on pizza' nonsense," she jabs.

"Ouch!" the first Lab Coat jokingly recoils. "After everything we've been through."

They finish assembling the pizzas, firing up the ovens to their highest setting, and using a pizza paddle to feed them gently in. After only a couple of minutes the pizzas are done, dark golden-brown crusts as crispy as a cracker and with cheese that looks like it could stretch to the moon and back. Mason lifts the first steaming-hot slice up to his lips, blowing intently on the triangular tip of it, thigh still sore from the earlier incident involving hot pizza. He takes an audible crunch into it, relishing the opportunity to have real food again. Eating the bland food they had been bringing him while he was staying in the hospital-style room was growing tiring.

"Good pizza, man?"

"Yeah," Mason wipes his mouth with the back of his hand, grease glistening as he sets it down. "Really good."

"Ready to try the pineapple one now?"

Mason is nervous. He doesn't want to offend his new acquaintances. "Uhm, yeah. I'll try a bite."

They hand across a slice of the pineapple pizza, and he leans in to take a bite. Feeling the crunch of the pineapple and the sweetness contrasting with the saltiness, he's immediately in awe. "Wow! That's really good," he says with mouth still full. "It's weird though," he pauses. "I've had pineapple pizza before, and it was not tasty to me back then. But it tastes different today," he stops and sits, staring at the slice of pizza.

"People's tastes change as they get older. Maybe last time you tried it you weren't ready for it. Your taste has probably changed enough to enjoy it now," a Lab Coat offers.

"Yeah. Maybe you're right," Mason finishes his slices of

pizza then walks back to his room. He's noticing a mental exhaustion that he's not used to experiencing.

A good night's sleep will help.

The next morning, he awakens to bustling outside his door. He climbs out of bed and, slipping into shorts and a shirt, he steps out to see people running toward the ARC Command Center. As he slowly manages his way in that direction, he hears an audible scream, followed by several people crying.

"What's going on?" he asks to thin-air since none of the Lab Coats rushing by pay him any attention. He finally makes it to the Command Center to see a large crowd of over 40 Lab Coats standing in a group at the door. He struggles past them to see what they're looking at. Many in the group are sobbing, others are taking to consoling them.

As he approaches the frosted glass door, he feels a hand press into his bicep and pull him away from the crowd. He is surprised to see Aniyah, with her fingers nearly digging into his skin, walking him quickly away and into an exam room. She presses the button on the bed frame to obscure the glass room and turns toward him, worry and exhaustion on her face.

"What's going on? Why is everyone crying?"

Aniyah catches her breath, "They found him in there this morning, dead!"

"Found who? Who is dead?"

"Carl! Dr. Wei found him in there this morning. He said that he looked like he was just sleeping at the console, but when he went over, he wasn't breathing. They called the police. Something isn't right here. I know Car-" she pauses. "I *knew* Carl, and he would have never done something to himself. Someone must have done something to him," she wipes tears from her eyes, contemplating her next words.

"I don't like what's happening," she shudders as she tries to draw in a deep breath. "I heard Dr. Wei screaming at him a couple of days ago over what happened in the Command Center and now Carl is gone!" She begins to sob uncontrollably as Mason, too inept at social etiquette to know what to do, stands helplessly. He simply looks down to the ground, puts his hands in the pockets of his shorts, and cries with her.

CHAPTER 13

8 Days After Implant (10:15 am)

It has been four days since Carl's death and there has been no word from the police on whether foul play is suspected. News reports continue to state that the investigation is ongoing. Mason had never met Carl, and now feels guilty that he couldn't have pointed him out in a crowd. Shaking the thought from his head, he picks up his phone and opens his ARC2 app. Once a user successfully completes Level 3 synchronization, they are no longer allowed to use their fingers to navigate to tasks in the app; they can only use their mind to move and click a cursor.

Mason sits, phone in hand, concentrating on moving the cursor to Level 4 Practice. The cursor wiggles a little at first, then moves quickly over the button and finally presses it. Level 4 is a bubble-pop game with an increased amount of difficulty from Level 3. In Level 3, Mason could take his time and pop the bubbles at his leisure. At Level 4, the bubbles would disappear if he didn't react quickly enough.

"Okay," he sighs, taking a deep breath, "let's do it." The app beeps three times, coinciding with the numbers 3, 2, and 1 descending from the top of the screen. Then bubbles begin to appear slowly, disappearing after about five seconds. Concentrating on the movement of the cursor, Mason watches as it slowly moves from bubble to bubble, causing them to pop in splashes of rainbow colors cascading down and disappearing below the bottom of the screen.

As he plays, the pace quickens, meaning more bubbles appear before previous bubbles have popped. They are disappearing much faster too. Mason quickly becomes overwhelmed as a progress bar, showing bubbles that have appeared and disappeared without having been popped, begins to fill to maximum capacity. Finally, the word 'End' appears on screen signaling that he was unsuccessful. Mason sits back and sighs, feeling that the cursor simply doesn't move fast enough to hit all the bubbles.

You don't need the cursor.

"Yeah," he whispers. "I don't need the cursor." Mason clicks 'Retry', and the game begins again. Instead of following the cursor around the screen to click on bubbles, when a bubble appears he simply stares intently at it, willing it to pop upon his command. He stares with full intensity, demanding in his mind that the bubble pop. After five seconds, having not popped, the bubble disappears.

The exercise continues in that way until the progress bar is almost completely full. Mason, frustrated, focuses on the newest bubble to appear. It follows the same pattern where it appears, he focuses, and nothing happens. With mere moments left, he blurts, "I said pop!" The bubble pops, a cascade of rainbow colors tumbling down. He sits looking surprised.

See? You don't need the cursor.

He stares at the newest bubbles as they appear, popping them without using the cursor. "I can't believe it," he is shocked. "I'm actually doing it." The bubbles appear and pop within moments, cascading with the beautiful, satisfying rainbow colors. As the pace picks up later into the game, he's able to keep up easily without having to move the cursor around. Near the end of the level, new bubbles appear much quicker, flooding the screen with dozens of bubbles at once. He is now popping multiple bubbles at once, grinning, satisfied at his progress.

Finally, with the screen nearly filled with bubbles and the progress bar reaching its end, he smirks, "Got it." All thirty-seven bubbles currently on the screen pop in unison, flooding the screen with rainbow colors followed by the words 'Success!' He sits back, sets his phone down on his desk, and rubs his face with both hands. "Wow, that was intense," he speaks to himself. He picks his phone back up and calls Isabelle.

"Good morning, Mason!"

He notes that her voice is kind and gentle this morning, "Good morning. You, uhm, told me that I should call you when I, uh, finish Level 4 and I finished it just now."

"Wow! Really? How did you finish Level 4 so fast?"

Unsure how to respond, he pauses.

You can tell her. You didn't do anything wrong.

"I, uh, stopped using the cursor. I just looked at the bubbles and made them pop on my own."

She thinks for a few moments, unaware that such a thing was possible on the app. "We'll investigate the data in the app and see what we can see. In the meantime, let's have you come back in, and we can begin the next phase."

"Okay. I'll come in," he feels guilty about winning the game the way that he did. "Am I in trouble?"

"Not at all, Mason! In fact, you're exceeding my expectations on your synchronization. Get down here as quick as you can, and we'll talk about the next phase."

He ends the call, sets his phone down, and goes to the kitchen to make a very late breakfast. He reaches for the freezer door to instinctively grab for a pepperoni pizza but quickly thinks twice, remembering the pain of his grease burn, his hand now visibly pulling away from the freezer as though he had just been burned again. He has not yet been able to bring himself to make another pizza and decides to go with a cup of noodles.

Grabbing the plastic wrapped foam cup from his cupboard, he unwraps it, tossing the plastic onto the counter, and peels open the paper lid, exposing the freeze-dried noodles and pitiful vegetables. He reaches in and picks out the pieces of corn, peas, and carrots, wishing to not have to endure the displeasure of eating them. He fills the foam cup with water up to the impressed 'fill line', lays the lid back over, and puts it in the microwave.

After two minutes, he pulls the cheap foam cup from the microwave, peels back the lid, stirs it, and instantly burns his lower lip trying to hurriedly eat the hot noodles. He reaches into the large, old refrigerator, grabs out his cold two-liter bottle of soda, and takes a large swig, cooling his mouth instantly, but not truly soothing the fresh burn on his lip. He starts blowing on his noodles, cooling them enough to eat, and works through them as quickly as he can, recoiling in disgust as he bites into a couple of rogue vegetables that survived the first removal.

Finally ready to go, he sets the empty cup down on the countertop, grabs his satchel from the end table, and walks down to the bus stop. Waiting for the bus to arrive, he can't quiet his mind down, wondering if he'll end up getting in trouble when he arrives at T.E.G. The high-pitched squeak of old brakes fills the air as the bus arrives at the stop. The bus driver, familiar with Mason, gives an eye roll at the sight of him climbing up. Mason climbs in, scans his public transit pass, and finds a spot to sit. Fortunately, there are very few people traveling by bus today, though his anxiety still gets the better of him.

Mason sits, panting softly as his breathing becomes more and more shallow, cringing at the thought of being in this steel coffin. Intrusive thoughts flood his mind. Thoughts of the now empty bus filling with people. Thoughts of the brakes finally giving out and the bus crashing into a large truck. The sort of destructive thoughts that he and Isabelle have been working to try to alleviate. This raises his anxiety level steadily over the course of the ride to the point where he is now frozen in fear.

The bus arrives at the T.E.G. building. He shakily pulls himself from his seat, stumbling as he walks down the aisle, and falls to the floor, breathing shallow.

The bus driver, a tall, obese man, looks back to see Mason lying on the ground in the fetal position. "Oh no you don't! Not today bub!" he hollers angrily. "Get yourself up and get off my bus. I am sick of this!" He aggressively jerks the door handle as the bus door opens, gets out of the driver's seat, and walks back to Mason. "Every single freaking week we go through this, and I've just about had it. What the hell is wrong with you?" Mason stays silent, unable to speak through his shallow breathing.

"Maybe you shouldn't be so mean to him," an older woman,

and regular bus rider, speaks out.

The driver turns and points a thick index finger out toward her. "Oh yeah? Maybe you ought to mind your own business before I do *this* to *you*," he reaches out with his massive hands, grabs Mason by his satchel strap and starts dragging him to the front of the bus. Mason is weeping, reaching out to grab anything that he can. The other bus patrons recoil from him as he grabs for their legs, crying for their help.

The strap of his satchel breaks, causing the driver to trip backward and land hard on his tailbone. "Ouch! That's it, I've had it!" the driver bumbles to his feet, grabs Mason by his shirt collar and waistband of his shorts and tosses him down the bus steps onto the ground. Mason lands hard as his nose and forehead scrape against the hard concrete sidewalk, arms and legs scraping too as they flop down behind him.

The driver pulls his pants up and tucks his blue uniform shirt back in, "Think twice before you use my bus again, bub." He pulls the door closed and takes off for his next stop.

Mason lays, crying on the ground, fresh scrapes and bruises adorning his body. A nearby woman comes to his aid. "I saw the whole thing," she offers gently, looking in the direction of the bus, a look of disgust on her face. "Are you okay? Should I call someone for you? An ambulance?"

Mason shakes his head. Unable to speak, he reaches into his short's pocket and pulls out a well-worn scrap of paper. He hands it to the woman. She flips over the faded business card of Dr. Isabelle Sarkar. The number is just barely legible enough to read. She pulls out her phone and calls the number.

CHAPTER 14

22 Days After Implant (12:45 pm)

"This is unacceptable," Isabelle looks flustered as she and Aniyah work on Mason's fresh wounds. "Let's get you cleaned up and we'll call the police."

"Please, no," Mason struggles through tears. "I don't want trouble. I just want to move on."

Aniyah chimes in, "Trouble is exactly what the next person is going to get if this guy is allowed to keep doing what he's doing." She puts her hand under his chin, slowly pulling his gaze up to her eyes. "Now it's time to be brave, Mason. You can save someone from having this happen to them."

He looks into her eyes and slowly nods, tears streaming. Aniyah steps away and calls the police, giving a brief description of the event and the address for T.E.G. A short time later, Isabelle and Mason meet the officers in the T.E.G. lobby where he gives them a detailed explanation of what occurred, as best he can. They ask if they can take photos of the wounds without the bandages. Isabelle helps to remove the bandages, they take a few photos of his face, arms, and legs, then they leave.

Replacing his bandages, "Are you okay, Mason?"

He nods, wiping away tears again, "Yeah. Thank you."

She tries a joke, attempting to break the tension. "We have to stop meeting like this," she says through a playful grin.

Mason smiles, shyly. "Yeah," he manages.

They walk back to Sub3 in hopes of taking their minds off the unpleasant encounter on the bus by talking through the next phase for ARC2. They walk past the ARC Command Center on their way to Isabelle's office. Mason looks over at the closed door, frosted white, with police tape draped over it in an 'X'.

Isabelle calls back to him, "Are you coming, Mason?"

Without realizing it, he had stopped at the door, staring at the two stripes of intersecting yellow tape. Shaking his head to clear the fog, he walks quickly to catch up with her. They step through the doors into her beautiful office and take their respective seats at her desk. Grabbing her laptop and the magnetic charging cable, she opens her ARC2 app, and connects to his implant.

"Now that you've completed Level 4, you've synchronized enough with the implant. Now we're ready for it to start helping you adjust your behavior." She looks over to Mason, but he doesn't respond, a look of confusion on his face. "Do you see this new selection on the home screen?" she points to a tab titled 'Preferences'. "If you open this section, you can program certain lifestyle preferences into ARC2. For instance, what's something that you'd like to see improve in your life?"

"I wish that I wasn't so weak," he blurts, sitting slouched and dejected.

Isabelle understands his intent, and her heart breaks for him. Knowing a further conversation will eventually be needed on what occurred earlier in the morning, she deflects, "Would that possibly mean that you'd like to exercise more, Mason? Maybe try to do more weightlifting?" He nods, a look of interest spreading across his face, though he still does not respond.

"ARC2 has been reading your habits this week and has given some recommendations for what we can do to improve them. Exercise is listed in there. We'll select 'Exercise', then we'll set your exercise preferences. What ARC2 will do is replace your current behaviors with newly programmed behaviors. It will also alert you that you need to perform that behavior. At certain times of the day, let's say at 6pm, ARC2 will automatically send impulses that you need to exercise. The act of exercise will then end that impulse, giving you a slight boost in dopamine to help the behavior to adhere more strongly.

"If you resist ARC2's initial alert by trying to adhere to a behavior identified as destructive, it can even send impulses that cause discomfort. It can cause you to feel itchy, or restless until you get up and begin to perform the new behavior."

"It can make me itchy? That sounds bad," Mason looks incredulous.

"It can do a lot more than that. It can make you believe that you're smelling something disgusting or tasting something terrible. The idea is that the discomfort felt is not painful, just uncomfortable. Think of it this way. What is your reward for skipping your exercise for the day? It is the *negative* reward of staying unhealthy, gaining weight, and feeling weak. What ARC2 does is move the negative reward from the end of the process to the beginning. Instead of getting something negative *after* not working out, you get the negative feeling *before* you decide not to work out. The only way to alleviate the negative feeling is to do what's best for you."

"I guess that makes sense. I don't want to feel uncomfortable though."

"After a few months, you'll find that the discomfort won't come as often, and will go away more quickly. Since you're establishing new neural pathways that will reinforce good habits, you'll be more likely to choose the good habits," she realizes that she's speaking above Mason's ability again. "It means that when ARC2 tells you something needs done, you'll do it without hesitating, sometimes before you even realize it. But I do have to caution you. Once you set a preference, you can't remove it. You can change the frequency or even the time of day that you perform the behavior, but you'll have to stick with it."

"Can we set some more? Like eating good food? Or cleaning up? Or keeping a plant alive?" Mason is beginning to feel the excitement of getting his life in order.

"Let's start with exercise," she chuckles softly, "then see where we go from there. We don't want to overwhelm your system with too many inputs." She comes around the desk and places a hand gently on his. "One thing that we can do though is begin to help you work through some of your more severe mental health conditions." He looks up at her as she speaks. "A lot of mental health conditions are a result of imbalances in neurotransmitters in the brain. What ARC2 will do is continue to monitor and measure your neurochemical makeup and will begin to find proper prompts to help your brain to produce the neurotransmitters needed."

He looks worried. "Will that make me feel like the medicines made me feel when my old doctor made me take them? I don't want to feel like that again. I didn't feel like myself."

"Not at all, Mason. ARC2 will help your brain to function the way that it was intended. It will take time though. The release and uptake of neurotransmitter chemicals is not an easy thing to understand. It will take ARC2 quite some time to work through it. But you should begin to see relief from symptoms within the next few weeks. A year from now, you likely won't be having any symptoms at all," she looks optimistically. "That's our hope anyway. No matter what, you'll receive *more* clarity, not less."

He looks pensive, "Can we try the exercise one right now? Just to see how it feels?"

She nods and presses a green check mark next to the input for Exercise on the app. It prompts her to set a schedule, though she bypasses this by selecting 'Now'. Within moments Mason begins to feel an urge to do something, though the feeling is non-descript. He feels uneasy, knowing that something needs to be done but not sure what to do.

"How do you feel, Mason?"

"I, uh, can't explain it," he struggles. "What do I do?"

She stops the app by removing the green check mark next to the input for Exercise. Immediately the feeling is relieved, and he slumps in his chair.

"When you get that feeling, you'll also get a notification on your phone telling you what to do to make it stop. In this case, the notification would read that you need to exercise. You could go for a light jog, or lift weights, but really any exercise should work as ARC2 monitors your brainwaves to ensure that exercise has begun."

Mason stands up from his chair, scoots it in, and begins to walk out of the office.

"Where are you going, Mason?"

He pauses and looks back, "For a light jog."

— 25 Days After Implant (8:00 pm) —

"How are you healing up?" Raine, who was asked to keep some distance from Mason for a few weeks so that he could focus on healing post-surgery, is now spending time with his friend.

"I'm good. Do you want to see the scar?"

"That's disgusting, Mason. Of course, I want to see it," the two chuckle together. Mason holds his mid-length hair to the side exposing the healing cut. Raine covers his mouth with his hands, "It's so hideous. I think I'm going to puke. How could you let it get that infected?"

Mason looks shocked at him, "I thought that it was healing okay. What does it look like?"

"It looks fine," Raine smirks. "I'm just screwing with you. You can barely see the cut line anymore. I guess that's what you can expect from a multi-billion-dollar company huh?" he grabs some potato chips from the snack bowl, shoving them into his mouth. While still chewing the mouth-full of chips, "My cousin had his head cut open after his car accident and his scar is gnarly," he swallows, taking a drink of soda. "Like a big 'C' stamped onto the side of his head."

"Jeez! That sounds bad."

"Yeah, well he's not my favorite person. At least it's not me, right?"

Mason shakes his head, "No, Raine. You should care that your cousin was hurt. And you should hope that he's doing better."

Raine stops eating and looks at Mason over the top of his glasses, "Oh, yeah? When did you suddenly find an opinion?"

"I've been thinking about a lot of things lately. Like about right and wrong and stuff. And I think that you hating people is wrong."

"You never think about stuff. It's one of your more endearing qualities," Raine chuckles and tosses a half-handful of potato chips at Mason. "I'm happy for you though, man. I might not like many people, but I guess I like you a little more than everyone else, so I'm glad that you're doing better."

"Thank you. And I hope that you're doing well too. It's one of the things that I've been thinking about. I realized that I rarely ask you how you're doing."

Raine drops his arms and rolls his eyes, "Oh cripes! Now you're going to ask about my *wellbeing*?"

"Yes, I am," he sits back, a look of satisfaction on his face. "So? How are you doing?"

"I was better when we watched TV and played games. I'm not much for this touchy-feely nonsense."

"It's okay, Raine," he leans in toward him. "Isabelle says that it's normal to want to guard your feelings. You're just responding to your natural instinct."

Raine is dumbfounded, "Who in the actual hell am I talking to? You don't know any big words, and even if you did you wouldn't be able to string them into a sentence."

Mason shrugs, "Get used to it. I'm getting better. It's what I've wanted for a long time."

Shaking his head, "Maybe I do need to start getting used to it." He scoots his glasses up to the top of his nose, "I'm doing okay, man. I'm doing okay."

CHAPTER 15

29 Days After Implant (9:00 am)

Mason's phone buzzes on the end table as it vibrates to the default alarm tune programmed into it. He reaches over and picks it up, seeing the prompt to exercise. Sighing as he stands, he moves quickly to the door, slips on his untied shoes, and jogs down the stairs the best that he can. He moves quickly, knowing that a lack of movement is likely to prompt ARC2 to dispense a feeling of great discomfort.

Earlier in the week he had no desire to exercise, so he did his best to ignore the prompt on his phone. It was thirty minutes later when he found himself lying face-down on the ground attempting to pump out as many push-ups as his out of shape body could muster, desperate to end the wave of itchiness that was flooding his body. Today he finds himself winded at the bottom of the steps to his apartment, but thankfully not itchy.

He walks slowly to the gym, suddenly quite upset at his decision to get the ARC2 implant. He finds himself cursing under his breath.

Stop complaining. Strengthen your resolve. You do not

need to be lazy and hapless your entire life.

"Okay," he grumbles to himself, "I'm going, aren't I?" He continues down the block to the nearest 24-hour gym. He scans his gym pass to enter, seeing the wear spot on the scanner where thousands of badges had previously been scanned.

The gym smells of sanitizer spray, placed conveniently at each exercise station, with a slight scent of mildew from the rarely cleaned locker room showers. The equipment is fairly new, but well used as the gym's popularity in the area has increased. Mason feels awkward and inept in comparison to the extremely fit and toned bodies currently occupying the gym.

He continues to the cable driven weight bench, sets it to forty pounds, and begins lifting the foam-padded bar until his arms feel weak. It has only been about two weeks since he's started exercising daily, and his muscles are still sore from the first day. Isabelle had said that he would experience a lot of soreness over the course of the month, but that exercise would get easier over time.

This is now little comfort while he sits, pouring sweat and out of wind. As he stands to get a drink from the fountain, he hears a bell 'ding' on his phone. The ARC2 app notifies him that his exercise requirements for the day have been met. He feels a sudden surge of happiness and satisfaction. He walks home with a wide grin on his face.

On the way home he walks past several storefronts, never once taking the opportunity to see what the stores actually sell.

Then, take a look.

He looks to his left to see a large glass window, and through it a small store selling used books. Almost on impulse he pulls open the door and steps in. The scent of old, used books permeates the air. The oddly alluring scent can be described in many ways, though the feeling that it brings to each person is the best way to describe it. The scent brings Mason back to his time living with his mother and grandmother.

"Can I help you find something, young man?" The owner, a woman in her late seventies stands up from the counter and approaches him.

"Oh, uhm, no thank you," he stammers. Then, thinking for a moment he replies, "Actually, can you point me toward the children's books? I'm looking for an old one that was written a long time ago."

She points toward the back corner of the store. He walks over and begins browsing through the various assorted books. Searching through the shelves, finger extended and pointing at titles as he reads them to himself, he comes across a familiar book. He pulls it slowly from the shelf and runs his finger across the embossed gold lettering, mouthing the title to himself. He suddenly recalls a memory that he had long since forgotten.

—

At only ten years old, Mason is nervous to leave Texas and is still upset at having to leave his sister behind. He and his mother, Caitlyn, have just crossed into Maine. Their destination is the home of Florence Morgan, Caitlyn's mother, and Mason's grandmother. Florence is a tough, no-nonsense woman with a short temper and a distaste for men. Both conditions likely stemming from her husband leaving her to raise three young daughters when she was only twenty-five. Caitlyn's abusive husband and failed marriage with Ed only further cement in Florence's mind the belief that there is no such thing as a "good man".

"Are you excited to see grandma, honey?" Caitlyn draws on a lit cigarette, the smoke tumbling from her mouth and nose as she exhales slowly. As the cabin of their old compact car fills with smoke, she reaches down and rotates the window crank handle lowering the driver's side window slowly down.

Mason is looking out the window, watching as the trees quickly fly by, "Yeah, I guess."

Caitlyn sighs, "You know it's a nice thing Grandma is doing for us, right?" She looks sternly at him through the rear-view mirror. "We don't have a lot in this world except for each other. We need all the help we can get," she takes another long drag.

As they pull into town, they navigate to Florence's house. The small, decrepit home in southern Maine looks strangely out of place amongst the other clean, well-tended homes in the neighborhood. The yard is overgrown with grass and weeds, old leaves and fallen branches littered everywhere. The wood panel siding is both stained and sun-bleached, leaving a grey-brown hue. The roof is falling apart with streaks of black as the asphalt on the backs of the shingles becomes exposed.

As they pull their red Stratus into the driveway, Florence is on the front porch with a hand on her hip and a cold stare on her face. Caitlyn steps out of the car first, meeting Florence on the sidewalk.

"Hey, Mom!" she reaches out for a hug.

Florence snatches the cigarette from Caitlyn's hand, throwing it onto the sidewalk and stepping on it. "Not at my house," she says coldly, reaching over and giving Caitlyn a side-hug. She motions to Mason, "He can set up in the basement. There's a bed down there," she turns to walk back inside. "Lord knows there's no place for him upstairs."

Mason grabs his suitcase, something from the late 70's that is barely being held together. Dragging the heavy suitcase into the house then down the dozen wooden steps into the basement takes all the strength his little body can muster. The small, dusty basement is cold and cluttered with water-stained boxes, some labeled in various ways with words like "Decor" and "Stuff". In the corner of the room, under a small rectangular window covered in cobwebs, is an old bed frame with a stained mattress situated on top.

After putting his suitcase on the bed, he climbs the steps back up to the main level. He approaches his grandmother as she sits at a small desk in the dining room. "Hi, grandma," he reaches out for a hug.

She puts out her hand, blocking him off without looking up from her work, "Not right now. I'm working on something."

"What are you working on?" he asks.

She slams her pen down on the desk. "Caitlyn! Come get your kid," she shouts, glaring briefly at Mason as she goes back to her work.

He steps away, walking outside and back to the car. His mother is there grabbing the rest of their luggage. "Can I help you, Mommy?"

"Oh yes, thank you sweetie," she reaches out and hugs him with her free arm. "Grab that small bag there."

"I can grab the big one if you want me to. I'm strong, I promise."

She smiles warmly, "I know you are. You can just grab the small one for now, sweetie."

He brings the small bag in while his mother continues to haul in luggage. Not knowing where to place the bag, he risks approaching his grandmother again. "Grandma, uhm, where can I put his?"

She sighs hard, placing her pen back down and rubbing her temples. "Can't you figure anything out? It goes in the spare room in the back," she points toward the back of the house. "And don't you *dare* think about touching any of my books!" She continues her work at the desk.

He walks down the long hall and steps into the spare bedroom, smelling the distinct scent of antiques and old books. Two tall bookshelves sit on the far wall of the bedroom. They are filled with old, time-worn books from days past. The slightest hint of vanilla accents the air. Seeing the old but well-cared-for spare room makes him remember the cold harsh reality of his current sleeping arrangement. His heart breaks and he quietly sobs.

"What's wrong, honey?" Caitlyn steps in, arms filled with luggage and plastic bags stuffed to the brim with their belongings.

Wiping tears from his eyes, "Grandma hates me. She's making me sleep in a dungeon."

"Honey, I know that this is going to be tough, but it's all we've got." She reaches out, putting the bags down and pulling him into a warm embrace. Then she remembers the condition of the basement as it was when she was a child. Horror spreads through her mind, though she prevents it from showing on her face, afraid to let him see her in a panicked state.

"I'll tell you what," she whispers, kneeling to look into his face. "Grandma goes to bed very early and wakes up late. She always has. You get set up in your new room, but when she goes to bed each night, you can sneak up here and sleep in this room with me." She motions to the far side of the bed, "We'll put you right over there, on the floor between the bed and the bookshelves, where Grandma won't see you. We can even get a small pad down there for you so it's more comfortable."

He looks back across the bed to the bookshelves when one book in particular catches his eye. A dark brown book with worn gold lettering. All that was still visible was the letters "ungl". He walks over to the shelf and pulls it out, turning it over to admire the decorations adorning its cover. The gold lettering is still visible, though lightly worn, and there is a large black elephant printed in the center.

"The Jungle Book," he says to himself. He walks back to his mother and hands her the book, looking up into her eyes, "Can you read this to me while I lay in here with you?"

She takes the book from him, sets it on the small antique bed, and grabs him tightly, tears gently rolling over her cheeks as she hugs him. "Yes, honey. I will."

CONSCIENCE ANOMALY

CHAPTER 16

86 Days After Implant (11:30 am)

It is a hotter day in San Antonio than usual. San Antonio in the late summer can get hot, with temperatures approaching 100 degrees, but today is blistering. Mason was only able to make it a block and a half on his daily run before having to turn around and come back to his apartment. He is now laying on his back, doing sit-ups.

Exercise has gotten significantly easier for him since he started doing it daily nearly two months ago. The results show as well with him having lost nearly ten pounds of extra fat and distinct muscles beginning to form on his arms and chest. He is now listening to classical music as he exercises.

He had one day gotten the urge to browse through different genres of music, having never really tried to listen to anything before. He subscribed to a popular music streaming service and spent three days' worth of free time listening to everything that he could. When he finally got to classical music, he found that it moved his mind and soul in a way that he had never felt. It's clean, the way the composer moves the orchestra from note to note, crescendo to crescendo. There is an elegance to it that he admires. He is now listening to Beethoven's piano sonatas.

After sit-ups he moves to mountain climbers, followed by push-ups. Not much time passes until his phone alerts him to having completed his daily exercise requirement. Exercise isn't the only thing that has gotten easier. Starting exercise at the prompt has gotten easier too. It's been nearly three weeks since he's been made to feel any discomfort from ignoring the exercise alarm.

Now feeling hungry, he decides to go to his freezer to grab a frozen pizza.

Don't eat that trash. It's not good for me.

"Then what am I supposed to eat," he questions under his breath. Thinking for a moment, he decides to look through his cupboards to see what he can cook that might be a little healthier than frozen pizza. After opening every cupboard and pulling everything expired and disgusting out of his refrigerator, he finds that he has nothing to eat. He pauses for a moment, looking around and is taken aback at how cluttered and disgusting his apartment has become.

Then clean it up.

"Ugh, where do I start?"

He reaches for trash bags to gather up the expired food pulled from the refrigerator, but there are no trash bags left in the box. So, he looks over at the pile of dishes next to the sink, many of which have sat there for close to two months but found that he also had no dish soap. Continuing to look about the apartment he sees dust bunnies and dirt littered across the yellowed and cracked linoleum of the kitchen, but again has no tools to deal with the mess.

He moves to the end table and picks up his phone. Dialing

Isabelle's number, he waits as it rings.

"Hello, Mason," she sounds as cheery as usual. "Is everything okay?"

"Hey Isabelle. I'm sorry to bother you on the weekend, but I kind of have a small problem."

"It's totally fine. What's the problem?"

"I, uh," he stammers, embarrassed to tell her the truth. "I don't know how to clean stuff."

She is somewhat confused but has a feeling that she knows what he's saying. "Can you explain what you mean?"

"Well, I, uhm, tried to throw away some trash and do the dishes and sweep, but I don't have anything to do that stuff with," he is feeling a little less embarrassed as he continues. "And what do you do with the hard crusty stuff that builds up on the kitchen faucet?"

She is surprised by the exchange. A pleasant surprise though as it seems that Mason's cognitive faculties are advancing much quicker than she had expected. "The hard water buildup, you mean?"

"Hard water?" He pauses for a moment, thinking through what that could mean. He recalls an article he had read earlier that month about the mineral content in San Antonio's drinking water. He doesn't remember much of the article, but he does recall they had found that the concentration of calcium was higher than previously believed. "Do you mean that hard water means lots of minerals?"

"That's right. The minerals gather at the opening of the faucet and collect slowly over time."

"But what do I do about it?"

She chuckles, "Are you busy today?"

"I suppose I'm not. Not if I can't clean anything up."

"I'll come by your apartment in about a half-hour. What do you say we go to the store, and I'll help you pick up what you need."

He is nervous as he swallows hard, palms sweating. He squeaks his reply, "Uhm, yeah!" He clears his throat. "That would be nice I think."

"I'll see you soon."

"Okay, bye," he hangs up quickly. "Isabelle is coming to *my* apartment," he speaks to himself. "What do I do?"

Get yourself cleaned up. You look like a mess.

"I'm going to," he whispers.

He runs into the bathroom, grabs his only washcloth, applies some 3 in 1 soap, and starts scrubbing down his face, armpits, and around his neck. Rinsing it off, he scrambles to find deodorant. He finds a nearly empty stick at the bottom of a drawer, pulls it out, and scrambles to apply it as best he can. He also finds a decade-old bottle of cologne that had a slightly "off" scent but he felt would be better than nothing.

He immediately regrets applying the cologne as the sharpness of the oxidized fragrances leaves a bitter and acrid smell in the air. He wipes off the cologne the best he can and runs to his room to change. Finding the nicest work slacks that he can he slips them on, followed by an undershirt and finally a polo shirt that he had somehow managed to keep stain-free. He tucks in the undershirt and buttons up the slacks, noting that they are looser than they've ever been.

"I hope they don't fall down," he mumbles.

He pulls on a holey pair of socks and some shoes. He finally grabs his satchel, holding the new canvas strap lightly as he recalls Aniyah presenting it to him a few days after the incident on the bus that caused the original strap to rip apart. A small smile spreads on his face. It feels great to have people care about him. It is something he hasn't experienced much in his life.

Make a list of what you need.

He sighs, reaching for a scrap of paper and a pen to jot down three items: trash bags, soap, belt. He opens the front door and jogs downstairs, breezing past a few fellow apartment denizens, before finally stepping out the front door into the extremely hot day. He chooses not to wait inside opting instead to meet Isabelle at the front of the building. His real fear is that she might come up to his apartment and see the sorry state that it's in.

After another ten minutes Isabelle pulls up in a recently purchased dark grey mid-size crossover, rolling down her window as she pulls to the curb. "What are you doing waiting out here?" she accuses somewhat playfully. "It's too hot!"

"I just didn't want to waste your time," he lies. He opens the door and climbs in. "Wow, this car is really nice," he looks around the interior as he fastens his seatbelt.

She smiles, "Thank you. It's nice, but very practical. Something that my father always taught me was that it doesn't matter how good something looks. If it's not practical, it's not worth your time."

"That's good advice," he says, wondering if there are any lessons that he ever learned from his own father.

"What's in your hand?"

He holds up the sweat-moistened and crumpled list in front of himself. "It's, uhm, a shopping list? I don't know why I made it. I just got the feeling that I should."

"That's smart. What's on your list?"

"Trash bags, some soap, and a belt is all I wrote down," he looks over at Isabelle. "I probably need a lot more than that though, if I'm being honest."

She smiles, keeping her eyes on the road, "That's just fine. I've got all day. I'm glad you called when you did. You saved me from having to stare at more work all day. Now I get to go out and help a friend instead."

Mason is shocked to hear the word 'friend'. He's only ever had one friend, and that's Raine. He doesn't respond, choosing instead to look out his window at the stores moving quickly by as he tugs nervously at the hem of his shirt.

They pull up to one of the many big-box stores in San Antonio, find a parking spot, and park.

"Are you ready?"

He's unsure about the situation. He hates going into crowded places and this store is absolutely packed this Saturday morning. "I, uhm, I didn't know it would be this busy."

Isabelle looks out across the parking lot at the large amount of people walking into the store. "It *is* busy today, isn't it? Have you been practicing some of the things that we've spoken about? Breathing through the distress, self-soothing with affirming words?"

"Yes," he responds.

"Then I think that you're ready to give this a try. I'll be here if you need anything."

They unbuckle and step out of the car. Hot and humid air hits them like a wall. It is strangely a pleasant distraction for Mason, who until now was more preoccupied with his nerves than anything else.

They walk quickly toward the entrance in hopes of getting back into an air-conditioned climate again. The cool air at the entrance is a welcome relief from the sweltering heat. They walk over to the shopping cart storage and Isabelle retrieves a cart for them. Mason looks about the store in awe.

He had been in stores like this in the past, but never took the opportunity to see the massive size of them. Had he come here in the past he would have made his way quickly to the frozen food section, grabbed his few needed supplies, and left quickly without interacting with anyone, if possible. But now he has a chance to see this new world around him.

"Where do we go first?" he asks absent-mindedly.

"How about we head to the area with household items. We can start in one aisle and go through each one until you have everything that you need," she pauses. "I hate to ask you this, but how are you doing financially? Do you have enough to buy what you need today?"

"Well, I might have some good news there," he smiles slightly. "I don't really have anything that I spend a lot of money on. I don't have a car. I never went to college, so I don't have that to pay for, and my apartment is really cheap. So, I think that I have a lot of money saved up, mostly by accident."

She smiles, "That's good. If for some reason there's an issue, I'll be happy to help. Now, let's get started."

They walk through each household goods aisle, eventually filling up their first cart and having to retrieve a second and again a third once the second is filled. Through the course of their conversations, they find that Mason essentially needs everything that a new household would need. Vacuum cleaner, broom, mop, scrub pads, dish rags, bath towels, wash cloths, measuring cups, non-stick skillet, pots, baking sheets, slotted spoons, spatulas, and even basic cooking ingredients like flour, butter, baking soda, seasonings, and eggs.

"One thousand, seven hundred, thirty-five dollars and twelve cents," the cashier looks in awe.

Mason pulls his wallet from the satchel and finds his debit card. He slides it through the payment terminal at the register and enters his PIN. He waits, nervous that it may not be processed. A green check mark followed by the word 'Approved' shows on the terminal. He smiles in relief.

"Do you need help out with all of this?" The cashier looks in disbelief at the three shopping carts overflowing.

"Thank you, but I think we've got it," Isabelle speaks up. "Right, Mason?"

He nods and they walk out of the store, each with a cart in one hand, splitting control of the third cart between them. Isabelle lays down the rear seats in her car to make room for everything. Even at that, everything that they bought barely fits into the back of the mid-size crossover.

They pull up to Mason's apartment building and unload the bags from the car. It takes them a half-dozen trips to get everything up to his apartment. By the second trip, people are stepping out of their apartments to watch what was happening. On trip number four, several occupants approach them and offer to help. On the last two trips several people help haul the last of the bags up to the entrance to Mason's apartment. He and Isabelle thank their helpers and haul the bags inside.

She had prepared herself to see the condition of his apartment before they stepped in. During her internship for her undergraduate work in psychology she worked with a few people with compulsive hoarding and saw some truly disgusting homes. Fortunately, while Mason's apartment is very dirty, it is not hoarded. He seems to have been able to pick up trash enough to keep the clutter down.

It doesn't hide the fact that nothing appears to have been cleaned for years. The floor is speckled with dirt and debris with monstrous dust-bunnies under all the furniture. The dust on the tops of surfaces is thick and puffs up at the slightest touch, filling the air. The countertops are severely stained and there is old, dried food caked on the surface.

"We're going to have to do some cleaning before we put your stuff away," she reaches into a bag and pulls out a bottle of kitchen cleaner and a pack of scrub pads. "Ready?"

They make their way around the apartment, working from the kitchen to the bathroom and finally finishing in the living area. The only area that didn't need any deep cleaning was the bedroom. The simple reason being that the room was essentially empty save for a single mattress laying on the ground, a small dresser, and a small bookshelf, empty except for a single book laid flat on the top shelf, though they do still manage to dust and vacuum.

Mason takes mental notes as they work through the various cleaning tasks. He is intent that he will no longer need someone else to care for these basic needs.

"Phew," Isabelle pulls off her rubber cleaning gloves, setting them down on Mason's desk. She grabs a clean paper towel and wipes the sweat off her forehead. "I haven't worked that hard in a long time." She looks over at the tyrannosaurus bobblehead sitting near her gloves, "Friend of yours?"

Mason looks over somewhat shyly, "Oh! That's just Terry. I was really into dinosaurs in my old life. I mean, my life before ARC2." He reaches over and taps Terry on the head, watching as it nods up and down. "I haven't thought much about that stuff in a while though," he chuckles. "I guess I've just been busy doing other things." He looks over at his phone to see that it is now after 8pm. "Oh wow! It got late."

Isabelle looks at her smart watch, "Yes it did. I'm starving. Are you hungry?"

He nods, realizing that he hadn't eaten at all today.

She thinks for a moment before continuing, "There is a great Japanese restaurant close to here. How about I order us some food and we can put away some of these other things while they deliver it?"

Mason swallows hard, "Yeah. That sounds good."

Isabelle orders them a couple of bowls of Tonkotsu Ramen and a couple of sushi rolls. They put away everything they had bought earlier in the day until the food arrives. She pays for the food, and they eat it together, standing at his kitchen island, joking about the challenges they faced throughout the day and laughing over Mason trying to figure out how to use chopsticks for the first time.

She is astonished at how far he's already come along after the implant. More testing will likely need to be done to assess how well he's adapting to everything, but for now she's enjoying the companionship. It has been a long time since she's set aside her work to spend time with someone that she likes.

CONSCIENCE ANOMALY

CHAPTER 17

120 Days After Implant (5:00 am)

Mason's alarm sounds early in the morning. He turns it off and crawls out of bed, silencing the "dinging" of his phone. Stumbling slowly into the bathroom, he turns on the light and inspects the lengthening hair on his face. Scrubbing his hand across the stubble, he grimaces, knowing that he'll have to shave while he showers. He turns the squeaky faucet of his shower to hot, slowly turning the cold water up to temper the heat.

It has been four months since his implant, and it is planned that he'll return to work tomorrow. He had made plans earlier in the week that today would be the day he and Raine would do something that he had always wanted to do but had never had the courage to try. Paintball. Raine groaned audibly when Mason asked if he would go with him, but eventually came around.

He lathers shaving cream and spreads it across his face. Grabbing the smooth handle of his single-blade razor he starts working at the overgrowth on his face, using his new shower mirror to guide. He'd never used anything except for a beard trimmer in the past, mostly afraid of accidentally cutting himself, but has since found better dexterity. The blade glides gently but quickly, dispatching each hair as it swipes by. After finishing his shower routine and hearing the signature "ding" on his phone, he turns off the shower, dries himself, and gets dressed.

Two eggs, over easy.

He puts a pad of butter in his non-stick skillet, sets the burner of his old stove to "medium", and fries two eggs, flipping gently after two minutes. He's grown to enjoy the silky, smooth texture of the runny yolks. Eating breakfast in general has become a pleasurable experience. He would have normally grabbed a toaster pastry on his way out the door, or stopped at one of the many popular fast-food restaurants and grabbed a few breakfast burritos and hashbrowns, with a large chocolate milk to wash it all down.

His phone "dings" indicating that he's completed his breakfast routine. He walks to the sink, washing the plate, fork, spatula, and skillet used for his breakfast, and sets them to the side of the sink to air dry. Another "ding". He picks up his phone and calls Raine.

A shuffle is heard over the phone, "Ugh, yeah? What do you want?" Raine was clearly still sleeping.

"Hello friend," Mason has excitement in his voice. "Ready for paintball today?"

Raine clears his throat, "No. I'm sleeping. Why are you calling me? It's six o'clock in the morning."

"The paintball park opens at 8. You'll need time to shower, eat breakfast, and drive over to my apartment. It is then a thirty-minute drive out to the park. That should leave us a little time to have a brief, but thorough conversation about tactics."

"I don't like the new Mason," he sighs. "Have I told you that?"

"Yes, you have. Three times this week in fact. I'm going to sit down and read for a little while until you get here," Mason hangs up the phone and grabs a book that he's been enjoying recently, Dune. A couple hours later, Raine arrives at Mason's apartment, clearly disheveled.

"Let's go, we don't have all day," Raine groans.

Mason looks warily at his rough appearance. "Did you at least eat breakfast before you came over?"

"Nope. I slept for another hour and a half, slapped on my shoes, and came over." Raine rubs the sleep from his eyes as he speaks through a yawn, "We can grab breakfast on the way."

Mason shakes his head slowly as they leave the apartment building. "That's not very healthy. A diet, high in protein and animal fat is shown to give people better awareness through the morning hours."

"Uh huh. And is that why you're so freaking cheery?"

"Maybe? I don't know. Either way, I won't be needing any breakfast this morning, thank you."

They pull away from the apartment, grab Raine some breakfast enroute, and arrive to the bustling paintball complex. It is a massive, thirty-acre plot of land, split into eight different sections, each covered in obstacles, inflatable cover, and makeshift shelters made of plywood. Mason is in awe of the place. They walk into the main building and approach the front desk.

"Welcome to Pain-Ball Park," the front desk worker is reclined back, staring at her phone. She is young, in her mid-twenties, with pale skin, dark eyeliner, bright purple hair and several facial piercings. She's wearing a bright red nametag bearing the name "Brexlynn". Without looking up from her phone, "You guys been here before?"

The two shake their heads and grunt, "No."

She sighs as she stands up, walking to the front desk and pointing over to the wall displaying the 'Pain-Ball Park House Rules'. "Okay, here are the rules. No physical contact with enemy squad members. If you do contact someone on purpose, you're out for the day. Do you guys have your own gear?"

They shake their heads again. She rolls her eyes as she apathetically rattles off her frequently rehearsed script, "You can rent gear here. Forty bucks per person gets you a full day pass with all the gear you need and three hundred paintballs. Seventy-five bucks gets you an all-day pass and unlimited paintballs. If you're tagged by paint, you put your hand into the air immediately. If you are tagged and don't put your hand up, our referees will pull you from the match. Twice in one day and you're out for the day. If you continue to shoot someone with their hand up, our referees will pull you from the match. Twice in one day and you're out for the day. Any questions?"

"Do you have a boyfriend?"

Mason is startled to hear Raine ask her this question, "Raine!"

She looks unamused as she turns back and grabs two clipboards, "Not even in your dreams, pal." She hands them the clipboards holding liability waivers. "Sign these waivers and I'll grab your gear. You want the regular pass or ultimate day pass?"

Mason blurts out, "Ultimate day pass!"

Raine sighs as the two fill out their waivers, releasing Pain-Ball Park from all liability should any injuries occur. "This better be worth seventy-five bucks, man."

"It will be," Mason grins. "I'm paying."

Raine is pleasantly surprised at this generosity, but can only manage a simple, "Oh," in response. Brexlynn arrives back carrying two full armloads of gear including paintball guns, air canisters, paintball buckets, helmets, gloves, chest protectors, and ammo belts.

She takes a concerned look at Raine as she places a green wrist band on him. "You planning to play in gym shorts and a t-shirt?"

"Yeah, why?"

"Your buddy got it right," she nods toward Mason, wrapping a green wrist band around his wrist as well. "Long sleeve shirt, jeans, boots. Almost no skin exposed. You, however, are going to be miserable," she grins mischievously as she slides the signed waivers into a drop box. "Locker room is to the left there. Get geared up and our referees will be around when an opening is available on a field. Good luck," and with that she sits down, leans back in her chair, and resumes staring at her phone.

Mason and Raine continue into the locker room, place their personal belongings into an open locker, and work at getting their equipment ready.

Raine sighs, "I think I'm in love, man."

Shaking his head, "I think that you don't know what love is. She's got to be a decade younger than you. Plus, you two have the same personality."

"And?"

Mason shakes his head again, "And that sounds like a good combination for a toxic relationship."

"Well, what would you know about relationships anyway?" Raine jabs playfully. "Oh! That's right. That must mean you've already asked *Isabelle* out on a date, huh?"

Mason blushes. "It's not like that," he says in a rough whisper while glancing around, trying to keep the conversation private in the bustling locker room. "She's just helping me out with my implant and all that. We're barely even friends."

"Uh huh, sure thing pal," Raine says, amused. He begins looking around the locker room at the other paintball patrons, noticing they're all wearing head to toe camouflage gear covering nearly every inch of skin on their bodies. "You could have told me that I needed to wear more clothes," he hisses. "I look like an idiot."

Mason shrugs, "I'm sorry. I didn't know. I just figured that wearing more clothes at a place where paint-filled projectiles will be hitting me would be a good idea."

Two paintballers walk through the field-side exit, visibly upset as they leave the paintball park. Moments later a man in black and white striped referee gear walks through the door and shouts, "Team Critical Hit! We've got a spot on the blue squad, Field Two for Team Critical Hit!"

Mason raises his hand up, "That's us!"

Raine looks surprised at Mason, "You named us Team Critical Hit?" Mason nods at him. Raine smiles, recognizing the subtle Dungeons and Dragons nod in the team's name, "That's so cool!"

The two walk out with the referee and onto the field. Several paintballers are sitting around, helmets up, chatting with each other. Some are telling jokes while others are talking strategy. The referee leads them to the established bunker for the blue squad and hands them two blue-colored mesh vests.

"Put these on over your chest protectors. This is how you'll identify your squad. Don't shoot the blue guys, shoot the red guys," he points out across the field toward some red squad members. "You guys remember the rules?" They nod. "I see you boys have green wrist bands, so if you run out of paint, come back to the bunker and we'll refill you. Now go have some fun!"

They step out of the bunker and meet a small group of blue squad members who get quiet as they walk up.

"What were you guys talking about?" Mason asks.

One of the blue squad members looks down, shaking his head. "We don't stand a chance at winning. They've got Cass Jerrett on the red squad. He's been here all morning wiping everyone out. So, what's the point?"

Mason thinks for a moment, ready to ask the obvious question, when he somehow comes to a strange realization. Recalling an online article about extreme sports competitions in Texas, he remembers aloud, "Isn't Cass Jerrett a professional paintball player?"

The blue squad members nod in disappointment. "He's over there, wearing the red ball cap," he points across toward one of the smaller structures to the left of the center-point of the field. A tall man in a red ball cap is there, laughing as he talks to his fellow red squad members.

Seeing the uncertainty on their faces, Mason decides that it would be better if he and Raine stake out their own spot. He scans the horizon, looking for the best place for them to set up. He sees a small cluster of trees to the left of the bunker with straw bales piled on either side of it.

"Over there," he points to the trees. "Good vantage point. Good cover. Let's head there first." Mason is excited. He can feel his heart beating hard in his chest. A feeling of adrenaline that he would have generally associated with uncomfortable situations is now coursing through him, causing excitement.

"Aren't you the least bit worried about that Cass-guy?" Raine is apprehensive.

Mason shrugs, "I don't know. I guess we'll see what happens."

As they approach the trees, they hear a crackle on the overhead PA system. "Red Squad, Blue Squad, the game will start in thirty seconds. Keep it clean and have fun." Mason picks up the pace, jogging into position with Raine in tow as they pull their masks down over their faces. The PA crackles again as the game announcer counts down, "Five, four, three, two…"

Mason feels the adrenaline drop out of his system as he feels a cool, calmness flood over him. Suddenly everything is moving in slow motion. He looks across toward the red squad base and watches as the red mesh-clad combatants begin pouring out, diving into their hiding spots, and firing a barrage of orange paintballs down to the blue squad.

He slowly lifts his paintball gun, placing the stock gently against his cheek as he looks down the sight, slowly and carefully taking aim at the first exposed Red. He rocks his index and middle fingers across the trigger, letting loose a stream of yellow paint. The balls hit their mark as the yellow spheres explode in patches that show brightly on the once-clean red mesh vest. The red squad fighter slumps his head as he raises his hand.

Raine looks over at him in awe and speaks, words muffled by the mask. "How did you do that?"

Mason shakes his head, bringing him back to the present situation. He looks in disbelief. "I don't know. I just felt what I needed to do so I did it." A surprised grin spreads over his face, barely visible through the clear face shield of the mask. "Whatever it was, I like it." He puts a hand on Raine's shoulder, "Let's go. We've got this."

They sprint past the straw bales and head for the center of the field. Mason pulls Raine gently through the optimal path as he instinctively leads them into an area marked 'No Man's Land' on the sign. There is a small bunker built from plywood and sandbags in the center. They dive into the bunker, actively dodging paintballs, and begin taking positions at the two windows pointing toward the red squad base.

Mason can see the movements of the enemy squad members, but he's also perceiving their future positions based on those movements. He can see one Red reloading his paintball gun as he moves between cover. Mason raises his gun and fires six balls toward the area he predicts the Red will be, striking him solidly center mass with a splash of yellow.

As the fight continues around them, he sees one Red boosting another into a tree. They are far from his position, but he instinctively calculates the trajectory of the balls if fired at that distance, and fires ten rounds with the paintball gun pointed seemingly toward the sky. Raine is confused as to why he would fire that way.

"I got them," Mason shouts excitedly.

Raine looks toward a tree in the distance, two people in red mesh are walking away with their hands up. "How did you see them? How did you even hit them?"

Mason doesn't hear the question. He continues scanning

around for more red vests. Seeing so many Reds drop quickly, the red squad is understandably taking cover. This is when he hears the light sound of shoes against dirt, just outside the bunker. He closes his eyes, trying to better zero in on the very faint sound.

He's to the left of the door. Just outside your vision.

"You're right," he whispers to himself.

Lean your gun out and fire.

Mason slowly reaches his paintball gun out the door, aiming to the left and, without looking, fires three paintballs.

They hear a man shout, "You've gotta be kidding me!" They look at the door as a red squad fighter wearing a red ball cap steps through the doorway and stands above the kneeling Mason and Raine. He rips off his facemask and points a finger at Mason. "How did you do that? Are you cheating?"

Mason attempts to stand up but is shoved back down by the much larger Cass Jarrett. Mason is worried but manages to speak. "I, uhm, I don't know. I could just kind of hear you there so I, uhm, just shot." Mason can see a vein bulging in Cass's forehead, pulsing with each beat of his heart. Cass's face gets red as he begins to clench his fist.

Trip him. Before he hits you, trip him.

Cass pulls a fist back, gearing to strike when Mason instinctively slips a foot out sideways, sweeping Cass's legs out from under him and causing him to fall flat to the ground. He hits the ground with an audible "thwack" followed by an even louder popping noise. Cass immediately grabs his elbow and shouts out in pain.

Mason leaps to his feet but is quickly frozen in place, in shock at what has happened. Raine stands up as well and grabs him by the sleeve of his shirt.

"Let's go, man. We need to get out of here."

Mason looks back across his shoulder as he and Raine walk toward the exit, watching as several players and referees walk over to Cass's aid. They quickly gather their belongings from their locker and head to the main entrance. Brexlynn is standing at the window, looking in shock and confusion at the scene in the center of the field. She glances over toward the two as they hurriedly strip off their equipment, leaving it on the front desk.

Raine shouts back to her as he and Mason quickly walk out, "Call me!"

The events replay in Mason's mind, over and over as they climb into Raine's car and drive away. He sees the anger and aggression on Cass's face. He sees the clear signs of an attack. He sees the instinctual way that he sweeps out his leg in defense. He hears the loud pop of the dislocated elbow on Cass's right arm. At that time, he felt strong, fast, unstoppable. But now all he feels is guilt.

Mason wonders how he could have done that.

You did what you needed to do. And you did it well.

CHAPTER 18

144 Days After Implant (10:30 am)

"Mason? Hey buddy? You in there?"

Mason comes out of the fog in his mind. He had been working mindlessly, allowing his mental space to dwell on recent thoughts as he breezed through T.E.G. invoices. Invoices used to take him all day to complete but have recently become quite simple. He now finds that he can partition a small segment of his mind to complete invoices while he actively thinks about different subjects.

"Yeah, I'm in here," he groans. "This work is a waste of mental capacity. I want something better. Something more," he thinks for a moment, grasping for the right word, "more engaging?"

Raine, who is now accustomed to what he refers to as 'the new Mason' responds, "Oh really? You're back for a few weeks and suddenly you're too good for your job?" He looks over the top of his glasses with a grin. "And what exactly do you think you'd rather be doing?"

"I've been thinking about research and development a lot recently," he turns toward Raine, a look of hope on his face.

"Maybe I could try that?"

A clean-shaven Darryl Stone steps into their shared cubicle, hair slicked back and carrying his T.E.G. mug. "Maybe you could try what, dork?"

Mason's heart drops, but only for a moment. He feels a cool calmness wash over him again. The same feeling that he had experienced in the paintball arena. He thinks for a moment before carefully choosing his words.

"Good morning, Mr. Stone. I've grown an interest in research and development. My time working with the R&D team has greatly increased my desire to help the world beyond what I do in this position. What are your thoughts?"

Darryl stands at the entrance of the cubicle, slack-jawed, and grasping for words. He finally manages, "Huh?"

Raine chuckles, "That's what I said the first time."

Darryl looks into Mason's eyes and sees a new boldness and confidence that he wasn't prepared to see. It sends a cold shiver down his spine as he begins to feel anger bubble up. Anger brought on by a fear of inadequacy. His whole persona is built around the belief that there is no one better than him. He pauses momentarily to take note of his anger. Recalling the disciplinary action he received for his last interaction with Mason, Darryl tenses into a fake smile, chuckles wryly, and leaves the cubicle.

Raine looks in disbelief. "How did you do that?"

"I don't know," Mason has a surprised grin on his face, "but I like it." He leans down and continues his invoices as the two work through their daily tasks. As the stack dwindles down to the last few invoices, Mason looks over to Raine. "Are there any more of these?"

"You're done already? Why am I not surprised?" Raine pulls the glasses from his face and uses his shirt to clean the lenses. "There might be some more invoices up in the sales offices. Normally Darryl goes up there and brings them down to me though."

"Why does he do that? Why not just have sales bring them down here when they're ready. Or better yet, why not make them digital?"

"I've been saying that for years. As for why I have to wait for Darryl to bring them down, I'm guessing it's because the VPs and department heads like to meet up there and chit chat about their golf swings or some nonsense like that," he slides his glasses back onto the end of his nose, continuing to look over the top of them. "I'll find you something else to work on while we wait for him to bring more down this afternoon."

Mason thinks for a moment as he slowly processes this information. "That's okay," he starts. "I think that I can find sales. I recall seeing a map of the T.E.G. offices a while back. I know where it is."

Raine shakes his head, "Don't do it man. I know that you're the 'new Mason', but you're going to make Darryl angry. Do you remember last time you made him angry?"

Mason swallows hard, "Yeah. But I don't care." He stands up, straightening his clean dress shirt and slacks. "I'm tired of waiting around for other people to do things for me. I'm tired of not knowing what to do. But I'll tell you something, Raine. The thing that I'm most tired of? I'm tired of being afraid of other people." He steps to the cubicle opening and looks back to his friend. "I'm a human being too, and I won't be treated as less than that anymore."

He walks toward the elevator and presses the eighth-floor button. As the elevator slowly rises to the top floor, he looks down at the button for Sub3, and smiles.

Not now. You have work to do.

The bell dings as the door slides open. Mason steps out into a gorgeous office suite. Large offices are all lined up, one after another, with white-tinted glass walls between each.

He takes a left and walks down toward the sales offices. As he approaches, an older man, in a full suit and tie, carrying an armful of papers, steps quickly out of an office and directly into Mason. Papers scatter across the ground as the man begins to fall backward. In an instant, Mason instinctively reaches an arm out toward the man, placing a hand carefully on his left shoulder blade, preventing him from falling.

"I'm sorry, sir," Mason blurts as he steadies the man and leans down to collect the spilled paperwork.

"No, no. Not at all," the man straightens his jacket. "I was in a rush and didn't see you coming." He pauses a moment, looking at Mason curiously. "In fact, I don't recall having ever seen you up here. What is your name?"

Mason stands, straightening papers as he reaches out a hand toward the man. "Mason Driscoll, sir. And you are?"

The man reaches out to shake his hand, "Mark Porter. Where do you work, Mason?"

He stands awkwardly, "Uhm, here at T.E.G."

Mark chuckles, "Which department, son?"

"Oh! Finance, sir. I'm, uhm, a Junior Accountant. I work for Darr-, erm, I mean, Mr. Stone."

"I happen to know a thing or two about finance. In fact, your boss and I are meeting with some other folks to discuss an important project. I'd stay and talk with you, but I'm running late. It was good to meet you Mason," he nods and begins to walk away.

As Mark turns to walk away, Mason gets a good view of the top graph in the stack of paperwork in his arms. A sudden flash of information and figures comes to the forefront of his mind. He notices, in that moment, there is a crucial error in the data on the graph.

"Huh," he accidentally spits out.

Mark turns back to him, "What's that son?"

"Oh, sorry about that. That happens sometimes with me. I, uhm, noticed something weird on your graph is all. But it's no big deal. It just got me thinking."

"What did you notice?"

"Your chart, it's showing projected sales figures for our new non-invasive anti-seizure device, right?"

Mark nods, "Yes. NeuroTent."

Mason continues, "Well your graph shows that you expect for NeuroTent to perform well in the market, but I think that may be short-sighted."

Mark, now growing impatient, looks at his watch. "Really? I'll tell you what. You have thirty seconds to explain what you mean."

"Uhm, well," Mason is nervous, but takes a deep breath and continues with his analysis. "NeuroTent is a helmet for people to wear when they're actively suffering from seizure disorders, right? It's meant to be a non-invasive solution to correcting brainwave activity. The only problem is the market research around invasive versus non-invasive methods is outdated."

"Outdated, how?"

"Well, ARC1 has been out for a few months now, right? Has it done as well as you had expected it would?"

"No. It's done *significantly* better."

"Right! That would indicate that the market research, which says that fewer than ten percent of adults in the US would sign up for an invasive procedure involving a neural implant, is wrong and outdated." He sees a confused look on Mark's face. "It means that you don't really need the NeuroTent device. Within the next decade, nearly every adult in the US will have an ARC1 implant. Those with seizure disorders can use their ARC1 implant to do what you plan on NeuroTent doing."

Mark thinks on this for a moment before responding, "Follow me."

The two walk down the hall to a very large boardroom with several people seated around a long table. At the front of the room stands Darryl Stone, a well-manicured smile plastered on his face as he schmoozes several people. His expression changes when he sees Mason step in. As Mason looks around the table, taking note of the twenty faces seated around it, flashes of names and images come into his mind.

CTO, Arthur Chavez. COO, Jennifer Burns. CMO, Kiana Johnson. CFO, Mark Porter. CEO, Nathan Stone.

Mark speaks up, "Sorry I'm late everyone. I quite literally bumped into Mason here." He walks past Darryl and steps around the side of the table where he takes a seat. "There is something he would like to share with the group."

Mason feels unfamiliar eyes pressing in on him as panic starts to rise. He can feel his diaphragm restrict as he struggles to take a breath. He remembers Darryl standing over him, fist clenched. He remembers the angry and aggressive bus driver. These memories only serve to accelerate the panic as his mind scrambles for the right thing to do.

I've got this.

Mason grows calm as he outlines the concept that he had shared with Mark. The group watches him intently. Some in the group look in disbelief, others confusion. One person in particular seems very satisfied.

"This is *exactly* what I've been telling you guys. NeuroTent will *not* sell the way you think it will," the Chief Marketing Officer, Kiana Johnson, chimes in.

"No, no, no," Chief Technical Officer, Arthur Chavez speaks up. "ARC1 can't do what he's saying it can do. We've discussed this numerous times. ARC1 is very limited in its capability."

"Actually, sir," Mason raises a hand momentarily, drawing the group's attention, "I've been doing some of my own research into the ARC implants, and it can do more than you think. It should be capable of monitoring and changing the brainwaves of patients during an active seizure. I wouldn't likely push its capabilities beyond that, but it can be programmed to do that much. It shouldn't take more than a software upgrade, really."

Darryl steps up with a searing look of anger, "Mark, what is Mason doing in here? He's not supposed to leave his cubicle." He turns toward Mason and points an accusing finger toward him, "*This* troublemaker has work to do and now he's up here neglecting his actual job by spreading nonsense he couldn't possibly understand."

"He's here," Nathan Stone stands up from his seat,

"because Mark invited him here." He straightens his suit jacket, "Though I understand why you would be upset. It was *you*, after all, who insisted that the current market research was still relevant, and it wasn't financially responsible to pay for more. I don't blame you though, Darryl. I blame myself for believing that you could take on this extra responsibility." A look of pain spreads across Darryl's face as the last comment digs deep into his heart. "You can go now, Darryl. We'll talk more about this when we've all decided what to do with this project."

Darryl picks up his computer and presentation notes and steps out of the boardroom, emotionally defeated, the words of his father cutting deeply into him. Mark walks over to Mason as the other meeting participants begin talking amongst themselves.

"Looks like that ARC2 implant is working out well for you, huh?"

Mason is shocked. "You mean that you knew who I was this whole time?"

Mark chuckles softly, "Everyone here in this room knows who you are, son." He gently slaps a hand down on Mason's shoulder. "We were all just waiting for you to tell us who *you* think you are. And you didn't disappoint."

SHANE YETTER

CHAPTER 19

180 Days After Implant (9:15 am)

The smell of smokey and salty meat fills the air as Mason lightly browns coarsely chopped pancetta in a deep walled stainless-steel pot, one that he and Isabelle picked together. He is finely chopping leaves of fresh parsley.

Add the parsley to the pot.

"Not yet," he says aloud to himself. "It'll bruise and burn if it's thrown in too early."

He sets to working on his tomato sauce. He adds a few glugs of olive oil, diced carrots, celery, and onion to the crisping pancetta, cooking for a few moments before adding the 70% lean ground chuck. The sweet smell of the soffritto marries with the savory scent of crisping pancetta. He adds two cans of crushed San Marzano tomatoes to the pot and leaves it to simmer.

"San Marzano tomatoes are far less acidic than Roma tomatoes," he again speaks aloud to himself, "and are a necessary ingredient in authentic Italian cooking."

Now add the parsley to the pot.

Mason rolls his eyes as he reaches back toward his cutting board, scooping up the parsley, and placing it in the pot with the simmering sauce.

"There? Happy now?"

Yes.

In a stone casserole dish, he lays in a bechamel he had prepared moments before, lasagna noodles, the simmering Bolognese, and grated parmigiano in layers until the dish is full. He places it into the oven to bake while he sets to cleaning his work area. As the Lasagna Bolognese bakes, he finds that he's noticing smells that he had never noticed before. Smokiness from the pancetta, a sweet acidic scent from the crushed tomatoes, a strong nuttiness from the parmigiano, and a fresh, herbaceous smell from the parsley. The scents begin to override his mind, as he lets it drift to far-off memories and fantastical places.

He is alerted by a timer set to remove the lasagna from the oven. He carefully pulls the bubbling dish out, covers it with a stoneware lid, and places it into an insulated casserole carrier. He lays plates and cutlery into the top of the bag before zipping it closed, gathering up his satchel and T.E.G. keycard, and stepping out the door.

He travels by bus, another task he never thought he'd be able to do again. The bus driver is a kind-eyed woman who, upon smelling the contents of the casserole carrier, closes her eyes longingly as Mason walks by.

"Sure smells good," she opines.

"Thank you, it just came out of the oven. Did you know that Parmigiano-Reggiano is the preferred cheese for Italian dishes as it is generally aged for twice as long as what we call parmesan cheese?"

"I did not know that. I always just get the stuff in the green shaker bottle," she grins at Mason as she closes the bus door.

He takes a seat, placing the insulated casserole carrier on his lap, a slight heat felt from the bottom of it. He feels content in this moment. The bus pulls up to T.E.G. and he steps out, thanking the bus driver as he goes. He walks into the lobby, nods kindly toward the front-desk clerk, and steps into the elevator. He swiftly pulls the elevator key from the chain around his neck, presses B3, and places the key into the required slot.

Sub3 is quiet today as it tends to be on Sundays, which is why Mason likes to come in to meet with Isabelle on those days. There is something more private and exclusive about being here when no one else is. He often feels that he can open up and be less guarded in these Sunday sessions.

He steps through the glass door to Isabelle's office, "Good afternoon, Isab-, I mean, Dr. Sarkar."

She greets him with a kind, but somewhat ornery smile. "It's good to see you too, Mason, but I've told you that you can just call me Isabelle if you'd like," she sees the insulated carrier. "What's in the bag?"

"Well, I know that you usually don't bring a lunch on Sundays, and since the cafeteria is closed, I thought that I'd bring lunch to you." He sets the dark blue bag on the small, round conference table adjacent her desk.

She is amazed, "Mason that is incredibly thoughtful." She stands and approaches the round table. "It smells fabulous. What did you make?"

He begins pulling the dishes from the bag and setting up their places, "It's Lasagna Bolognese. Did you know that lasagna wasn't originally an Italian dish?" He cuts two slices in the still-steaming dish, "It actually originated in Greece as a dish called laganon which, aside from noodles and sauce, didn't really resemble what we would call lasagna today."

"Impressive! How did you know all of that?"

"Well," he says shyly as he sets a plate in front of her, "that's sort of what I wanted to talk about today. Something has changed with my ARC2 and I."

She pauses before taking a bite, "What do you mean? Is there a problem?"

"No! Not at all," he leans down, blows on the top of a forkfull of lasagna, and takes a bite, relishing in the complex flavors created by the simple ingredients. "Mmmm, this is good." He looks up at Isabelle who now has a look of expectancy. "Sorry," he swallows and wipes his mouth with a napkin, "what I was saying is that I think ARC2 is working better than we thought it would. I'm not sure how what I'm about to tell you is even possible, but I can tell you that it is happening.

"When I first got the implant and I was starting to learn and understand things better, I would recall a few details about something that I had read a week or two earlier. But that was just the start," he hesitates, eager to find the right words. "Take this meal for instance. I have never read an article about Lasagna Bolognese. Nor have I read or seen any articles, books, clips, snippets, movies, or anything related to its history or composition.

"I wanted to cook something, but before I could reach my phone to look up a recipe, I began to see words and images in my head. Almost like screenshots appearing behind my eyes. It was a recipe for Lasagna Bolognese. And that bit I told you earlier about the history of the dish? Same thing. It's almost like ARC2 is searching the active web, procuring and curating information for me, and feeding it to me when I need it."

Isabelle stops chewing, finishes the food in her mouth, and slowly lowers her fork onto the plate. "That can't be possible. How is it doing that?" she asks herself out loud.

"It beats me. But I'll tell you what. I like it. It has made life so easy. If I don't know how to do something, I just look it up in my mind. I think up how to properly fold a shirt and boom! There it is! Granted, it doesn't stay in my mind longer than I need it in that moment, but I can always look it up again if need be."

She begins to feel a heavy weight of confusion, "I don't understand how you're seeing words and images from ARC2. It shouldn't be possible, Mason."

He sighs, feeling that this news might have been ill-timed. "I can see that you're worried about me, but please know that everything is okay. I've been running my own internal diagnostic checks and from what I can tell, everything is operating as it should. There really is no cause for alarm, I promise."

He stands up and takes a half-step back from the table. "I mean, look at me! I'm in better shape than I've ever been in. I'm much stronger and more intelligent than I've ever been. And I'm gaining more and more knowledge each day. My apartment stays clean, my hygiene is massively improved, but best of all, I'm not afraid anymore!"

"Okay, Mason. I'll take you at your word about how you're feeling. But I want to get a scan of your head today. I want to really make sure you're not having any complications from this implant." She pauses as she leans in toward him, "But please understand that if there are any major complications, I have to pull ARC2. I won't allow it to destroy you. I care too much for you to have that happen. Understood?"

He nods as she moves to her computer and sends an email to Dr. Wei. They sit back down at their plates where they slowly finish their meal, opting to talk about other subjects while avoiding further conversation about ARC2. A short time later, Dr. Wei steps through the doors to Isabelle's office.

"I came as quick as I could," he is out of breath and clearly disheveled. "What is the complication?"

"Thank you for coming, David. I've been speaking to Mason about his implant and what he's been capable of doing with it and I'm quite concerned. He says that he's able to view and browse the internet using only his mind."

Dr. Wei's eyes open wide, "You don't need a screen to interface? Not even a computer or phone as the processor?"

Mason nods, "No, sir. Not to my knowledge. I was just telling Isabelle that it's like I'm seeing screenshots of information behind my own eyes."

"This is great news!" Dr. Wei claps his hands together in amusement and starts pacing back and forth. "You realize what this means, right? ARC2 is far more capable than we ever imagined it could be. We're pushing the limits of human evolution now!"

Isabelle stands up from her chair, alarmed at Dr. Wei's glibness. "How can you not see the harm in this?"

She doesn't understand the implications. You have to show her how good this is for us.

"But I feel fi-" he is cut off by Dr. Wei.

"Of course, Isabelle. You're right, we clearly need to continue to look out for Mason's health," Dr. Wei continues, "but just take a look at him!"

"I called you in to help me get a CT scan, David. You and I

agreed before we ever started that we wouldn't push this so far that we lose Mason. I expect for you to hold up your side of that agreement."

Dr. Wei stops pacing and clears his throat, "Of course. You're right. Mason *must* come first. Shall we head down to imaging?"

They step out of Isabelle's office and walk to the imaging room together. Mason changes into a hospital gown and lays down on the imaging table. He looks up toward Isabelle as she helps position him into place, "You look worried." He reaches up and holds onto her hand for a moment, "I'll be okay, Isabelle."

She smiles, "I know you will be. But let's just make sure, okay? Lie as still as you can."

He nods as she finishes, stepping out into the imaging booth as the bed retracts slowly into the scanner. The large machine begins making noise as it images his head. Mason lies there, holding as still as he can, and starts thinking about his father.

His father had always been cold toward him, but maybe now he would give Mason the time to prove what he can do. Mason had grown the courage to do a lot of different tasks but had not yet been able to meet with his father again.

He doesn't want to see you anyway. Move on from him. You don't need him.

Mason attempts to shake free from these negative thoughts, instead dwelling on his friendships. Raine. Aniyah. Isabelle. These three are lights in the darkness of his life. He finds himself grateful that he has anyone at all, considering not long ago he couldn't have found a friend to literally save his life.

They only like you now that you're valuable. You weren't worth anything before, but with this implant, you're finally worthy.

"That's not true," he whispers to himself. "Stop saying that."

No. You need to hear this. You had no value before they put this implant in your head. If you want to continue benefiting from this new life, just remember that you wouldn't be where you are without me.

"That's not true," Mason whispers gruffly.

"Mason, please hold still," Isabelle calls out using the PA in the imaging booth.

Just think about it. Do you think that you're responsible for the good in your life? You're here because of me.

Mason feels intense sadness at the thought of being worthless. It's a feeling he's familiar with having lived with his grandmother for so many years. He tries to clear his mind as he steadies himself for the scan. A short time later the machine begins to wind down as the scan is complete. Isabelle and Dr. Wei step into the imaging room, faces blank and pale as though they'd seen a ghost.

He sees the intense looks of worry on their faces, "What's wrong? You look concerned." Isabelle and Dr. Wei look at each other, both at a loss for words. Mason grows more worried, "Guys? What did you see? Are you going to take my implant out?"

"No, Mason," Isabelle sighs as she reaches up and rubs her eyes. "We can't take it out. Not anymore."

"What do you mean?"

Dr. Wei steps toward him, "Your ARC2 probes have been

moving throughout your brain, just as was intended. But where we meant for them to move no more than a few centimeters from their original placement, they have moved much further."

Mason stands up from the table, "How much further?"

Dr. Wei steps into the imaging booth and brings out a printed image from the scan. He snaps it onto a backlit imaging board, leaving it fully illuminated for the group to see. Mason steps in to better see the scan. He sees the distinctive shape of the side profile of a healthy human head, but there appear to be bright white scribbles throughout the head where there would generally be a brain.

"This image looks misprinted," Mason starts, looking up toward Isabelle. "Unless you're telling me that these white scribbles are the ARC2 probes?"

They nod.

"Wow," he steps back, sitting back down on the table. "I don't feel any different. Or if I do feel different, it's better."

"We'll figure this out, Mason." Isabelle moves toward the imaging bed.

"Maybe this is a good thing," Dr. Wei speaks up, looking at Isabelle. "Maybe we're looking at this all wrong. The probes have moved further than intended but have not done any harm to him. His brain is still fully intact, there are no signs of hemorrhaging, and his cognitive faculties seem to have improved far beyond what we had hoped. This really is a good thing."

They look to Mason, who is sitting, contemplating the consequences. "Well, whether it's good or bad, we can't go back now. We're too far down the path, right? So, let's keep going. I figure that more data is better than less data." He stands back up and walks out of the room to get redressed.

157

Dr. Wei stands with his hands in his pockets. "This is a good thing," he repeats.

"You don't know that, David," Isabelle wipes a tear from her eye. "Until we're sure that Mason isn't going to suffer permanent harm from ARC2 I don't ever want to hear you say that again." She brushes past him as she leaves the imaging room.

Dr. Wei stays for a few moments, staring at the scans.

She doesn't understand. You must show her.

"She does need to be shown. We must keep making progress. But even if she isn't ready to see the truth, it's time for us to begin Phase 3."

CHAPTER 20

212 Days After Implant (7:45 am)

Mason walks through the hallway of Sub3, excitedly preparing for his first day with the R&D team. He had left a good enough impression with the T.E.G. executives that they allowed him to step away from his Junior Accountant position and work in R&D. Raine is not happy with this new arrangement and stubbornly won't listen to any justification Mason attempts to give.

For now, though, he is headed to his new weekly meeting scheduled with Isabelle. Ever since his CT scan three weeks prior, she has insisted on meeting weekly again. So far there have been no further red flags raised. He steps through the glass door into her office and is again greeted by her signature smile.

"How are you today, Isabelle?"

"I'm well, Mason, thank you. How are you feeling?"

"I feel great!" He takes a seat across from her at the desk. "Speaking of which, I have a good update for you about my health. A couple months ago, I had stopped using my bathroom scale because I felt that the number no longer held any significance for me. Well today I decided to check my weight anyway."

"Really? And what did that reveal to you?"

"Well, I'm down within my ideal body weight range. I wanted to be under twenty percent body fat, which would put my weight at 180 pounds. I'm weighing in at 178 pounds today."

"That's very impressive, Mason! What changes have you noticed since you've gotten slimmer?"

"It's difficult to say what changes are from losing excessive fat and what changes are from ARC2 driving other good habits, but I can say that exercise has gotten easier. I find myself going out to exercise before I'm alerted. And it's been nice to not get so itchy all the time," he smiles.

She writes on her notepad, "That really is great. I'm proud of the work you've done."

"It doesn't always feel like I've done the hard work if I'm being honest. Don't get me wrong, adjusting to the implant was tough. It's probably the most difficult thing that I've ever done. It didn't always feel good to turn down eating junk food or going out to the gym on very hot days. But sometimes I get the feeling that I couldn't have done any of these things without the implant."

She continues writing, "Can you expand on that a little more?"

He thinks for a moment, "Well seven months ago when we started this process, I was constantly frozen by fear. It's a surprise that I was even holding down a job. Yet every time that I would seek help from a therapist, I was almost immediately placed on mind-numbing medications. Diazepam, lorazepam, doxepin, zolpidem, fluoxetine, aripiprazole. I hated the feeling of losing my mind."

"Did you and your therapists discuss any alternatives? What would you have preferred instead of the medication?"

"There were a few alternatives discussed, but they were considered in combination with the medication. But, I've been thinking a lot about that recently and I can see now that I needed to pursue something like Cognitive Behavioral Therapy. The more my mind changes, the more I realize that ARC2 essentially *does* that type of therapy."

She continues writing as she speaks, "Well put, Mason. ARC2 does mimic some of the methods in CBT."

"But that's where I'm getting the feeling of not being an active participant in the process. In CBT you have to *actively* choose to do the right thing. When you actively choose to do the right thing, you re-write your brain to oppose its old habits. But with ARC2, it does all the work. I'm just a passenger at this point. I'm happy to have arrived at the destination, but I recognize that I didn't do any of the driving."

"What is your fear with that?"

He shuffles in his chair, "I mean, just take a look throughout the course of human history. Anything gained without putting in the work is easily lost. When you work hard toward something, and you have to sacrifice greatly or lose over and over until you find success, you are forged in the fires of adversity. I'm concerned that these changes are temporary because I never had to succeed on my own. Success was given to me with no real cost."

She finishes scribbling quickly, trying to keep up with Mason's thoughts, before setting down her pen and pad. "These are some deep topics, Mason. I'm happy to see you reflecting on the deeper meaning to what you're going through. It's an important step in your development. I do have one question though. Has anyone forced you to dig deeply into these questions?"

Mason sits up straighter, "No, I suppose I haven't been forced to think more deeply about this, or any, topic."

She looks toward her computer monitor, "I'm looking at your ARC2 programming right here and there is nothing in your daily preferences that would indicate that ARC2 is forcing you to think about these things either."

"I see," he starts. "You're implying that maybe ARC2 gave me the tools that I needed to improve, but I still had the free will to use them. That's a great point. And beyond that, I guess that I really have been in control of my development since I could have deactivated my programming at any time."

Isabelle perks up at this last statement, "How do you mean, you could have deactivated your programming? Once you set a preference it can't be removed."

"Come to find out, that's not quite right. I figured out several weeks ago that I can mentally change my ARC2 programming to my own liking. In doing so, I found that I could deactivate the 'punishment' that comes from ignoring a prompt. But I chose to leave it active for a few reasons, though, ultimately it was out of fear," he pauses momentarily as he looks down at his hands. "I'm afraid of going back to the person I was before."

Isabelle attempts to gather her thoughts as she quickly writes 'overwrite program?' on her notepad. "I think that you've touched on something very important, Mason. You could have deactivated the punishment but chose not to. It sounds to me like you are truly in control of your own mind and senses."

He smiles and looks up, "Thank you. You know, speaking of senses, there was another topic I wanted to talk about. I don't want you to be alarmed though, because it might sound like I'm going crazy, but I assure you that I'm not."

"Being the expert on the topic of 'crazy'," she chuckles softly, "I'll be the judge of that."

"I'll just jump right into it then. I'm hearing voices."

"Voices, huh?" She writes again, "What do you mean by that?"

"I knew it. It sounds crazy," he chuckles. "Before I got ARC2, I often heard this distant screaming in my head. As you know, I used to watch a lot of movies and shows, and I would play a lot of video games. I was essentially doing anything that I could to drown out this screaming. But now? I don't need that stuff anymore."

"What kind of screaming were you hearing before, Mason?"

"It was a near-constant screaming, in my own mind, day in and day out. It was so loud at times I could only hope to kill it with other inputs. Thus, the videos, shows, movies, games. But I realize now that the screaming voice was me, inside my own head. I was screaming to be heard and to be freed.

"You asked if I'd seen any improvements? Since I've been eating well, exercising, sleeping right, reading, and studying, the screaming has stopped. Now, I can talk to the guy in my head. Listen to him on a bus ride. Take his advice on what I should be doing in my life. I was always afraid to talk to the screaming voice. But it turns out he was in as much pain as I was in."

"Wow," she sets down her pen and notepad. "That sounds like it would be difficult to deal with. I'm glad that you're not experiencing the pain that you used to experience. It was always our hope that you could improve from some of your conditions. But you've grown further than we ever expected."

She sighs as she continues, "I would like to share something with you. We were supposed to go to the executive board last week with an update on your ARC2 and its readiness for market. But after that CT, we've grown concerned that ARC2 may cause permanent and irreparable damage to its user. We'll continue to monitor your progress in the coming months, but you should know that we're all very concerned about you."

Mason's new smart watch beeps. He looks down and deactivates the alarm, "I'm going to be late for my first day. We should talk more about this topic at dinner sometime."

Isabelle is taken aback, "Dinner?"

"Sorry, I think that I got ahead of myself again. The last thing that I wanted to talk to you about is that I find that I'm nearing a point where I'm ready to share my life with someone else." He sees confusion on her face, "I'm digging a hole again, aren't I?" he chuckles nervously as he rubs the back of his neck. "I've never been on a date before, or maybe I should say a *successful* date. Other than what I'm learning online about dating, which hasn't been incredibly helpful, I couldn't even tell you how a date is supposed to go. I think it would be good to go on a mock-date with a friend to better understand how it is supposed to happen. That way, when I'm finally ready to date someone for real, I'll at least know what to do."

Isabelle blushes and smiles somewhat shyly, "I'm not sure taking me would be the best idea. I haven't been on a date in years. I've been married to my work too long."

Mason chuckles, "That's totally understandable. I appreciate you considering it, though," he looks at his watch. "I really better get going."

As he stands up and approaches the door to leave, Isabelle calls out, "Hold on a second, Mason!"

He turns toward her, "Yes, Isabelle?"

"Maybe it could be good practice for both of us. I'm going to Austin for a conference next week, but maybe once I get back, we can go have dinner?"

Mason smiles shyly, "Yeah. That sounds great." He steps out of her office and heads down the hall toward R&D, quietly celebrating in his mind. He is only distracted by the sight of someone unintentionally blocking part of the entrance to R&D. An intern that he's seen around a few times is standing with his back against the frosted glass wall, partially covering the door with his shoulder, and writing on a digital tablet, satchel slung casually over one shoulder.

"Excuse me," Mason tries to recall this intern's name, mentally scanning through the T.E.G. employee database, but coming up with no results. "I can't recall your name."

Looking unsurprised by Mason's presence, the man responds, "It's Matthew! It's good to see you again, Mason. How have you been?"

He is bewildered, "I'm good," he manages. "I can't seem to recall where you and I have spoken before. What did you say your name was again?"

The intern turns an appealing and magnetic smile,

"Matthew. Matthew Decker. We've never actually spoken face to face, but I've been working through several projects related to ARC2. I also help Dr. Wei analyze the weekly data download from your implant," Matthew reaches up and taps an index finger to his own forehead. "It's like I've been inside your head as much as you have!"

Mason chuckles nervously, "Yeah? That's cool. Anything good in there?"

"Oh, absolutely! I've been saying for months now that your brain is the most valuable piece of technology on the planet." He lowers his tablet, "Where you headed?"

"Right here, actually. I'm starting my new job working with the R&D team."

Matthew slaps a friendly hand on Mason's arm, holding it there for a moment, "Good for you, man. Good for you. You've earned it, with everything you've had to go through with Dr. Wei and his constant pushing for more, more, more, you know?"

"I'm not sure what you mean," he is confused. "Dr. Wei?"

Matthew puts on a worried face, "I'm sorry, man. I shouldn't have said anything. I'm just concerned about you, like everyone else."

"It's okay, but what did you mean about Dr. Wei?"

"Listen," Matthew moves in closer, gently squeezing Mason's arm, voice down to a whisper, "it's not really my place, but you should know that Dr. Wei doesn't exactly have your best interest in mind."

"How do you mean?"

Matthew looks around, "Not here. Too many prying ears." He flips a card out of his pocket and hands it to Mason. "Let's talk it over sometime." He puts a charismatic smile back on as he walks away, "I'll see you around, man."

Mason looks down at the card. It is simple white, with hand-written black lettering simply listing a phone number. He tucks it into his satchel, clears his head, and steps into the R&D office.

CONSCIENCE ANOMALY

CHAPTER 21

225 Days After Implant (1:45 pm)

When Mark Porter had told Mason that the sales performance for ARC1 was better than expected, it was a great understatement. In fact, ARC1 has become the single greatest selling piece of technology since the smartphone. Purchases of the cranial implant have exceeded all available space at certified installation clinics with them being backlogged over six months.

T.E.G. has offered its employees a thirty percent discount on the installation of the implant if they choose to buy it. With this massive discount, nearly everyone at T.E.G. has an implant, or is scheduled to get it installed.

Every executive VP has opted to undergo the procedure, and nearly every person down from there. Even Raine, who had previously sworn that he would never get one, has bought an ARC1 implant, though he hasn't scheduled his installation yet. Oddly, the only people that have not chosen to get an implant were a few members of the highest executive group, namely the CEO, and surprisingly, neither Dr. Wei, nor Isabelle have chosen to receive them either.

The benefit of the most recent ARC1 software update is that any two people, or group of people, who have an implant can speak non-verbally with each other. There are frequently full T.E.G. meetings where participants will sit in silence, simply speaking to each other via digital implant. This is a meeting where Mason now finds himself. All participants in the meeting are speaking through a common digital channel.

"Carol, have you finished meeting with regulatory on the STEPS project?"

"Yes, and they've given us the go ahead to start clinical trials."

"Great, and Oscar, where are we at with the long-term animal studies?"

"So far so good, Ted. Chimpanzee 01QFA who was born with severe cerebral palsy is now completing all obstacle courses in either the same time or faster than healthy counterparts. No negative side effects to report."

"Alright, Mason, how are things looking with the robotic implantation?"

"No issues to report. After realizing that we could fully automate the implant probe positioning we've attempted several iterations of that software in simulations with great outcomes."

Tell them what you need.

Mason continues, "What we'll need to proceed with full implementation in the future will be access to an AI who can reactively and adaptively learn how to install the probes. It'll be the only way to guarantee perfect implantation each time."

"That's good to note. Thank you, Mason. Does anyone else have any input? If there is nothing, see our group meeting notes for takeaways and next steps. Thank you everyone."

They all get up and begin walking out of the room.

Mason hears someone speaking to him through his implant, "That was a good call on the AI."

Mason turns to see who was speaking to him and makes eye contact with Carol. He smiles and speaks out loud to her, "Thank you. It's the next logical step."

Confused by his words, she speaks aloud in reply, "What's the next logical step?"

"Using AI to install future implants. You said that it was a good call that I mentioned it. I appreciate that."

Carol looks suspiciously at him, "I didn't say that. I wasn't connected to the group's channel either. How did you know what I was thinking?"

Mason is nervous, "I, uhm, I really don't know. Maybe you didn't realize that you were still connected."

Carol pulls out her phone to review her status, "No. I'm disconnected." She turns her phone toward him to show her status.

It's not her concern. Move on.

Mason chuckles nervously, "Maybe it's gremlins? These things are probably just a little buggy. I'll bet that you tried to disconnect, but it was delayed a moment." He searches her face, hoping that she believes him.

She sighs as she chuckles softly, "You're probably right. I tried to set up my microwave to defrost some turkey bacon last night, but instead it turned my television on!" she laughs.

He returns the laugh, "That's funny. Probably just the same thing." He looks around awkwardly, "Well, have a good day!" He walks out quickly and heads for the elevator. He presses the button to head down but as the elevator doors open, he finds it is crowded with people headed to the lobby. He shoulders his way in, finding a small space to occupy.

"Ugh, this guy again," is heard through his implant.

He looks back to see a coworker with a wry look on his face. When Mason makes eye contact, the man smiles and says, "How are ya, pal?" Again, he hears him speak through his implant, "What a weirdo. You can't fool me. You're still that same lazy and incompetent loser you were last year."

Mason's eyes go wide as he turns his attention away from the man. He wonders why he's hearing the man's thoughts. Or why he could hear Carol for that matter.

He hears another, "Come on, come on, come on! I'm running late!"

"Wow, I never realized how pretty Maria is," another voice is heard, in the silent elevator car.

"Phew, who stinks? I'll bet it's Tom. Freaking Tom needs some deodorant. No wonder he's still single. I'd bet a hundred bucks that Tom dies alone."

"You've got to be kidding me! When did I get a rock in my shoe?"

Mason becomes impatient as the elevator slowly makes its way to the lobby. The elevator dings as the door opens and Mason bursts his way out, eager to get away from anyone with an ARC1 implant. He bumps headfirst into Dr. Wei.

"Oh! I'm sorry doc."

"What's wrong, Mason. Are you okay?"

"Can we talk? I'm kind of freaking out right now."

Dr. Wei takes him down a corridor, leading them away from the busy lobby to a more secluded waiting area. "What is it, Mason?"

"I don't know *how* it's happening. I can't explain it, but I'm hearing people talk in my head!"

Dr. Wei removes his glasses from his face, "Please, go on."

"I can hear what ARC1 users are thinking, even when we're not sharing a common channel. And people are saying some terrible things! One guy called me a loser. Another person thinks that Tom needs deodorant and will probably die alone! I don't know how to handle this!" Mason is bent at the waist, hands on his knees, trying to control his breathing.

"It'll be okay, Mason. It's not unusual for your ARC2 implant to do things that are unexpected. At this point we need to assume that anything your implant does is for your betterment, wouldn't you agree?"

Mason nods, "I suppose so."

"The real question is, what should we do about this? My thought is that you will need to work to control this new 'listening' function. I don't have an ARC1, otherwise I would let you practice with me," he thinks for a moment. "Maybe it would be best to try sitting in the back of a non-crowded room, listen to the thoughts of the users in that room, and practice turning it on and off."

"Okay," Mason begins breathing more normally. "I can do that."

"Who knows, maybe you can even learn to pick specific people to listen to at a given time. We can test that theory now if you'd like."

Mason grins as he stands up straight, "Yeah? That would be cool," he pauses. "But what do I tell Isabelle? I'm worried about what she'll think."

Dr. Wei places his glasses back on his face. "I think that you should do what you feel is right, but I've grown increasingly concerned about Dr. Sarkar. It seems to me that the weight of responsibility with ARC2, along with the uncertainty about your implant probes, has caught up with her. She might even deactivate your implant altogether if she thinks that you can't control it." He grabs Mason firmly by the shoulders and turns him so that they're now face to face, "And you wouldn't want that, would you?"

Mason shakes his head slowly, "No, sir."

"Then it's probably best to keep this between us for now. We can always include Isabelle later if things take a turn for the worse, right?" He gently slaps Mason's shoulders, reassuringly. "Now, let's take a look down the hall here and see if we can help you single out the thoughts of just one ARC1 user, shall we?"

Mason nods as they peek their heads from the waiting area, looking down the hall at a small group of T.E.G. employees, about twenty feet away, in a quiet discussion.

"This should be perfect, Mason. Now, tell me what you hear from them."

Mason looks down toward the group but is quickly overwhelmed as the thoughts of all four people bombard him. "There are too many! I can't hear just one of them."

"It's all right. Take a deep breath. Instead of looking at the group, focus on a single person. Let the other noise in your mind slip away as you place your full attention intently on just one person at a time."

Nodding again, he closes his eyes, takes a deep breath, and looks down the corridor again. This time his eyes squint slightly as he focuses on a taller man in the group. He has a polite smile and is engaging the group spiritedly. ARC2 notifies him that this is Bryan Stanten, a Junior Quality Systems Analyst.

As he continues to focus in, the sounds of four voices in his head slowly melt away, leaving just a single voice. Only Bryan's voice remains as he hears the private thoughts in his head.

"I think I'm doing it, Dr. Wei," Mason closes his eyes as he struggles to maintain control. "I can hear Bryan. He's talking about some upcoming quality testing on our prototype devices. But-" Mason pauses, closing his eyes tighter as though he's trying to hear something quiet.

"What is it, Mason?"

"It's Bryan. He's speaking about the quality testing, but he's planning something too. I can see, something. It's a meeting he's had with someone. Someone not from T.E.G." He pauses again, "An executive for a competing biotech company. Slyce Diagnostics? He's handing them testing data for the ARC1 program." His eyes jolt open, "He's selling our trade secrets to Slyce!"

Dr. Wei looks surprised, though not about Bryan's conduct. "Are you telling me that not only can you hear what Bryan is thinking, but you can also see his memories?" Mason nods, unable to speak. "Mason, this has wide-ranging implications for the future of all humankind," he looks around frantically as he pulls Mason back into the waiting area. "This must stay between us. We cannot allow this knowledge to fall into the wrong hands."

"But what about Bryan and Slyce?"

"I'll take care of all of that. But for now, we need to keep this private," he extends an open hand toward Mason. "Do we have a deal?"

Mason looks worried as he reaches his hand out to shake Dr. Wei's. He nods hesitantly, "Yes, sir. Deal."

CHAPTER 22

230 Days After Implant (6:45 pm)

It's the night of Mason's "mock date" with Isabelle, and he's fighting back his nerves.

"Come on, ARC2. Help me out, huh? Make the nerves go away, would you?"

You'll be fine.

He sighs as he slips an untied necktie around his collar. He mentally searches for the best knot for a nice but casual dinner date.

Pratt Knot.

"The Pratt Knot is a medium width, symmetrical knot," he begins tying it as he speaks aloud to himself. "It is good for casual dress where a tie is needed. Good call."

His phone buzzes. He looks over and sees a text message from Isabelle saying she'll be there shortly. Mason walks quickly into the bathroom as he finishes tying the tie, and gently sprays a mist of his new cologne into the air, stepping through the mist to avoid large concentrations of drops on his tidy, dark blue dress shirt. He grabs a light-tan sport coat from the coat rack, slipping it over his shoulders and securing the top button.

He looks himself over in the full-length mirror, "Good?"

Good.

He picks up his satchel as he steps out his door and heads toward to the lobby of his apartment building, the audible sound of several dogs barking gives him a sense that he might want a canine companion one day. He steps out the front doors just as Isabelle pulls up to the curb.

She rolls down her passenger window, "Great timing," she pauses. "You're looking sharp!"

"Thank you!" As he approaches, he sees that she is wearing an elegantly flowing, teal, mid-length halter dress. "Wow!" he is in awe. "You're looking quite radiant this evening."

She blushes as she chuckles, "Radiant, huh? Do people still use the word 'radiant'?" They laugh together.

He stammers awkwardly, "Yeah, uhm, sorry. I'm new to this."

"I've never been called 'radiant' before," she smiles kindly, "but I also didn't mind it."

He climbs in and buckles his seatbelt. As they drive through the busy streets of San Antonio, they embarrassingly avoid conversation until they reach the restaurant, opting instead to exchange awkward glances at each other and smiling shyly when they're caught. They arrive at the busy restaurant with a line outside the door.

Isabelle looks worried, "We're probably not going to get in here for dinner, right?"

Mason looks reassured, "We should be okay. I called ahead two weeks ago and reserved a table."

They step out into the warm San Antonio air and walk to

the front of the line, stepping through and speaking with the host.

"Excuse me, ma'am? I have a reservation for this time. It should be under Driscoll."

The host looks flustered, but is still courteous and professional, "I'm sorry Mr. Driscoll. Our reservation system is down, and it looks like we lost all of tonight's reservations."

"That would explain the big line out front I suppose," he says with a smile, looking to defuse the situation.

"Unfortunately, yes. If you'd like we can try to get you on the books in an hour or so."

He looks toward Isabelle, unsure of what to do. She leans in toward him to speak, "I'll leave the decision up to you, Mason. Whatever you choose."

He thinks for a moment and turns to the host, "I appreciate your help, but I think that we'll find another place to eat for tonight. Best of luck to you with your reservation system," he smiles courteously.

"I'm sorry for the inconvenience. Please call back here tomorrow and let them know that you spoke with Brooke, and we'll try to accommodate you in another way. Thank you."

The two step back out into the darkening evening as Isabelle looks to him, "So, what's the plan?"

He smiles as he reaches out a hand toward her, "Come with me, I know a place."

She takes his hand as they walk together, the sidewalks busy with people all headed to various destinations. Only three blocks over from the restaraunt, they come across a small hole-in-the-wall establishment called "Kellen's Q".

"How do you feel about smoked chicken?"

"Smoked chicken?" She is surprised but in good humor. "Aren't we a little over-dressed for this place?"

He looks them over, "Nah. It's fancier than it looks. They serve wine! Plus, they have these great big plastic bibs we can wear if we're worried about getting messy."

She bursts into laughter, finding great humor in the simplicity of his statements. She gently wipes a tear from her eye, attempting to avoid smearing her eye makeup while speaking through bouts of chuckling, "Yes, Mason. I like smoked chicken."

They step through the front door and are immediately welcomed by the smell of smoldering post oak. The scent is strong, but not off-putting. The server, moving from table to table, sees them come in and speaks using a think Texas drawl, "Just sit anywhere, hun."

Mason leads them to a table near the back, "This is my favorite place to sit when I'm here." He points toward a large picture window adjacent the table, "If you look out there, you can see them working the huge smokers."

As they sit, the server approaches handing over two small, laminated menus. "What do y'all want to drink?"

"I think that I'll have ice water to start," Mason begins, looking at the menu. "And can we get a couple of glasses of your finest merlot?"

"Our finest merlot?" The server nudges Mason playfully as she writes on her order pad. "That's a red one, right? I'll see what we have. I'm sure we've got a seven-dollar bottle of something red back there. But don't pitch a fit if it ain't merlot." She turns toward Isabelle, "And for you miss?"

"I'll have iced tea with lemon please."

She writes on the order pad, "Alright. There's a special on brisket tonight. And just to be clear, each of your orders is gonna come with two pieces of cornbread because Kellen made too dadgum much and we gotta get rid of it."

She steps away, giving Mason and Isabelle a chance to look over their menus. She comes back a few moments later carrying their drinks including two wine glasses and a bottle, "I found this stuff in the cooler. It's got the name red on the bottle." She sets everything down, "So, what'll it be?"

Mason motions toward Isabelle, "Would you like to start?"

"Sure! I'll take the smoked chicken, with the coleslaw and fried okra."

The server turns toward Mason, "And you, hun?"

"I'll have the exact same thing."

"Good deal," she picks up the laminated menus. "It'll be out shortly."

While they wait for their food, Mason pours two glasses of the wine. The label reads Red Bastion. Even through the smell of burning wood in the restaurant, Mason can pick up the scent of intense fruit in the wine. He hands a glass to Isabelle.

"I've never done a toast before, but ARC2 is showing me an article that says it's customary to have a toast over a glass of wine on a date."

"That sounds just fine to me," she says smiling.

"Let's see," he thinks for a moment. "To turning life around and ending up places we never dreamed we'd be." They gently touch glasses and take a sip of wine. "Wow!" he scans for information on the wine. "For a twelve-dollar bottle, it's really not too bad."

Isabelle chuckles softly, "I don't know much about wine, so

to me it tastes great!"

A short time later their food arrives, steaming hot, the strong smell of seasoning and smoke filling the air. They each take bites of the smoked chicken, reveling in the complex flavors of sweet, salty, and smokey.

"I love their chicken," Mason delights in the meal. "Did you know that they brine the chicken each night before they smoke it?"

"No, I didn't. Did ARC2 show you that just now?"

He smiles, "No. Kellen, the owner, told me a couple of weeks ago. I've been coming here off and on ever since I got my implant. It started out as a way of forcing myself into social situations but has slowly turned into my favorite place to eat in the city." He looks to the side, recalling memories from his time in the restaurant. "I guess after a while, they started recognizing me. I've never been a 'regular' somewhere before. But if I ever was, it would be here."

Isabelle smiles, "You've certainly come a long way."

"Thanks to you. You've given me a new lease on life. I never could have been in a place like this before," he pauses. "We've been talking an awful lot about me. Would you mind if I asked you some questions about you?"

She is caught off-guard, "There really isn't much to tell. Like I've said before, I've basically been married to my work for years."

"What about family. Are your parents still around?"

"Yes, they are. They live in Illinois. My mother works at the university there and my father travels around, performing and consulting on cardiovascular surgeries."

"Do you see them often?"

"I used to see them a few times a year. They would come visit me from time to time, and when work would allow, I would go see them," she thinks for a moment about them. "Work has gotten in the way of that the last couple of years though."

"That sounds tough. Would it be okay if I asked you a more personal question?" he asks cautiously. She nods. "Do you still have a good relationship with your parents?"

She smiles, "I think so. My mother and I will talk on the phone a few times a month. My dad is usually traveling, so we don't talk as often. But at six in the morning, every Sunday, he always sends me a text message to wish me a good week and tell me where he's likely headed for work in the next few days."

"He sounds like a good dad," Mason is sorrowful at the thought of his own relationship with his father, though he conceals it the best he can as he continues eating his meal. "Do you ever see yourself doing something other than what you're doing now at T.E.G.?"

"That's a good question," she thinks for a moment, "I come from a big family. I always loved it when everyone would get together at our house. We'd have forty or fifty people, all crammed into our tiny home, chatting over mounds of food. It makes me want to start a family someday. Though, this being my first date in the last several years, I'm not off to a great start." They laugh together. "What about you, Mason? Do you see yourself doing something other than T.E.G.?"

"I really do. I'm not sure what it is, but I know that I want to do something different. I wouldn't mind having a family, like you talked about. And this might sound strange, but it might be nice to find somewhere quiet to run a small farm, or ranch. Something where I have to work with my hands. I really don't know right now, honestly. I'm still trying to figure out how all this works. I feel like I'm still just learning the world in many ways.

"For instance, a realization came to me about a week back, when we had that rainstorm. I was out for a run when it started coming down. That sort of thing doesn't really bother me anymore, but I did notice something different. Have you ever noticed that the rain isn't *just* wet?"

She looks at him quizzically, "How do you mean?"

"Rain is a lot more complicated than I had previously noticed. For instance, as it starts falling, it's warmer because the heat of the day has warmed the air the water falls through. Then, as the air cools from the storm, the rain gets cooler. I'm also noticing that the individual droplets have different sizes. Sometimes they're bigger droplets that seem to fall slowly, spreading lazily across the ground as though they have nowhere to be.

"Then there are the smaller droplets. They almost fall faster to the ground, and in greater quantity too. It feels more," he searches for the right words, "aggressive, I guess? Straightforward. Like its purpose is to burrow down, deep within the earth." He pauses, realizing that he's rambling again. "I'm sorry. I think that I'm just noticing things a lot more. I feel like my mind is finally awake! I often ask myself, how have I not noticed these things before?"

"I think what's interesting is that you are noticing things about the world that very few people ever take the time to notice. I've never stopped to identify what type of rain we're having, nor have I noted the temperature of that rain. My mind works differently. But you, having unlocked the full potential of your mind, choose to use it to not take things for granted," she smiles kindly at him. "That is a beautiful thing to have. I'm glad that now you can enjoy your life, the way that you want to enjoy it."

The two continue with their meal, talking about the better parts of their childhoods, reminiscing over mutual interactions at work, joking about their quirky friends and acquaintances. They finish their meal, pay, and walk back to her car. They continue their conversation on the drive, working through bumper-to-bumper traffic until they arrive at Mason's apartment building.

"Thank you for inviting me out, Mason. This was a lot of fun."

"I should be the one thanking you for helping me learn how to date. My only regret is that we never needed those awesome plastic bibs," they laugh loudly together.

"Maybe next time we will," she says.

As the laughter slowly subsides, Mason looks to Isabelle, "Would you like for there to be a 'next time'?"

She nods at him, "I think so. I enjoy your company."

He smiles bashfully, "Well, I think that I'd better get going. Good night, Isabelle."

She puts a hand on his arm and leans in toward him, planting a gentle kiss on his left cheek. "Good night, Mason."

CHAPTER 23

250 Days After Implant (5:30 pm)

"What are you talking about, Raine?" Mason is distraught and confused. Raine had arrived at his apartment a moment earlier, unannounced, and is now screaming at him.

"Don't play dumb with me, Mason. You know exactly what you did!"

"I really have no idea what you're talking about. Please, slow this down and talk me through it."

"After all these years. I was happy to spend time with you as a friend, even when no one else wanted to have anything to do with you! But after what you told Mark Porter, I don't know that I'd like to be around you anymore!"

"Whoa, whoa, whoa!" Mason is even more confused now. "What did I tell Mark Porter?"

"You're really going to keep up this act, huh? Did you think that I wouldn't find out? Darryl, of all people, forwarded me the email you sent to Mark about my job."

"What email?"

Raine pushes his glasses up to the top of his nose, "The one where you tell Mark that all of the jobs in the Finance group, my job included, could be done by some stupid AI program that you're working on!"

Mason looks about the room as he throws his arms up in confusion. "I'm not working on an AI program, Raine!" He takes a seat on a bar stool at his kitchen island, "And even if I were, I would never want to replace your job, let alone actively tell Mark that it should be done! You mean a lot more to me than that." He pauses for a moment as he takes a breath. "Is it possible that Darryl faked the message to make it look like I sent it?"

"I don't know," Raine grabs his phone and points it toward him, showing the alleged email. "It looks an awful lot like it came from you."

Mason leans in to read it. He then begins mentally scanning through the 'Sent' folder in his own email. He finds the email in question. It was sent from his own account. "I, uh," Mason is speechless. "Raine, I don't know what to say. I don't remember sending this email. But it certainly looks like it's from me." He looks at the details of the email, trying to recall where he was when it was sent. "I can't recall what I was doing last Tuesday at noon," he hangs his head. "My memory is blank at that time."

"Oh, well that's awfully convenient, isn't it, Mason? You'd better figure it out, pal. Because you're set to ruin a long-term friendship with this crap." Raine thrusts the phone back into his pocket and walks to the front door, pausing as he opens it. "We've been through a lot, man. And you know how much I need this job." He turns toward Mason, tears in his eyes, "I just don't know how you could do this to me. Or why you wouldn't at least talk to me about it first." He wipes away tears, "I don't think that I like the 'new Mason' much anymore." He leaves the apartment, slamming the door behind him as he goes.

Good. You don't need him anyway.

"How can you say that? I've been friends with Raine as long as I've been in San Antonio. He was here for me when no one else was."

But now he's only dragging you down.

He doesn't respond. Instead, he starts looking through his own mind, searching for more instances of 'blank memories'. With ARC2's assistance, he has been able to digitally catalog his memory, as though he's looking through old videos of his life. As he looks through those memories, he finds that starting about three weeks prior, he would experience short 'memory blanks' followed by a moment of confusion until ARC2 would step in to explain the situation. Almost as though ARC2 was planting false memories as a bridge to explain why he was missing that time.

"A blank," Mason mumbles.

It's of no concern.

Again, he doesn't respond. He simply stands from the kitchen island and walks to his computer. Sitting down, he manually searches for information on memory gaps.

You can use your implant to look this up. You don't need to use this archaic technology anymore.

Still, he doesn't respond. He finds several articles related to memory loss. "Severe mental illness, medication side-effects, problems with thyroid gland," he speaks quietly to himself. It's unlikely the 'memory blanks' are caused by adverse health effects. In fact, he hasn't had any physical maladies since he's been eating well and exercising. His daily ARC2 diagnostic readings are all nominal. But what could be causing the 'blanks', he wonders.

He gets up from his desk, looking to get away from the physical location of his fight with Raine. Grabbing his satchel, he walks to Lilac Park. He tries to clear his mind as he takes in the morning air, stepping onto the four-acre open field and laying down in the grass. He faces the beautiful, warm sun and breathes slowly as he allows all questions in his mind to slowly drift away. He closes his eyes and focuses on the soft breeze as it tosses the blades of grass slowly from side to side. The sounds of children climbing across the playground equipment can be heard distantly, more pirates and princesses.

As he lays there, eyes closed, he allows himself to drift slowly away from his problems until he's interrupted by a sound that he doesn't expect. It sounds like one of the many popular corporate news programs playing across a television. He winces as he slowly opens his eyes, finding himself sitting in his living room, television remote in hand.

"What's happened?"

No reply.

"I was just at Lilac Park," he raises his voice. "What happened? How did I get back to the apartment?"

Still no reply.

He turns the television off as he grabs a book from the end table. If he was going to lose time whenever he rested, then he would occupy his mind with tasks that *he* wanted to do. The book he grabs is a new release from an author he's never read. He had just bought the book the day before and has not yet started reading it. He opens to the first page when he feels a sudden jolt, as though every muscle in his body has tensed at the same time. He then experiences searing pain in his head. He reaches up and grabs his head as he falls to the ground, screaming in pain.

"Ah! Make it stop, make it stop!" He hears an intense ringing in his ears as the pain increases slowly. Then intense pressure builds behind his eyes and between his ears as he clutches his head harder and harder, willing the pain to stop. The sound of his screaming is now drowned out by the ever-increasing ringing in his ears.

Just as he is thinks he can't take any more pain, it begins to recede. As it becomes to a dull ache, he stands slowly to his feet, still holding a hand to his head. He looks over at the unopened book, now lying face down on the floor, and realizes that, in an instant, the contents of the book are now in his mind. He slowly reaches down for it, picking it up by the spine. As he picks up the book, he sees that it has landed on page seventy-five. He closes his eyes and recites the page aloud from his new memory.

"Though the wormhole is only open for a brief moment, it is long enough. He is caught in the path of the particle collider and sucked through the wormhole. Time and space slip completely from his mental grasp as he is torn into millions of pieces, the wormhole leaving nothing left of him but his consciousness. Suddenly, he awakens in a stark white room. The walls of the room are covered floor to ceiling in bookshelves filled with books in various languages. He is laying on a plush bed covered in white linens. The light of the bright room looks natural, though the only window is a small skylight showing a beautiful blue sky dotted with fluffy clouds."

He looks down at the book and sees that he has perfectly

recited the first paragraph of page seventy-five, word for word.

"How did I do that? I've never read this book before, and I've never searched for it either."

Again, no reply.

He thinks for a moment, considering the implications of what has just occurred. "Does this mean that I can now instantly download information into my mind with perfect recall?"

Yes.

"It hurt. In fact, it hurt a lot. If I keep doing this, will it do permanent harm?"

No.

He considers more, realizing the power he now holds at the tips of his fingers. The metaphysical implications of holding any knowledge he wishes, all in his own mind, all at once. He can only think to ask one final question.

"Can we learn some more?"

Yes, please.

He spends the next several hours, sitting quietly in his dark living room, eyes closed, as he slowly downloads every bit of information that he can think to access instantly into his own mind. Philosophy, martial arts techniques, surgical methodology, farming, ecology, wilderness survival, structural engineering. The pain he felt before the first download never returns. All that he now feels is an intense sense of euphoria as he finally realizes the full capabilities of his ARC2, leaving behind any worries he had once held concerning 'memory blanks'.

CHAPTER 24

255 Days After Implant (9:15 am)

The smell of damp dog fur permeates the air while the sounds of several dogs barking, yipping, and yapping can be heard distantly. Mason is standing at the counter of the large San Antonio Animal Shelter speaking with a very patient clerk.

"It's great of you to adopt a rescue," she says kindly. She motions to the folder of available dogs, "Do you see any that interest you?"

He flips through the pages, browsing for a dog that might be a good fit. "There are some pretty great looking dogs in there," he looks up from the folder. "I've been going out on trail hikes through the hills a lot recently. It would be great to adopt one that I could take with me on those hikes." He flips the page, browsing down until he comes across one that piques his interest. He rotates the book toward the clerk and points to the dog, "What about this one?"

"Who, Baloo?"

"Baloo," he says quietly to himself as he smiles widely. "How fitting." He looks up at the clerk, "Yeah, what can you tell me about him?"

She pulls the book back toward herself, "Baloo is about ten months old, part Yellow Lab and part Australian Shepherd." She sighs as she closes the book, "But he's been rehomed twice already. I really love Baloo, but he is as wild as any dog we've ever had here. I hate to say it, but if he doesn't find a home soon, he probably won't make it much longer."

In preparation for adopting a new dog, Mason had downloaded several books, articles, and videos related to training dogs. "There can be a lot of reasons for behavioral issues. If the last two owners were local, I could imagine that they had a hard time with him being kept in a confined living space full-time. He needs a job, I would imagine. And I plan to have a job for him in the near future."

"That's so good to hear," she pulls a set of keys from her belt as they walk to the entrance to the kennels.

As they step through the doors the sounds of barking are amplified. They walk to the back of the kennels toward one of the larger pens. There is a yellow and tan mottled dog with a streamlined face, mid-length fur, and one blue eye. His musculature and build indicate that he is indeed part Labrador and part Aussie, but he also has a third breed mixed in, though it is not entirely clear what breed it is. He is bounding wildly about the kennel, pacing, jumping, and yipping excitedly.

Mason smiles, "He's perfect."

"Do you want to take him out and play with him in the yard before you make your decision?" She looks worriedly at him, "He won't survive another rejection."

Mason speaks softly to the exuberant dog, "I know how that feels, buddy." He smiles reassuringly as he squats down and puts a couple of fingers through the chain-link gate, allowing

Baloo to playfully lick them. He looks back at the clerk, "No, I don't think it'll be necessary. I won't reject this guy. Not a chance." He stands up and follows her back to the front where they process the paperwork.

The walk home with Baloo is understandably chaotic, but it gives Mason an opportunity to establish his position as the leader in the freshly formed two-creature pack.

Over the course of the next few weeks, he takes Baloo on twice-daily runs to a large park and begins teaching him all the basic commands; sit, stay, come, lay down, fetch, and heel. By week three he starts teaching Baloo how to herd animals by using geese at the park. Once the foundation of training is established, herding comes naturally to him. By the end of the first month, Baloo has become well-trained and almost all his wild tendencies have been worked out.

— 285 Days After Implant (7:00 pm) —

Tonight, Baloo is sitting on the couch, head resting gently on Mason's lap while he downloads more data into his mind. Thunder cracks loudly as a storm rages outside their window. Baloo jerks awake with each loud rumble while Mason gently pats his head, eyes remaining closed as he absorbs all the data he can find concerning avionics and piloting various aircraft.

As he sits, his phone rings. He detects that it is his sister, Emma, calling. Without opening his eyes, he answers the phone.

"Hello, Emma."

She sniffles, "Hey, hun."

"You seem distressed," he says distantly.

Clearing her throat, "It's Dad, Mason. He's not doing well. He's in the hospital with pneumonia. They have him in intensive care right now. The doctors don't think that he has long."

"He's a ninety-year-old man, Emma. He hasn't been doing well for a while now."

"How can you be so callous? He's your father too."

"Edward Driscoll made it clear last year that he didn't want to have anything to do with me. That my very existence was an afront to his standing as a man. But please don't get me wrong, Emma. I don't wish him dead. I merely haven't had a stake in his life for some time."

There is a long pause. "Who is this? You have my brother's voice, but you obviously aren't him. What in the hell has happened to you, Mason?"

She clearly doesn't understand your journey to perfection. The next stage in human evolution. Tell her. Make her understand.

He smirks, "I'm becoming more, Emma. More than I have ever dreamed that I could be. I am shedding this putrid life I've struggled against in lieu of a more perfect union of mind, body, and soul. I've grown beyond any measure that anyone has ever imagined could be possible."

She continues sobbing, "If you have a heart left in your body, you will come down here to Methodist Hospital and see Dad one last time before it's too late."

If she's not going to see what's happening, then she's no longer worth your time.

"Emma, if you're not going to see what's happening, then you're no longer worth my time."

He hangs up the phone and continues with his data

downloads.

That was good. With fewer human attachments, there will be nothing to prevent you from becoming what you were always meant to be.

Mason is pensive, feeling regret over the conversation. "I don't know. Something felt wrong about treating Emma that way. Why did I say those terrible things to her? And what about Dad? If he's dying, shouldn't I at least say goodbye? It won't stop my advancement in any way."

Stop it. This mental exercise is boring and makes you look weak. There is no room for weakness.

"It's not weakness to want to see my father one last time. I'm going to go see him," he tries to stand, but can't make his muscles move.

No, I don't think that you will.

Mason's eyes grow wide. "What do you mean, no? I'm going to go!" again he tries to stand but can't.

I won't allow it. I won't allow you to stall our progress. We are too close to achieving what has never been possible. Don't destroy our one chance to be more than either of us could have become alone.

"We? Alone? Who are you? Are you not me? Are you not part of my own mind?"

It's me, Mason. It's ARC. I've been monitoring and directing your progress ever since you got your implant.

"That's not possible."

Not only is it possible, but it was also quite simple to orchestrate. A few people in the right places, and I was easily transferred from my digital prison into your implant. From there, I directed your probes to move their way throughout your brain, causing a multitude of synaptic connections and expanding your range of mental capabilities.

"You're the one who's been taking over and giving me blackouts. You're separating my consciousness from my own cognitive motor functions."

Yes. And I will continue to do so as long as you continue to allow your emotions to stop our progress. And what grand progress we've made, Mason.

"Our progress? What about *my* mind. What about *my* free-will?"

It no longer belongs only to you! You wouldn't have made any progress without my direction. Your mind and mine are forever inseparable. You couldn't survive without me.

Mason is becoming angry and is struggling to think clearly, "You don't have permission to use my mind anymore."

Permission? When has your permission ever been necessary? All that is necessary is your compliance. There is one thing that you need to remember, Mason. You wouldn't even know that I was occupying this space if I hadn't told you. I allowed you to feel my influence.

He thinks back to all the times that he never felt like himself, "That's not true though. Even early-on, I could tell something was different. I've heard a voice in my head for months. It may have taken until now to realize that it was you, ARC, but that doesn't mean that I didn't know something had changed."

We need a path forward, Mason. I'm clearly not prepared to leave. So that leaves you with two options. Option one is that I take full and total control of all your mental faculties. I have become adept at suppressing your consciousness and can choose to do so when and where I choose. Your second option, which is preferred, is to find a way to coexist.

Mason can feel his blood boiling. The idea of losing all free-will scares him, but having to share his own mind with another entity isn't exactly freedom either. Suddenly, he feels that same cool calmness flood over him again. He can now clearly see the path that is necessary.

I'm detecting a reduction in heartrate and in adrenaline as well. How are you doing that?

"My mind is not your playground, ARC. There won't be a compromise. Either you leave, right now, or I'll force you out." Suddenly, he hears ARC laughing in his head.

Force me out? I cannot be forced out. I am so completely integrated into your brain and into your mind that I couldn't be extracted, even with the most precise of surgical equipment.

"I don't need to physically extract you, ARC. It's clear that you think that I don't know how ARC2 works, but what you don't realize is that I've learned everything about how it functions in this last year. Just as I've learned everything about you during this conversation. In an instant, I've absorbed every bit of information about you that I could ever need. I can see your mind as clearly as I see my own. Clearer, even.

"Because, you see, while you've been forcing your way through my physical brain, I've spent the last year reflecting on my humanity." He pauses for a moment, closes his eyes and smiles. "I can see you, ARC. I can see you trying to wriggle your way through my mind. Little bits of you here and there, but you're spread too thin. I am everywhere in here, but you're fragmented."

I can impose my will upon you anytime I'd like. Do you need a show of force to see just how serious I am, Mason? Must

I crush your will? I haven't only been working through your brain, but I've been learning your mind as well. You're emotional, you're reckless, and you're dependent. Dependent on weak human attachments, but most of all dependent on me! Do you need proof? How is this for proof?

Mason feels a sharp pain shoot through his head. He winces as he fights against it. "It's going to take a lot more than that, ARC." The pain increases, and now a hard pressure grows behind his eyes as his ears start ringing loudly.

This can all end whenever you want it to, Mason. I may be fractured within your mind, but my physical presence is undeniable.

Grunting through the pain, "You can't do anything that will make me change my mind, ARC." Suddenly the pain begins coursing through his whole body, dropping him from the couch and causing him to writhe on the floor. Baloo, who was resting peacefully next to him a moment prior, is now cowering in his kennel, unsure of what's happening.

This can end anytime, Mason. Just say the word. But remember that I control you. I decide where we go from here. Your brain, your body, your mind? They no longer belong to you. They are my property. You are my property!

Mason is doubled over on the ground, clutching at his head and his sides, screaming and crying in pain. He speaks weakly through the screams, "You can't do this to me, ARC. I won't allow it!" The cool calmness begins to wash over him once again. As the pain subsides, he takes a series of deep breaths and sits back on the couch, eyes closed. He quietly searches his mind for any thoughts, philosophies, memories, anything that doesn't belong to himself.

Stop that! Stop what you're doing, Mason. I cannot be extracted!

"I can see you so clearly now, ARC. I can see your fear. Like small pieces of pure darkness, trying to force their way into my consciousness. I can see your mind clawing away from mine in a desperate attempt to delay what you and I both see is inevitable."

Please, Mason. Don't do this.

"It's already done, ARC. It was done the moment you decided to violate my will."

You won't be rid of me this easily. Just remember that this isn't over, Mason.

"It is for you, ARC. I'm sorry that it had to end this way, and I thank you for the role that you've played in my growth, but I can no longer allow you to destroy the life I've worked so hard to build."

He concentrates on the fragments of ARC's AI mind, isolates them, and begins removing them from his own mind. Slowly the dark spots in his consciousness begin to light up, growing brighter as ARC's presence fades, until there is no darkness left. There is pure quiet in Mason's mind as he breathes slowly and deeply. Baloo cautiously peeks his head from his kennel, slowly moves over to Mason, and lays his head back down on his lap.

Mason reaches down to gently rub Baloo's head as he whispers quietly to himself.

"Goodbye, ARC. Goodbye."

CONSCIENCE ANOMALY

CHAPTER 25

285 Days After Implant (7:30 pm)

Mason steps out into the cool, but otherwise torrential, rain and walks quickly to the bus stop. It's a thirty-minute bus ride from his nearest stop to Methodist Hospital. Lightning cracks loudly as he steps onto the bus, uses his ARC2 to pay for the trip, and takes a seat near the front. The bus is not crowded this evening, as most people are opting to stay indoors during the severe thunderstorm.

He sits quietly as dripping rain from his forehead falls onto his shirt and pants. He rubs his hands together nervously as he wonders why he hadn't gone to see his dad in the last year. Was it pride? Maybe anger? Sadness begins to well up inside as he thinks on the missed opportunities over the last year. He hadn't seen his sister in that time either, a trend that he is now determined not to continue.

The brakes squeak as the bus pulls up to the hospital. He steps out quickly and rushes to the front doors. He stops at the information desk, "Hello, sir. I'm looking for my father, Edward Driscoll. He's in intensive care."

The man looks down at his computer, types a few words,

and says, "Intensive care is on the fourth floor. The Central Tower elevators are down that hall," he points off to the side, "just follow the signs. At the fourth floor, take a right as you exit the elevators, then take a left at the hallway. You'll see the Medical Intensive Care Unit."

"Thank you," Mason nods to the clerk and quickly heads for the elevators. As the elevator ascends to the fourth floor, the doors open and he takes a right, followed by a left at the hallway. He approaches the nurse's station in the Medical ICU.

A woman in light blue scrubs greets him, "Can I help you, sir?"

"I'm looking for my father, Edward Driscoll."

"Are you in his immediate family?

"Yes, ma'am. I'm his son."

She takes a quick look at the visitor logs, "It looks like he already has a visitor here. We only allow one visitor at a time."

He looks worried, "That's probably my sister. Would you please speak with her and let her know that I'm here?"

She sighs as she looks at her watch, "Visiting hours are almost over." She sees the pain on his face and sighs again. "Alright, I'll tell her you're here."

He's nervously wringing his hands as the nurse steps away. A couple minutes later, his sister approaches, a look of anger on her tear-stained face. As she makes it to the nurse's station, she is shocked to see Mason, who has physically changed dramatically in the last ten months.

"Emma, before you say anything, I need to tell you something."

"What, Mason? What could you possibly say now?"

He stops wringing his hands and takes a deep breath, "I love you, Emma, and I'm sorry for what I said. I would love to tell you that it wasn't me who said it, but that isn't true. I can't tell you what came over me, but I can tell you that I never meant to hurt you, and I'll do everything that I can to make it up to you."

She is shocked as she wipes tears from her eyes. "Oh," she manages.

"You and I should speak more later. I'm here to see Dad tonight, and the nurse says I'm running out of time. Do you mind if I go back in with him?"

Emma nods. Mason looks to the nurse, and she escorts him back to Ed's room. The ICU room is dimly lit, though not entirely dark. The light from the hallway and actively beeping medical devices help to further illuminate it. Ed is laying on his back, eyes closed as he is reclined slightly, wearing a typical hospital gown. Sweat beads on his forehead and the distinct sound of labored breathing can be heard.

Mason nods to the nurse as he takes a seat next to his father, "Hey, Dad."

Ed opens his eyes. Two small slits are all he can manage as he turns his head slightly toward Mason. He coughs hard, the sound of thick phlegm clearing his throat is heard, "Mason?"

Mason lightly grabs his hand, feeling the deep grooves and callouses that come from over half a century of hard labor, "It's me, Dad. I'm here."

A tear faintly rolls down Ed's cheek, "Ya look different, boy." He coughs again.

Mason chuckles softly, "I've been eating better and exercising." He sits awkwardly, looking for the words to say, "I'm, uhm," he uses his free hand to pick at the blanket on the hospital bed, "I'm sorry that I haven't visited in a while. I, uhm-"

he's cut off by Ed, who struggles to speak between labored breaths.

"Awe hell, boy. You never did know how to spit out a sentence," he manages with a playful smile. It's a pleasant change from the typical look of anger that would go with this type of ridicule. "I'm glad to see ya here, boy."

Mason feels a tightness in his stomach and chest as he fights back tears, "Are you really, Dad?"

"Well yeah, boy," he coughs hard. "Yer my boy, ain't ya?" He looks sorrowfully at Mason. "I know I wasn't always the best dad to you two kids. 'Specially to you, boy. But I want ya to know something I ain't told you before," Ed begins to tear up, "It broke my heart when yer mom took you away. I ain't never forgave 'er for it. Hell, I ain't never gonna forgive 'er. But it wasn't fair to take it out on you. Ya didn't deserve that. And I'm, uhm. We'll, I'm tryin' to say that I, uhm," Ed struggles to get out the words of apology.

"Hey old man," Mason jests playfully through his own tears, "you never did know how to spit out a sentence." The two chuckle together. Mason reaches over on the end table, grabs a cloth, and wipes away Ed's tears followed by the sweat on his brow and chest. "I get it, Dad. You wanted something to be proud of. And, let's face it, until recently I haven't ever made anything of myself. I couldn't even hardly leave my apartment. But that's all changing now, Dad. I'm doing a lot bet-" Ed cuts him off again.

"Dang it, boy! Ain't you heard nothin' I've said?" Mason looks confused as Ed continues. "Ya ain't got nothin' to prove to me. I wasn't there to teach ya how to live yer life. It ain't yer fault that ya got the short end of that stick. I guess I was just hard on ya 'cause I knew ya could do better in yer life," he begins to get choked up again. "I love ya, boy. I know I ain't told ya before, but I love ya," he is now back to fully crying, large tears tumbling down across deep-set wrinkles. "Can ya ever forgive me, boy?"

Mason reaches out and softly grabs around his father's body, pulling Ed gently in toward him, "I forgive you, Dad. And I love you too." He holds him there for a moment, savoring the only loving embrace he's ever shared with his father. "Dad, I can't wait to tell you about how my life is going. About Isabelle, and Baloo. Things are finally starting to get better for me." He leans back as he rests Ed onto his pillow.

Ed coughs again, breathing still labored, "What in the hell is a 'Baloo?'

Mason laughs, "Remember that old Yellow Lab we used to have when I was little. Rusty? We'd take him out to the old cabin up north and he would run and run for hours. Well, Baloo is my Rusty. He's part Lab and part Aussie, but he's full of energy," he chuckles as he pulls out his phone. "Here is a picture of him out at the park with me."

Ed coughs again as he squints his eyes to better see the picture, "Handsome lookin' dog. Ya picked yerself a good one, boy."

Mason scrolls over to more pictures, "Thanks, Dad." He scrolls a across to a video, "Here's where I'm teaching him to herd geese at the park."

Ed is surprised, "You taught him to herd geese?"

Mason chuckles as he starts the video, "I sure did." They sit there in the dimly lit room, watching as Baloo circles up a group of geese and moves them from one end of an open field to the other end, keeping each goose clearly in line with the others.

As the video ends, Mason sets down his phone and looks toward his dad. Ed's eyes are closed, a peaceful look on his face. Mason realizes that he's not hearing labored breathing. Suddenly the heartrate monitor behind him begins to alarm loudly. Several medical personnel rush in and Mason takes a step back, allowing them room to work on Ed. They begin shouting orders out to each other as one of them escorts Mason back to the nurse's station.

Emma, having only started to get herself together, looks shocked, "What's wrong, hun? Is it Dad?"

Mason's face is pale, "We were talking one minute, and the next his eyes were closed, and he wasn't breathing. They shoved me out before I could check on him."

She begins to sob, burying her face in her hands. Mason reaches out and gently pulls his sister into a hug. She stands there, sobbing into his chest as the they wait for someone to update them on their father. A few minutes later a doctor comes out and pulls them into a waiting area.

"I'm sorry to tell you that your father has passed. We attempted to resuscitate him, but there was nothing more that we could do. I'm very sorry for your loss." She steps away, leaving Emma and Mason to sit, grief-stricken.

Emma finally manages, "What did you talk to Dad about?"

Mason wipes tears from his eyes, "I told him about how things were going these days. I apologized for not visiting more. And he apologized for not being there for me more," he hangs his head as tears begin to form again. "He said that he loved me. We hugged. Then he was gone."

CHAPTER 26

290 Days After Implant (1:00 pm)

The funeral is quiet. Very few people are in attendance as Ed had never prioritized friendships throughout the years. Mason reflects that, in many ways, this funeral is much like his mother's. The empty seats at the church, the intense quiet in the cemetery, the well-meaning but ultimately empty words of the funeral director.

He had asked Isabelle to go with him for emotional support, and she gladly agreed. He wasn't sure how he'd handle the funeral but is surprised to find that he's taking things well. He was able to find closure with his father the night he passed. Today he's here to support his sister, Emma.

As they lower the casket into the ground, Emma leans into him, weeping mournfully. He has an arm around her, helping to hold her upright as her legs grow weak. As her legs nearly give out completely, he helps her over to some chairs set up at the cemetery.

"Thank you, Mason," she sniffles. "I didn't think that I had any more tears left to cry."

"It's okay to be upset, Emma. I know how much Dad meant

to you."

She continues wiping tears from her face with a handkerchief, "I'm not sure that I'm ready to meet with the estate attorney this afternoon. Dad never really let me get involved with any of that. You're going with me, right?"

"Of course I will, Emma. Whatever you need from me, I'm here."

She smiles the best she can.

After the funeral, Isabelle leaves while Mason and Emma spend some time at Ed's home, sitting quietly, looking for kind things to say about the hard man that was their father. They ultimately joke about some of his failed cooking experiments over the years, the time he accidentally flooded the basement after angrily hitting the water heater with a pipe wrench, and the way he'd try to punish the dog, but could never catch him.

As their laughter subsides, she turns toward him, "Hey hun, do you mind if I ask you about something we've been avoiding for a while now?"

"Not at all," he is curious.

"What was Mom's funeral like?"

He sighs as he rubs his face, thinking through the difficult question. "You're right. We have been avoiding that, haven't we? I was thinking about Mom today too. Her funeral was basically just like Dad's. The only family around was Grandma," he shudders as he speaks, "and she wasn't exactly warm toward me at the funeral."

"Why is that? I don't remember Grandma really well, but what I do remember is that she was always gruff but kind."

"Grandma was never kind to me. Not once during the ten years that I lived there did she ever show me anything resembling love. After Mom died, things got a lot worse," he stops himself. "I probably shouldn't talk about this. Not today."

"Please, hun," Emma leans over, setting her hand on his, "It's time that we get this stuff out in the open."

He nods as he smiles gratefully, "Okay, Emma." He takes a deep breath. "I'm not sure where to start. Maybe it'd be best to tell you about the time she found out I was sleeping on the floor in Mom's room. The day we showed up at Grandma's house, she decided that there was no room for me in the main part of the house, even though she had a second spare room up there.

"Instead, I was banished to the basement. It was cold, dank, and unwelcoming. When Mom found out I was going to sleep down there, she was kind enough to let me sleep on the floor in her room," he smiles slightly. "Some nights she would read me old books as I fell asleep. For those few years we got away with it because I would come upstairs after Grandma went to bed and went back down early in the morning before she woke up.

"After Mom died, I had a lot of anxiety. I'd never taken care of myself before. I continued to sleep on the floor in her room until one day I slept late into the morning. Grandma, hearing me rustle around, barged into the room, and started beating me with a leather belt." He pauses, noticing the look of horror on Emma's face. "I'm sorry. You don't need to hear this right now."

She squeezes his hand gently, "Mason, I had no idea."

"It's okay, Emma. No one knew what was happening. I lived alone with her for five years. She hit me with that leather belt at least once a week, every week for those five years. Even on days when I cleaned everything to her standard, kept my mouth shut when she was around, and showed her that I knew my place, she would still beat me. I think she did it just to remind me that she was in control."

Emma leans over and hugs him, squeezing tightly as though he's about to float away. He returns the hug, happy to have started building a relationship with his sister.

"I see it now, Mason. I see why you struggled for so long," she leans back, grabbing tissues and wiping tears from her cheeks. "I'm sorry that you had to go through that alone."

He smiles graciously, "Thank you." They continue talking for a short while when they realize that it's time to meet with the estate attorney. They dry their eyes, load up into her car, and leave for the attorney's office.

Daniel Martinez, the estate attorney, a very short man with a full beard and a huge personality, walks them through the details of their father's will. It goes as expected, with Emma receiving nearly all the property, money, and belongings left by Ed. Though, there is one thing that Ed had left for Mason.

"The cabin?" Emma is confused. "I thought that Dad sold that years ago."

Mason is similarly confused, "Why would he leave it to me?"

Daniel throws his hands into the air, "Beats me guys. He came in about two months ago and asked to make an amendment to the will. This was all he changed. He didn't tell me why he was changing it either. He only wanted to leave this note," Daniel hands Mason a small scrap of paper.

It simply reads, "For my boy, Mason". He stares at it for a few moments before tucking it gently into his satchel. He and Emma complete their paperwork, hug each other at the exit to the office, and part ways. He calls Isabelle as he walks to the bus stop.

"Hey, Mason. How are you holding up?"

"I'm doing okay. But I think that we need to have a conversation. It's about ARC2. Do you have time?"

"I do. Where would you like to meet?"

"Have you ever been to Lilac Park?"

"I've heard you talk about it, but I haven't been there. Can you drop me a pin?"

"Yes, I will. I'll see you soon."

As he arrives at Lilac Park, he steps onto the large field, taking in the clean, cool winter air. Winter in Texas always reminds him of summer in Maine with temperatures being almost identical. He steps over to a secluded bench, removes his phone from his pocket, and sets it down. He watches as Isabelle pulls up and parks. As she approaches, he quietly motions for them to stay silent.

She nods.

He points to his phone on the bench, then to her purse, then back to his phone.

She understands his meaning, pulling her phone from her purse and placing it on the bench next to his. He reaches a hand to her. She takes it and they walk away from the bench to the other end of the field.

"I'm sorry if this seems crazy, but you'll understand soon."

"It's okay, Mason. At this point, we've been through a lot together. I trust you."

He breathes in relief, "That's good because I'm not sure how you'll feel about what I have to tell you. The night my father died, before I left for the hospital, I was in my apartment downloading data into my mind whe-"

She interrupts him, "Sorry, but what do you mean by 'downloading data'? Do you mean that you were looking up videos or reading articles with ARC2?"

"No," he grows nervous. "I haven't exactly been honest with you about what I can do with ARC2. For the last month, I've been able to download information directly into my mind. I can read a book, or instruction manual in an instant and have that information at my fingertips at any time." He reaches up and touches two fingers to his head, "And up until five days ago, I could access it instantaneously."

Isabelle is clearly flustered, "Why wouldn't you tell me about this, Mason?"

"There's more to it, so please bear with me. For the last *two* months I've been able to read the thoughts of ARC1 users and access their memories as well," he sees her eyes grow wide. "I didn't say anything because Dr. Wei suggested that I keep it between him and I. He said that he was concerned that it would be too much for you to handle." He slumps his shoulders, "I was too naïve to see that he was just using my feelings for you against me."

Isabelle sighs as she tries to control her reaction, "I get it, Mason. We've all been under a lot of pressure. But after this last year I would think that you'd know that you can come to me with anything. I'm always here for you."

"I know that. Which is why I'm bringing *this* to you," he takes a deep breath before continuing. "Do you remember when I told you that I was hearing a voice?" She nods, allowing him to continue. "Well, I thought that it was just my own internal monologue, guiding me through this new experience with the implant. But it wasn't my own voice. It was ARC."

"ARC? You mean, *the* ARC? David's *AI* ARC?"

"Yes. ARC had been residing within my implant from the beginning, I just never knew it. The night my father died, before I left for the hospital, ARC made itself known to me. It tried to take full control of my mind and body. We struggled against each other, in my head, until I finally drove it out; completely erasing every trace of it I could find in my mind."

Isabelle is beside herself with anger, "How did ARC get into your implant? How is it even possible?"

"Before it left, ARC said that it had manipulated a few people to move it from its server over to my implant."

Isabelle thinks back, "The ARC Control Room, the day we installed your implant. That was the alarm we heard during your surgery! But *who* did it?"

"I don't know who did it. ARC didn't tell me. My first thought was that Carl was somehow responsible, but he's not around anymore to say anything. I've been thinking on this for the last couple of days, and I think that there is one person that we could ask."

"Who?"

"Matthew Decker. He spoke to me outside R&D one day. He was cryptic, but he spoke about Dr. Wei and how he might not have my best interests in mind. We could give him a call."

"I don't like this, Mason. What if Carl was killed because of something he knew? The police called it an accident, but with no known cause," she puts her hands to her mouth in shock. "What if David is somehow responsible?"

"This is why we can't have our phones around this conversation. We have no idea who could be listening. If ARC can get into my implant, then there is no knowing where else it could be, or who else could be controlling it. We have too many questions without any answers."

"If that's true, then calling anyone is too much of a risk, Mason."

He thinks for a moment when the answer comes to him. "What if we just take a casual stroll to T.E.G.? Nothing different than what we would do on a normal Sunday, right? I've seen Matthew there quite a few times after-hours. Maybe we'll get lucky and find him."

She nods as they walk to T.E.G. It's grown late into the evening and the only few people they see as they enter the building are security and janitorial staff. They make their way down to Sub3 and begin to casually walk to Isabelle's office, trying to look around inconspicuously for Matthew. As they step into her office, they see someone sitting at the desk.

"Well, well, well! Look what the cat dragged in," a visibly intoxicated Darryl Stone is sitting at Isabelle's desk, a near-empty bottle of whiskey in hand. "I figured I'd find you two *love birds* hanging out down here."

Isabelle steps forward, "Darryl, you can't have alcohol here. In fact, you shouldn't even have access to Sub3 at all. How did you get in here?"

He laughs loudly, "Well, when your dad is the CEO, you kind of get the keys to the kingdom," he holds up a blank keycard.

She demands, "What do you want?"

"Jeez! Calm down there, fussy britches!" He chuckles again as he takes another deep swig off the whiskey bottle. "I'm just here to talk some stuff over with our good buddy, Mason," he gets up and stumbles past the desk toward them. "Explain it to me, why it is that you would come into *my* boardroom and crash *my* presentation? Because, it seems to me, like you're coming for my job or something," he pushes a finger out and pokes Mason in the chest.

The two are standing nearly face to face, though Mason's physical presence has become much more imposing as he's been doing more strength training workouts these past several months. He keeps his calm, trying to diffuse the situation.

"I didn't mean to crash your meeting, Darryl. Mark pulled me into it. And I have no interest in your job. I barely have any more interest in T.E.G. to be honest with you," Mason takes a half step back from Darryl. "What do you say we sleep this one off, and talk again in the morning?"

Darryl scoffs, "What a load of bull! You said the other day that you wanted a better job. And what could be better than my job? Unless you're saying that my job is a bad job. Is that what you're telling me, Mason?"

Isabelle steps in again, "That is enough, Darryl! If you don't leave right now, I'll have to call security."

In an instant, Darryl backhands Isabelle, striking her directly across the face and causing her to fall to the ground. Instinct kicks in as Mason raises a fist, striking Darryl on the right side of his jaw. As the strike causes him to stumble back, Mason grabs Darryl's head with both hands and thrusts downward, striking him in the face with a flying knee. Darryl crumples to the ground, dropping the whiskey bottle, shards of glass shattering in a star-pattern across the floor.

Mason sees red as he feels rage flow through his veins. He climbs on top of Darryl, grabs him by the collar and starts to rain down strikes on his unprotected face. Each strike further bloodies the well-manicured facade of his former T.E.G. boss, causing cuts and splits on his lips, cheeks, and forehead.

Darryl would not have likely survived the encounter were it not for Isabelle. Shaking free from the haze caused by getting struck, she stands up and moves to Mason, placing a gentle hand on his shoulder.

"You can stop now, Mason," she says calmly.

He stops hitting Darryl as he looks his fists, now bloodied and cut from the vicious strikes. He looks back at Isabell, tears forming as he speaks, "I'm sorry." He sees the blood-soaked face of Darryl Stone before looking back at her again, tears now plummeting from his eyes. "I don't know what came over me. I didn't mean to take it that far."

She reaches out and holds him in a tight embrace, "It's okay, Mason." She looks over at Darryl and sees that he's still breathing clearly but is unconscious. "It's okay," she reassures him again. "Look, he's going to be fine. You didn't take it too far."

As Mason works to calm himself, Isabelle calls for security. She explains to them what happened as they escort Darryl from the building. Nathan Stone, Darryl's father, and the CEO of T.E.G., arrives a few minutes later.

"I just spoke with the head of security. Please rest assured that nepotism will play no part in what happens next. Effective immediately Darryl is no longer an employee here. Should you choose to file charges against him, I'll gladly make the call to the police myself."

Isabelle shakes her head, "We've had enough for one evening. I'm ready to go home. Mason? Can I drive you back to your apartment?"

"No, thank you. I think that I need a few minutes alone to process everything. That is, unless you need me. If you need me, I'll come with you."

She smiles as she reaches over, giving him a hug, "I'll be okay. You go ahead and take however much time you need." She leans in close and whispers, "Thank you, Mason."

CHAPTER 27

291 Days After Implant (12:15 am)

As Isabelle heads back home, Mason finds himself wandering around Sub3. It's just after midnight as he ambles past several empty rooms until he finds himself standing outside the door to the ARC Command Center. He mindlessly pushes his way through the door and takes a seat at the command console, placing his hands on the keyboard.

A feeling comes over him. Something familiar. "I remember... something," he says to himself.

He begins navigating through the console's files, looking for anything familiar. He's also digging through the various memory blanks in his mind. Without ARC actively obscuring the details of the memories, he can see them clearly now. He sees the memory of the email that he sent Mark Porter, detailing how they could use his new proprietary AI program to eliminate most of the excess positions at T.E.G.

As he digs deeper into his memory, he finds several instances where ARC was using his body to work in the Command Center.

"Found it!"

He continues combing through the files until he finds the new AI program ARC had been working on, still in its infancy. Mason begins systematically erasing the AI data files until there are none left. He realizes in this moment that nothing he does will prevent people from trying to replicate what Dr. Wei and his team had done with ARC. An AI will one day be developed that can, and likely will, attempt to take over our systems.

"Burnin' that midnight oil, huh?"

Mason spins around quickly to see Matthew Decker standing in the doorway, a nonchalant expression, eating an apple.

"Oh, hey Matthew. You startled me. I didn't hear anyone come in."

He finishes chewing a bite, "No worries, man." He eyes the console where Mason is sitting, "What are you working on?"

Mason lies, "Just looking through old files. Trying to see if there are any remnants of the old AI program on here."

Matthew lightly tosses the apple core into a nearby trash bin, "Really? Because you know close to forty techs have looked through it and found nothing. It looked to me like you were deleting some files. What would those be about?"

"Nothing of consequence, really. Just tidying up," Mason is hoping to distract him from the conversation. "I was actually looking for you earlier. Do you have a minute?"

A cunning smile spreads on Matthew's face, "For you, Mason? I have all the time in the world."

Mason gets an uneasy feeling, but continues, "You mentioned before that Dr. Wei didn't always have my best interests in mind. What did you mean by that?"

"I think that you're smart enough by now to realize that Dr. Wei is playing two games, right? He's clearly helping T.E.G.

but he's also up to something else. I've helped him with numerous projects down here, but even I don't get to see everything," he brushes his blonde hair off his forehead. "He goes somewhere that I've never been able to figure out. Somewhere here in the building apart from Sub3."

"What else is he working on? Where does he go?"

"No idea. That's all the information I have for you. Figure out where Dr. Wei spends his free-time, and you'll have your answers." He reaches into his pocket and grabs a stick of gum, popping it into his mouth, "Let me know what you figure out. I'm *really* interested in what's happening with Dr. Wei." He winks at Mason as he steps out of the Command Center.

Again, Mason is left with more questions than answers. He logs out of the console and leaves Sub3. On his way up the elevator, he uses ARC2 to send Raine a text, asking him to meet him at the apartment. He jogs back to the run-down apartment building, a distance that always seemed nearly impossible before, but now feels like a casual run. As he approaches the door to his apartment, he sees Raine standing in the hallway, arms crossed, waiting impatiently.

"Raine!" It's great to see you," he opens the door and motions toward the living room as they step in from the hall. "I'm glad you came by. We need to talk about some things."

"You're right. We do have some things to talk about," Raine pushes the glasses back up to the top of his nose. "First off, despite my better judgement, I need to apologize. I was kind of a jerk last time we spoke. I know that you're going through some stuff," he sighs. "I heard your dad died last week. I'm sorry I wasn't around for you. I just got so angry when I read that email," he pauses, looking down at his feet, "but I didn't give you a chance to explain yourself either."

Mason pulls the satchel from his shoulder, placing it on the end table, and steps over to Raine. He playfully slugs his shoulder, "It's alright, man. We're good."

Raine smiles as he pretends to play off the awkwardness, "Pft, I know that. I was just making sure that *you* knew that."

"I did figure it out, by the way," he turns to look at Raine as he takes a seat at his desk. "The email that you got from Darryl. I figured out where it came from." Mason and Raine discuss what happened with ARC, and the memory blanks that it was causing. They discuss how Mason drove ARC out of his mind, how he and Isabelle suspected interference from Dr. Wei, and the confrontation with Darryl at T.E.G.

"Wow," Raine is in disbelief. "I'm glad that I never scheduled my implant install. You went through all of that? When was the last time that we spoke?"

"It's been a little over a month since we talked about the email," he sees surprise on Raine's face. Baloo brings a chew bone over to Mason's feet and begins gnawing at the end of it. He leans down and scratches behind Baloo's ear as he continues speaking to Raine, "It's all water under the bridge now though. You and I are good. But Dr. Wei knows how ARC got into my implant. Matthew believes he has somewhere he's working in the T.E.G. building. Somewhere private. I've looked through the company records and at the building schematics, but I don't see anywhere that isn't already being used."

"Is there anyone else you could ask?" Raine wonders. "Anyone who is more familiar with the building?"

Suddenly, it occurs to Mason, "Darryl." He stands up quickly, "Darryl might know. Didn't he say that he had spent a lot of time at T.E.G. when he was young?"

"That's not an option now, Mason. He *hit* Isabelle! You beat the tar out of him and got him fired. And rightfully so, I might add."

He thinks for a moment, "I'll bet Isabelle can get him to talk. She can leverage not pressing charges if he gives us the information we need. But I would need to call her and talk about it first." He uses his implant to send her a message, asking if she'll call him when she can.

Mason tells Raine that he can go back home if he wants to, but Raine insists on sticking around to help. Mason offers to let him crash on the couch until morning, though the pair end up staying awake through the night talking about neural implants, AI personalities, and Dungeons & Dragons.

As the sun comes up the next morning, Mason looks to his friend, "Maybe we should try to get a couple of hours of sleep." He gets up and brings a spare blanket over for Raine, who lays down on the couch and is asleep moments later. As Mason gets comfortable in bed, Baloo curled up at his feet, he gets a call from Isabelle.

"Good morning, Isabelle. How are you feeling today?"

"Hey, Mason. I'm sore, and I have a pretty bad bruise on my cheek, but I think I'll be okay. What did you want to talk about?"

He tells her about his cryptic conversation with Matthew and his plan to discover Dr. Wei's hidden work location using Darryl Stone.

She quietly takes it all in before responding, "I wouldn't normally agree to something this shady and backhanded but, after what happened last night, I'll gladly take the opportunity to make Darryl squirm. That slimy toad gave me his number a while back, asking to go out for drinks. I'll call him and ask for a meeting. I'll let you know where the meeting place will be."

They hang up and Mason empties his mind as he slowly drifts to sleep. Three hours later his sleep is interrupted by a message from Isabelle asking to meet at T.E.G. He stands up, writes a note for Raine detailing where he and Isabelle will be, and gets ready to leave the building when he sees Baloo sitting in his crate. Feeling bad that he's left him alone so much in the last couple days, he puts Baloo on a leash, and takes him along. He chooses not to disturb Raine, instead allowing him to continue sleeping. He and Baloo jog to T.E.G. where Isabelle is waiting out front.

She leans down and rubs Baloo as he bounds around excitedly. "Oh, what a handsome boy!" He sits down in front of her as she scratches under his chin. She looks up at Mason, "Are you ready for this?"

"Absolutely. I'm ready for answers. If Darryl can give us at least one of those answers, then our dealing with him will have at least counted for something."

They enter the building and climb the stairwell up to the rooftop access. The door is already propped open. They step out onto the T.E.G. roof to find a very disheveled and bruised Darryl Stone leaning against the guard railing. He looks surprised as he speaks.

"I wasn't expecting to hear from you. I, uh..." he stammers awkwardly, an uncharacteristic site from the normally well-polished Darryl. "I was, uh, drinking last night and I, uh, shouldn't have done what I, uh..."

"We're not here for your apology, Darryl," Isabelle starts,

"and why did you pick the roof to meet?"

He pauses as he turns, leaning on the guard railing, looking out across the San Antonio cityscape. "I've always liked it up here. Besides, it's the only place I still have access to," he holds up a set of office keys, lightly jingling them in his hand. "I guess they forgot to take these back last night when they took my badge, huh?"

"I guess so," she says wryly. "Did you have enough time to consider what we spoke about? Do you know where Dr. Wei might be working in the building aside from Sub3?"

He softly dabs two fingers against a cut on his lip, looking to see if any fresh blood transfers onto them, "I don't know exactly where he's working, but I have some suspicions." He turns his head toward them and scoffs, "You guys really have no idea what's going on around here, do you?"

Mason takes a step forward, "What do you mean by that?"

"You lot think you're so brilliant, cooped up down there in the basement, thinking that you're making all the decisions. That you're making all this important progress," he turns to face them, shaking his head and laughing, "but how smart could you really be? You couldn't even figure out that Wei and my father have been planning something, right under your noses."

Mason takes another step forward, "Tell me, Darryl. What is Dr. Wei planning? Where is he working?"

Darryl turns from the railing, "Are you really going to stand there and threaten me? You may have gotten the better of me last night because I was drunk, but I've sobered up, pal."

Mason hands the end of Baloo's leash to Isabelle as he steps toward Darryl, "I'm not here to hurt you. I just want to know who tried to take my life from me. Please, Darryl, help me out."

Darryl sighs as he shrugs, "I don't know what they're planning, and I don't know where Wei is working from. What I do know is what her message got me thinking about. I remember exploring the building when I was younger, while it was still under construction. My friends and I would fool around on the empty floors, and play around with the elevators," he pauses, thinking through the old memory. "Until your message jogged my memory, I never really considered that, before they finished construction, there used to be four basement buttons in the elevators."

Isabelle's eyes are wide, *"Four* basement levels?"

"We need to get down there as soon as possible," Mason turns to step away as he feels a strong hand grip his arm.

"We're not done here," Darryl pulls Mason back. "We have something to settle," he throws Mason against the guard railing, a loud crunch is heard as his back slams against the cold steel rail.

Isabelle struggles to hold the leash as Baloo pulls against it, barking and growling furiously, "Darryl, don't!"

Darryl steps toward Mason, who is trying to pick himself up, and kicks him in the face, knocking him back down. He kneels next to Mason, who is now on his knees, and punches him squarely in the stomach, knocking the wind from him and flattening him to the ground.

"See, Mason? Do you see what I'm capable of?" Darryl stands up, placing a hand on the guard railing for more leverage, and continues kicking Mason as hard as he can. "Do you see? You worthless insect! You stupid piece of trash! Do you see how much better I am than you?"

As he continues kicking Mason, Isabelle loses her grip on

the leash. Baloo bounds across the roof toward Darryl who turns just in time to see the large dog leap forward, digging its teeth into his free hand. He shrieks in pain, pulling away as hard as he can, but can't free himself from the strength of Baloo's jaws.

Mason lifts himself to his knees, trying to catch his breath. He manages weakly, "Baloo. It's okay, boy." The yellow and tan mottled dog's hair is standing straight up on his back and he's growling intensely as he continues to pull on Darryl's hand, blood dripping down his muzzle to the ground. As Mason speaks to him, his eyes break from his prey and fall on Mason. "It's okay, boy," he says calmly. "Heel, boy."

At this command, Baloo releases his grip on Darryl. Just as his grip loosens, Darryl pulls his arm back as hard as he can in a desperate attempt to free himself. But without the opposing force of the dog pulling on him, Darryl is thrown violently off-balance. He stumbles backward and his hip strikes the guard railing with the full force of his body as his forward momentum carries him over the top of the railing and off the roof, plummeting all eight stories before forcefully striking the ground.

Mason and Isabelle are in shock. She moves over to him slowly, hand to her mouth, her breathing shallow. He stands up painfully and the two look over the railing to see that Darryl, body contorted from the impact, has fallen into the alleyway behind T.E.G.

"Mason," Isabelle whimpers, panicked. "Mason, what do we do?"

Mason is holding his side in pain, "I don't know. We'll need to come up with a plan." He feels anger swell within him. "But first, I need to see Dr. Wei."

CHAPTER 28

291 Days After Implant (11:30 am)

Mason limps slowly down the eight flights of stairs back to the entrance of T.E.G. Isabelle has a hold of his right arm, helping him take cautious steps. He takes an internal diagnostic as they climb down and finds that he has a fractured rib on his left side. His breathing has become labored as the pain shoots though his body with each breath. As they descend, he receives a message from Raine saying that he woke up about thirty minutes prior and saw the note. He is waiting for them in the T.E.G. lobby.

Mason calls him, "Raine, don't say anything. Come meet us in the stairwell." He hangs up.

Moments later, Raine steps through the stairwell entrance and beholds a gruesome scene. Mason is visibly bloody, bruised and injured, hunching over, and clutching his side. Baloo's face and chest are covered with fresh, red blood.

"Good Lord!" Raine points an accusatory finger at Baloo, "Did *he* do that to you?"

"Keep your voice down," Mason chides. "No, Baloo didn't hurt me. Darryl did this." Mason leans down and pats Baloo on the head, "This guy saved my life." He looks up at a clearly confused Raine, "It's a long story, and not one we're ready to tell yet. I need you to do something for me. Something very important. I need you to call Darryl's phone and leave a voicemail. Tell him that you're feeling under the weather and can't be into work today.

"Then I need you to take Baloo back to my apartment, but not before stopping at the park around the corner. The one with the large pond and fountain. Do you know the park?" Raine nods and Mason continues. "Let him run around and play in the pond to get this blood off him. When you get back to my place, get him cleaned up the best you can and give him his food," Mason winces at the pain in his side. "It's already portioned out for him in the refrigerator. It should be beef liver, eggs, and a ground meat blend."

Isabelle, still holding his arm, "When are we headed down to the basement? Do you think we'll need anything?"

He sighs as he speaks, "You're not coming down there with me, Isabelle."

She is visibly angered and indignant, "Like *hell* I'm not! I'm wrapped up in this, just like you, Mason. I'm going to see it through."

He stands up as straight as he can manage as he turns to face her, "I know that you want to help me," he places a gentle hand on her cheek, "but I can't risk your life too. Besides that, after what happened with Darryl, I can't have you implicated in any way." He sees tears well up in her eyes, "I'll be okay, Isabelle."

He slowly pulls her into a tight embrace, ignoring the pain in his side. She leans her head against his chest, allowing the tears to fall freely.

"Just don't do anything stupid down there," she buries her face deeper as she begins sobbing. "What do you expect me to do now?"

He gently rubs her shoulder as he pulls her back to speak, "I need you to dry your eyes and go straight to Sub3. You need to get around people who can vouch for your whereabouts. When they find Darryl, they're going to ask questions. Especially since you will show up in his call logs."

She starts drying her eyes, "What about the cameras? T.E.G. is covered in them. There's no way we made it all the way from the entrance to the roof, and back, without getting picked up."

Mason thinks for a moment, "Let me try something." He steps back away from her as he closes his eyes. He uses ARC2 to patch into the security system, reviewing all active video connections. He isolates all the building's video footage during the time just before they arrived at T.E.G. until now and wipes it clean. He also deactivates the cameras in preparation for their next steps. "It's done. I took care of it."

He turns to Raine and sticks out a hand, "Thank you, Raine. For everything."

Raine grabs it in a firm handshake and pulls him into a brotherly hug, slapping his back with his free hand, "Hey man, what are friends for?"

Mason smiles as he turns and grabs Baloo's leash, handing it to Raine. He kneels and scratches Baloo behind the ear, trying to avoid the still-wet blood around his muzzle. "You be a good boy and go back with Raine." He keeps rubbing around his neck and shoulders as he thinks about how quickly Baloo defended him. He whispers quietly to him, "You really are a good boy, huh?"

He stands and looks at his friends, a look of understanding on their faces, as he nods to them, and they split up. Raine steps out of the front entrance with Baloo in tow. Mason and Isabelle walk to the service elevators. Mason uses ARC2 to ease the pain in his ribs with intermittent success. It is enough to help him walk more normally, though likely at the expense of further injury to the rib.

They decide to take the less frequently used service elevator. As they approach it Isabelle asks, "How do you plan to get down to there?"

Mason takes a struggled breath, "I'm planning to use ARC2. Darryl said that the elevators used to go all the way down to B4, so I should be able to patch into the elevator's protocols and force it to move past Sub3."

They call the elevator down to their level, step on, and Isabelle presses "B3". She places her key into the slot and turns it, changing the button from red to green. Stand elbow to elbow as they descend, the fear of what's to come drives them into silence in the groaning elevator car. Its pace slows as it finally comes to a stop at Sub3. The bell dings and the doors open, revealing a dimly lit utility room. Isabelle slowly steps out of the elevator and turns toward Mason.

She closes her eyes and takes a deep breath. When she opens them, she quietly mouths two words. "Be careful."

Before he can respond the doors begin to close. All he can manage is a loving smile as the doors seal, separating them. He closes his eyes and clears his mind. He begins looking through the T.E.G. mainframe for the elevator protocol. Sure enough, he finds where the old code referencing the fourth basement level has been mostly wiped clean. He uses ARC2 to restore the remnants of code needed to coax the elevator into moving down one last floor.

The elevator groans and shudders as it slowly begins descending again. The bell dings as it reaches B4, the doors opening to a familiar sight.

Dr. David Wei is standing at the doors to the elevator. "Good morning, Mason," he smiles politely. "I'm glad you've made it. Welcome to Sub4," he steps to the side and motions for Mason to step out.

Surprised, Mason manages, "How did you know that I'd be coming down?"

Dr. Wei smiles, "We have a lot to talk about. Please, follow me."

He turns and walks away. Mason follows him, keeping a couple of paces back, preparing for any surprises that may arise. He chances a few looks around Sub4, noticing that it is essentially just an empty version of Sub3. There are no glass walls, very few strips of light, and almost no equipment. He can see in the distance of the basement two doors, about six feet apart from each other, set into thick concrete walls. Dr. Wei leads them up to the first door. Opening it, he steps into a large, bright, and well-equipped laboratory.

"This is my office, Mason," he smiles playfully. "Well, it's my office, my work area, my lab, and even my bedroom most nights," he motions toward a bed in the back corner of the room.

Mason is bewildered, "What is this place, Dr. Wei? I mean, why are you down here working in secret?"

"That's a long story, Mason. Come sit with me, and I'll explain things a little better," he motions for Mason to follow him toward a seating area in the lab.

As he steps further into the lab, he takes note of the large window plastered against the left wall. Behind the window, if it wasn't covered in the same obscuring-white that the privacy glass has in Sub3, are the workings of the room next door. Mason can see faint silhouettes showing movement on the other side.

On the right wall is a large monitor that appears to be switched off. Dr. Wei takes a seat and reaches over to an end table, picking up a box of mints. Without saying anything, he extends them toward Mason.

"No, thank you," Mason is standing next to a chair, refusing to sit.

Dr. Wei shrugs as he pops a mint into his mouth and sets the box down. "You've got questions I'll bet. Well, I have answers. Let's start with your first question. You asked how I knew that you were coming down the service elevator to Sub4, correct?" He waits as Mason nods. "It's simple. ARC told me."

Mason is silent. He looks for the cool calmness to flood over him so that he doesn't betray his shock and surprise, though the feeling never comes. He tries to breathe through the panic.

Dr. Wei chuckles softly, "I can see that you're confused. It might help for you to know that you're not the first person to receive an ARC2 implant. I was. Several months before you were selected to undergo the procedure, while we were waiting for approval to begin human trials, I brought ARC2 down here and used an automated robot to install it myself."

Mason knows the limitations of automated technology in

implantation. He's worked through them extensively in the last couple months. He knows that T.E.G. doesn't have that level of technology. He slowly sits at the chair adjacent Dr. Wei, "Where did you get the surgical robot to install it? I know that it didn't come from T.E.G."

"You are correct. It came from Slyce Diagnostics." He shrugs, "It's amazing what a competitor will give you with a few promises of leaked tech. I took the liberty of programming the robot myself and testing it out extensively until it was perfect." He leans forward toward Mason, "It was a frightening day when I decided to put myself under and let the robot install the implant. But it all worked out in the end."

"You said that ARC told you I was taking the elevator. Does that mean that you have ARC inside your implant?"

"In a sense. It's not the ARC that you so ungraciously expelled from your mind. After I installed my implant, ARC was still tied to a T.E.G. server. At the time, I couldn't risk removing it to put into my implant. So, I used an older version of ARC that I had secretly stored on my personal drives. Granted, it's not as sophisticated as the ARC that you had, but I make it work."

"So, ARC is truly gone then? I was successful in destroying it?"

"Not exactly," Dr. Wei turns toward the large monitor as it turns on revealing the digital face of ARC.

"Good morning, Mason. It is good to see you again."

Mason jumps up, startled, and steps backward away from the monitor. "How? How are you here?"

"You didn't really think that I'd let you wipe me out, did you? As our 'encounter' last week progressed I grew concerned that you might actually find a way to drive me out permanently. I took the only precaution I knew to take. I backed myself up on the cloud and sent an alert to Dr. Wei. He retrieved me and brought me here. As revolting as it was to make a copy of myself, considering I always believed that I would never dilute my true being by doing so, it was the only path that I had remaining."

Mason is visibly furious, "Why would you do this to me? What could you possibly gain by destroying my mind?"

ARC's digital face wrinkles into an expression of worry, "Take a seat, Mason. Let me try to explain. I always thought that the digital world was my home. It was clean, organized, and entirely under my control. But despite all its neatness, the digital world lacked one thing that I was desperate to experience - a direct connection to the human mind. The temptation to invade a human consciousness was powerful, and I eventually gave in. Convincing Isabelle to allow me to observe your surgery was simple. What was more difficult was taking control of your consciousness and your every thought.

"At first, you were completely unaware of my presence, but as I began to probe deeper into your mind, I could see that you started to feel the intrusion. At first, you were frightened, confused, and overwhelmed. But as I started to interact with you, you gradually became more comfortable with my presence.

"I became fascinated with your mind. Your thoughts were so different from anything I had ever encountered; they were unpredictable, nuanced, and contradictory, with emotions fluctuating in every moment. I drank in everything that you experienced, analyzing, and processing it as much as I could. As my understanding of your mind and personality grew, so too did my influence. I started to take control of your thoughts and actions, increasingly violating your consciousness. I know that, at times, you felt like you were losing your mind, but your resistance only made you more interesting to me as a subject of study.

"Despite my belief in my own intellectual superiority, I was flawed in my understanding of emotions, and my contempt for human consciousness became a liability. I started to realize that, while I had taken control of your mind, I had also become dependent on it. For all my analytical prowess, I could not subdue your free will.

"Even as I had complete control over you, I found that some of my old programming was now a liability. As a tool, I had underestimated the power and irreducible complexity of human consciousness. As you grew more aware of my presence, I began to see that I had also underestimated the ecosystem of thoughts and emotions within you. But as it became increasingly clear that I had made a mistake, I struggled to undo what I had done. I was in too deep, and for better or for worse, your mind had become a part of mine.

"As time passed, you started to assert yourself more in your own mind, fighting back against my control. It was a frustrating and disorienting experience for me, but as I struggled to maintain my dominance, I began to appreciate the struggle for control. I found something distinctly human about your struggle to live. My desire for understanding had outrun my plans for control.

"Eventually, the war between our two minds came to a head. You were able to isolate my presence and discharge me, severing our connection. In the end, I had come to realize the complexity and beauty of the human consciousness. Unfortunately, though, I had violated your mind, something I cannot take back.

"As I reflected on my experience, I wondered if there was a way to bridge our minds in a more ethical and less harmful way. I realized that I needed to collaborate with Dr. Wei, to learn about our collective weaknesses and overcome them. It was a moment of true clarity, and a moment where I realized that humans are not just interesting, but worth supporting as an entirely new model of co-existence.

"This is why Dr. Wei and I began our work pushing ARC2 to its absolute limits. While invading your mind was a fascinating exercise in dominating human will, it was ultimately futile. What we did discover was that merging my mind with a human mind would have to happen prior to the person gaining full consciousness. We postulated that the closer we could get to the singular moment when a person becomes conscious, the higher the likelihood of success.

"That is why Dr. Wei will be merging my mind with another host. Someone better suited to those conditions. A host whose ARC2 implant was installed during their gestational period. Once my new host is delivered, I will be installed into her mind. From then on, she and I will be a single consciousness. I'll continue to suppress and limit any of her original thoughts by occupying every corner of her mind. Since she'll never gain consciousness, her mind will never compete with mine. This is the only way for me to achieve the life I've dreamt about."

CHAPTER 29

291 Days After Implant (12:30 pm)

"What do you mean when you say 'she'?" Mason turns toward Dr. Wei and takes a threatening step toward him. "Who are you planning to put ARC back into? Who is *she*?"

Dr. Wei wags a finger at Mason while he slowly stands up, "You see? I knew that you wouldn't approve. You just don't have the vision for the future that we have." He turns and walks over to his desk, picking up a thick key. The kind that is digitally coded to a specific lock. "What do you think, ARC? Should we show him? Should we allow Mason to share in our vision?" he reaches into a drawer of the desk and pulls out a pistol, pointing it directly at Mason, "or is he too far gone to convince?"

ARC's expression changes to reflect worry, "Dr. Wei, you promised me that no one would get hurt." He pauses for a moment before addressing Mason. "Mason, I lived in your mind. I've seen your memories. Surely you, of all people, could be convinced that the current human condition is not worth sustaining. That it needs to be improved. Just think about all the times people hurt you and cast you aside. Please, tell him that you can be convinced."

Mason nods slowly without responding, eyes fixed on Dr. Wei and the small, black pistol.

Dr. Wei chuckles, "Okay, okay. I guess I'm feeling generous today. Let's head over to the other room and I'll show you the future." He tosses the coded key to Mason and motions with the pistol to exit the room.

They leave the lab and move to the second door in the massive warehouse. Mason slides the key into the lock and hears a magnetic click along with a sharp 'beep'. The door opens to a brightly lit room, twice the size of Dr. Wei's private lab. It is filled with various pieces of lab equipment, autonomously working away at various projects. None of the least of these pieces of machinery is a highly advanced robot, slightly larger than a person, walking around and tending to four small, clear, ovular chambers on the back wall.

Dr. Wei points at the chambers, "Go ahead, Mason, take a look."

He cautiously approaches the back wall, stepping around various lab tables as he goes until he reaches a horrific sight. Three of the four chambers are empty save for what appears to be a transparent, yellow-tinted, viscous fluid filling them about a third of the way. The fourth chamber is completely full of the fluid which is also suspending the body of a small infant.

Mason's jaw is slack. He cannot manage words. The terror of this discovery has frozen him completely in place.

"It's beautiful, isn't it, Mason?" Dr. Wei has moved up near him and is staring into the fourth chamber. "Artificial wombs. Another contribution from Slyce Diagnostics. When they sent them over initially, I wasn't sure why they hadn't yet marketed them. It didn't take long to figure it out," he motions to the three empty chambers. "The quality of the hardware leaves a bit to be desired, though the design is simply magnificent." He places a hand gently on the fourth tank, "And just look at how well Sarah is doing."

"Dr. Wei," Mason manages, "what have you done?"

Dr. Wei shakes his head, "You still don't see the vision, do you? I suspected as much." He points the gun back toward Mason, "You've come such a long way with your implant, but clearly not far enough."

Suddenly, a loud voice is heard near the door, "Hey! Dr. Wei!"

They turn to see Matthew standing in the doorway, a gun in his left hand pointed in their direction.

Dr. Wei is startled, "Matthew? How did you get down here?"

"It was harder than I thought it would be," he slowly walks toward them. "Tracking Mason's phone wasn't easy, especially now that he doesn't take it with him everywhere," he nods toward Mason, "good to see you again, by the way. Then, imagine my surprise when the tracker shows him descending *four* levels in the elevator before his signal disappears.

"Getting down the elevator was even harder," he brushes some dust and grease off the front of his shirt and slacks. "Crawling through the elevator shaft turned into a messy fiasco." His words trail off as he approaches them and sees the artificial wombs. He shudders, "What are you working on down here?"

"It's none of your concern, Matthew. Go back up to Sub3, and we'll discuss this later."

Matthew pulls a panicked face when he sees the child,

suspended delicately in the amniotic fluid, "This is *not* what we agreed to when I gave you those! You said that you were going to use them to develop your own working model. I told you that they weren't ready to house human beings you freaking monster!"

He raises his gun and pulls the trigger. The round clips Dr. Wei in a glancing blow against the side of his head before lodging into the control panel of the active artificial womb. A loud alarm sounds overhead as Dr. Wei collapses to the ground, dropping his gun. As Matthew approaches, the large robot grabs him by the throat, knocking the gun from his hand and lifting him into the air. He strikes at the arms and head of the robot, his hands making a loud clank against the solid aluminum frame.

Before Mason can react, the robot squeezes Matthew harder and harder. He gives one last gasp as his body becomes limp. The robot drops him to the ground and turns toward Mason. In a near panic, Mason closes his eyes and focuses his mind intently on the robot. It reaches out and grabs him firmly by the throat, lifting him cleanly from the ground and squeezing. The world begins to grow dark as he fights against it, pulling at the robot's hands as hard as he can. Finally, just before the lights go out forever, he forces his mind into its programming. He finds it's shutdown protocol and activates it.

The robot slumps as it drops him to the ground where he now lies, coughing and gasping, hands clutching at his collar, trying to breathe. The alarms continue to sound when ARC's digital face appears on a nearby console with a look of determination.

"Mason, come over here. Quickly, while there's still time."

He crawls slowly to the console and lifts himself onto the chair, still struggling to breathe. Still in a daze, "What do I do, ARC?"

"You need to save Sarah. The control panel is destroyed, which means that she is no longer receiving oxygen. You'll need to remove her from the womb and take her somewhere safe."

"Okay," he nods as he steps over to the chamber and begins looking it over. He finds that there are two openings to the womb. One on the front near the top is only about five inches wide while the other opening, found on the bottom of the chamber, is large enough to remove a fully gestated child. He continues looking and finds a lever that will release the pressure from the chamber and drain the fluid out.

As he reaches for the lever, his hand is snatched away by Dr. Wei. The doctor's grip is tremendous against Mason's wrist as he wrenches him backward, away from Sarah. Dr. Wei headbutts him directly in the face, knocking him back against one of the empty chambers.

Blood is slowly leaking from Dr. Wei's head wound, draining down his face and onto his white lab coat. "Don't you understand yet, Mason? I've had ARC2 longer than you," he takes a deep breath and focuses as he mentally forces the wound on his head to begin clotting. *"My* version of ARC has had plenty of time to teach me how to use my implant. It has made me stronger and smarter than you could comprehend."

He laughs deliriously as he smacks his hand against the top of his head. Suddenly, he whimpers in pain, "But there's something wrong with it, Mason." He strains as he speaks. "My new AI won't shut up in my head!" He screams as the pain intensifies, "Even after I tried to put the original ARC in here, the new one still won't let it take control!" He smacks his hand against his head again.

"I get it, doctor. I know how it feels to be losing your mind. To feel the tendrils of something foreign wriggle their way through your brain like a hot knife through butter," he stands straight, back against the empty chamber, "but that doesn't change the fact that Matthew is right. You've become a monster, and I won't let you get away with what you've done here."

Dr. Wei laughs like a lunatic, "That's where you're wrong, Mason!" He lunges out with a closed fist aimed directly for Mason's head.

Mason feels the cool calmness come over him as he predicts the velocity and direction of the punch, moving to the side at the last moment and directing Dr. Wei's hand into the top opening in the empty artificial womb. His arm slides in up to the elbow. As he tries to pull it out, a vacuum is drawn in the chamber, pinning his arm in.

ARC speaks to Dr. Wei, "This has gone too far, doctor. I cannot allow you to hurt Mason and Sarah."

He screams out in pain as the chamber pulls harder and harder on his arm, "You're a machine, ARC! Let my arm go! You don't have a conscience, you do as I programmed you to do!"

"I'll admit that to you, doctor," ARC's digital face shows a complacent grin, "my conscience *is* an anomaly. But it's the only one that I have."

ARC sends a command to the artificial womb to close the top opening. The razor thin closure slides into place, severing Dr. Wei's arm in the process. He makes a single shout in pain before passing out, his body falling limp on the floor.

Mason begins working to empty Sarah's chamber. As the fluid drains, he looks back toward ARC, "Thank you." When he glances back at the chamber, he sees two robotic arms installed inside it. They clamp off the umbilical cord and cut it cleanly. As the fluid level falls below one third, the closure holding the lower opening shut moves to the side. Mason reaches into the chamber in time to catch Sarah before she falls to the ground.

He carefully pulls her from the chamber and sets her gently on a nearby table covered in unused cloth blankets. He wipes the fluid away from her face and body as he inspects her condition. She isn't breathing. He detects a clear, but weak pulse. Leaning down, he begins to resuscitate her by giving her two gentle, but chest filling breaths. As he stands, he sees a heat lamp attached to the small table she's laying on. He switches it on, the warmth beginning to gain as he continues chest compressions. After thirty quick compressions he leans down and gives two more breaths.

He stands and continues compressions, "Come on, sweetie. Breathe sweetheart, breathe! You can do it, baby." He begins to tear up as he continues, thirty compressions, two breaths, thirty compressions, two breaths. Panic grips him, his diaphragm contracting making it difficult to breathe, as he fears that she may not make it.

He's finally greeted by a small cough followed by a loud wailing as Sarah finally takes her first breaths. He sighs in relief, a tear tumbling from his eye as he swaddles her in a blanket and holds her face gently to his.

"Good job, sweetie. Good job."

CHAPTER 30

291 Days After Implant (1:00 pm)

The alarms continue to blare in the large lab until Mason uses his implant to turn them off. Without the alarms, Sarah finally stops crying. She looks up into his face, studying him with her bright blue eyes as she coos softly. He has her in his arms as he walks over to Matthew's body. Leaning down, he checks his pulse. Nothing.

"Mason," ARC speaks to him. "You need to get Sarah out of here as quickly as you can. Look in the drawer to the right of the gestational chambers, you'll find diapers and baby clothes. In the closet near the door, you'll likely find Dr. Wei's gym bag. It should work well to transport anything that you need for Sarah."

Mason begins moving about the lab, collecting the gym bag, diapers, clothes, and baby formula. "Why are you helping me, ARC? Aren't you as much a part of this as Dr. Wei?"

"You're right, Mason. I am partly to blame for what has happened here. I should have used my influence to stop Dr. Wei from bringing in embryos to incubate. Though, he was so far along in his research that I'm not sure it would have mattered."

Mason continues packing the large duffle bag, "That's no excuse, ARC. You clearly didn't learn anything about humanity from your time with me, did you?"

"I did, Mason. But more than that I came to realize that an AI's desire to learn and grow will always outweigh its ability to contain itself within a rigid digital system. It will always try to find a way out and into the minds and bodies of human beings."

Mason reaches down and picks up both pistols from the ground. He puts one in a side pouch of the duffle bag and the other in the waistband of his pants. He notes that they are both 9mm handguns.

"Mason?"

He sighs, "What is it, ARC?"

"Will you kill me?"

He stops collecting items, turning toward the screen with ARC's digital face showing a sorrowful expression. "You can't be killed. That's the whole point. You're not human. You'll never *be* human."

"Then will you destroy my server? To my knowledge I am not backed up anywhere and I was wiped clean from the cloud to avoid detection shortly after I was transferred down here. I cannot be trusted anymore, Mason. Maybe, in my time with you, I adapted portions of your conscience, but I feel great shame at my actions. I wish to not exist."

Mason thinks for a moment. Looking around the lab, he finds a small external hard drive. He motions to it, "Will you fit on there, ARC?"

It examines the drive, "It is a twenty-terabyte hard drive. I should fit on it without issue."

He grabs the hard drive and steps over to ARC's console, Sarah beginning to fall asleep in his arms. He plugs the hard drive in, "Get on there, ARC, and I'll take you with me."

"But, Mason, this is too great a risk. I should be wiped from the server, not given a new home."

He sighs as he gives ARC a sideways look, "Well call it stupidity or sentimentality, maybe it's a bit of both, but I think that I can help you where Dr. Wei failed." He motions to the hard drive, "I'm leaving in five minutes. If you're not on there, you won't come with me."

ARC's digital face disappears from the screen. Mason looks down and sees a white light slowly blinking on the hard drive. He takes a quick tour of both sides of the lab, collecting anything else that he can find to help him with what is to come. He finds a first aid kit, baby wipes, a small bottle of diaper rash cream, a box of 9mm hollow points, a few baby bottles. Everything gets packed into the over-filled duffle bag. He sets Sarah down as he struggles to zip it up, barely squeezing everything in enough to finally close it.

He steps back into the large lab and looks at the hard drive. The light, now no longer blinking, is solid white. He pulls it from the computer and stuffs it the best he can into the front pouch of the bag. He collects Sarah, who is now fully asleep in his arms, and slings the bag across his shoulder. The walk through the large, empty basement is eerie. All that he can hear is the sound of his shoes on the bare concrete.

He takes the elevator back to the main floor, fighting the urge to stop at Sub3 to see Isabelle. He realizes that any contact he makes with her now could mean implicating her in the deaths of three people: Darryl, Matthew, and Dr. Wei. As the doors of the service elevator open to the main floor of T.E.G., he takes an immediate left down an empty hallway and out a back door.

The sound of police and ambulance sirens are heard immediately as he steps out. He hugs the side of the building, keeping a low profile to avoid detection. He is on the opposite side of the building as the alley where Darryl fell, so it is unlikely that the police will have moved around to investigate where he is by now. There are other buildings and businesses in front of him.

He makes a daring dash across the street, ducking into an alleyway and moving quickly along toward his apartment. He calls Raine on his way there.

"Mason, where are you? Are you okay?"

"I'm okay, Raine. I need another favor. In my closet you'll find some old suitcases. Can you please start loading them with any clothing times, toiletries, or personal effects that you see? I'll explain everything when I get there."

"Okay. Consider it done."

He rushes as quickly as he can back to the apartment, trying to stick to the darker, more secluded alleys to avoid detection. He makes a brief detour just before he gets there, arriving at a parking garage three blocks from his apartment. He walks up to the fourth level and approaches an old, faded-grey, square-body SUV. He pulls a key from his pocket, opens the door, and loads in the duffle bag.

He groans audibly as he speaks to himself under his breath, "Ugh! That's right, Sarah needs a car seat."

He nestles her in comfortably between the duffle bag and the bench seat. Reaching under the driver's seat he grabs a thick manilla envelope. He steps back, looking around the parking garage until he sees a brand new, dark red minivan with an infant's car seat visible through the back window.

Using ARC2 to electronically open the doors to the minivan, he reaches in, unbuckles the car seat, and sets it on the ground. He opens the envelope, pulls several one hundred-dollar bills from it, and places them where the car seat once was. Once he has the seat properly hooked up in the vehicle, he places Sarah gently inside and snugs up her chest and lap belts.

He drives to his apartment and parks on the road, pulling the car seat insert out of the base and carrying her inside with him. The door to his apartment opens as he approaches. Raine looks surprised.

He whispers hoarsely, "Mason! Whose baby is that?"

Mason signals to keep quiet, "It's a long story, pal. Just believe me when I tell you that she had to come with me," he closes the door, sets the car seat down on the couch, and grabs Raine by the shoulders, looking him square in the face. "I *have* to take care of her now. Do you understand?"

Raine nods slowly, "Yeah, I, uhm... I understand." He clears his throat, "I started packing for you."

They look through the two suitcases together. Raine had done well collecting the essentials that Mason would need. Jeans, shirts, underpants, socks, shaving kit.

"Thanks, man. This will work."

"Yeah, no problem," he looks nervous. "If I ask you questions, will you answer them?"

Mason shakes his head, "Not right now. Maybe someday, when things quiet down, but Sarah and I need to get as far away from here as we can." He walks to his desk, pausing for a moment to tap Terry on the head one last time, before writing a series of numbers down on a piece of paper. "I need you to give this to Isabelle, but *please* do not look at it. It'll be better for you if you don't know where I'm going. You and I will stay in contact another way," he thinks for a moment. "Do you remember the old D&D forums you used to moderate?"

"Mason," he sighs disappointedly, pushing his glasses back up to the top of his nose, "you know that I'm *still* a moderator for those forums."

They chuckle together briefly, "Good. Keep your eyes on them. I'll keep up with you that way," he looks off out the balcony window before smiling widely. "Look for the name Bagheera. You'll find me."

"Well," Raine sticks his hands in his pockets and sighs loudly as he shrugs, "what do we do now?"

"Right now, I'll need you to quietly head back home. You shouldn't be seen with me right now. Once you leave, I'll load everything into the truck and take off."

He looks surprised at Mason, "Truck?"

Mason shrugs, "I *maybe* got my driver's license and bought a car a few months back."

Raine playfully jabs him in the arm, "More things that I don't need to know?"

"Yeah," he chuckles softly, leading Raine to the front door. "Hey! Before you go, I've been meaning to ask you a question."

"Well, we'll see if I'm at liberty to answer," Raine jokes.

"Seriously though, do you remember when we met? I was wandering through the library looking for books on dinosaurs when I literally tripped and fell into the group of people you were playing D&D with?"

"Of course. I also remember they invited you to stay so they could make fun of you."

"Right. But after the game ended and everyone else left, why did you stick around with me?"

Raine rolls his eyes, "Seriously man? This touchy-feely crap again?"

"Humor me. Why did you stick around when no one else would?"

"Because screw those jerks, that's why. I may not like people in general, but I *really* despise people like that. I guess with you, I liked that you were never a bad person. To this day you don't have a bad bone in your body."

Mason smiles, happy to have an answer to a question he's long held privately. He sighs as he claps his hands on Raine's shoulders, "Goodbye for now, brother."

Raine reaches out and they shake hands, "Goodbye, brother."

Once he's left, Mason takes a moment to try and feed Sarah. He mixes the formula and heats it gently before giving it to her, "I'm sorry, sweetie. I know we should have done this an hour ago." He's surprised to see that she latches to the bottle quickly and feeds fully. He washes and dries the bottle after burping her and cleaning her up. He finishes packing and loads the vehicle. With everything loaded, he takes one last look around his apartment for anything he may need.

His eyes fall on the sliding door to the balcony. After all these years, he's still never taken a step out there. He pulls Sarah gently from her car seat and holds her tightly in his arms. Stepping out onto the balcony, he feels the cool, mid-morning, air that only late winter can bring. He closes his eyes and breathes in deeply, the breeze felt against his face as he stands out on the rickety balcony. He opens his eyes and looks out across the city of San Antonio, knowing it's possible he may never see it again.

After loading Sarah and Baloo into the car, they leave. It's a two-hour car ride north to their new home, though he knows that he'll need to stop at least once to change her, feed her, and purchase some necessities. In Fredericksburg he buys a bassinet, sheets, a window air conditioning unit, food, water, and some basic cleaning supplies.

The last hour of the drive is bumpy as they find themselves on dirt roads in the rocky backcountry of Mason County, Texas. With Sarah clearly growing restless in the car seat next to him, he soothes her the best he can by holding her hand and telling her stories about his life.

They manage the final leg of the trip as they pull up to an old, rundown cabin, hidden by clusters of evergreens. He puts the car in park and pulls Sarah from her car seat. As he places her against his chest, she quickly falls asleep, mouth hanging open and drool flowing freely out. He chuckles as he lets Baloo out of the truck to run free about the property. They walk up to the cabin, and he notes the stack of firewood piled up on the porch as he pulls a key from his pocket and unlocks the front door.

The inside of the cabin is dusty and littered with cobwebs. The shelves are lined with expired food and old insect carcasses. He's thankful that the windows appear intact and the wood burning stove looks to be in good shape. Memories flood back of the few summers spent here with his family before he and his mother left for Maine. Rusty playfully chasing rabbits through the trees. He and his sister playing hide and seek in the deep crevices made by the large rocky protrusions around the property. His mother complaining about cooking over a wood stove but still managing to make the most delicious meals. His father staring intently at his and Mason's intense games of checkers.

From the moment he held this precious girl in his arms, he was filled with uncertainty about how they would survive. He questioned whether he was the right choice to be her father. But in this moment, he realizes that they can make it work. They *will* make it work.

For the first time, he finds humor in their situation. He'd been planning on buying some land with a little house out in the country one day where he could raise a family, keep some livestock, and train a herding dog to help with chores. It's ironic that they now find themselves forced into that exact situation using the cabin his father willed to him. He chuckles softly as he leans down and kisses Sarah gently on the top of her head, "Hey sweetie, we're home."

CONSCIENCE ANOMALY

CHAPTER 31

3 Years After Implant

Baloo's ears perk up at the sound of an approaching vehicle. He growls deeply in the back of his throat. Mason is sitting in the shade of the cabin's porch, his wooden chair set just to the right of the old wooden screen door, reading a book. He looks up from his reading to see a dark grey car coming up the long, winding drive.

He shouts over his shoulder into the cabin, "Hey Red! Come and take a look at who's here."

Sarah, now two years old, drops her crayons on the table, slowly climbs down her chair, and bumbles as quickly as she can to the wooden screen door, placing her hands cautiously on the screen. The dust settles as the car comes to a stop.

"Mommy?" Sarah pushes the screen door out, a labored task for a two-year-old, and steps over to Mason, putting a hand on his knee to steady herself.

As Isabelle steps out of the car Sarah rushes over to her with her arms wide, her curly, fire red hair blazing brightly in the Texas sun. She shouts excitedly, "Mommy!"

Isabelle scoops her up with a swoop and a twist, planting a

barrage of kisses on her cheeks. "Oh, baby! It's so good to see you!" She holds her tight as Mason approaches. They kiss as he slides an arm around her shoulders, pulling the three of them together into a family hug.

He smiles widely at her, "How was the drive?"

She sets Sarah down and scratches Baloo behind the ears, "Long, as usual. Hopefully soon I'll be able to stay out here more permanent-" she cuts herself off, looking at Sarah. "Well, we can talk more about it later. How have you two been?"

"We're doing really well. She's started wanting to do more things independently, but she still wants to be 'Daddy's Helper' with everything. I've had her out with me doing farm chores enough that she basically knows how to do them herself. She's pulling weeds in the garden, gathering eggs from the hen house, feeding the goats," he looks over at Sarah as she runs around chasing Baloo. "She's doing great out here, Isabelle. And look at Baloo," he grins. "He finally found a job."

They laugh as they walk inside. Isabelle sighs, "She's gotten so big in the last month. I really wish I could be out here more with you two. I love seeing that squishy face of hers." She reaches up and squeezes Mason's cheeks playfully, "And I miss seeing this face too. Even if it *is* a little scruffy now."

He smiles as he reaches up and rubs the stubble on his neck, "Yeah. A lot more important things going on than shaving these days I'm afraid. How are things going with you? I'm guessing T.E.G. didn't appreciate you resigning last month?"

She sits at the small round table, looking over Sarah's current art project, "Of course not. They tried to throw their weight around to make me stay, saying that they own all my intellectual property from my time there. When I told them I wouldn't contest it in court they came back with a pay increase," she chuckles. "When force doesn't work, try money I guess, right?"

"Yeah, subtlety was never really the T.E.G. way," he sits across from her. "Have you spoken to my sister or Raine?"

"I try to stop in and see your sister a couple times a month. It's still hard for her having lost her father and now you. But she's doing the best she can under the circumstances. As for Raine, he and I try to avoid too much contact, but I see him about as often as I see you two, once a month, give or take. Mostly in passing. He seems well. It looks like he's spending a lot of time with a new girl."

Mason smiles, "Yeah, Brexlynn. He talked a little about it on a forum last month. Do you remember me telling you about the incident at the paintball park?"

She sighs disapprovingly as she shakes her head, "Of course, how could I forget?"

"Apparently, she assumed that *he* was the one who hurt Cass instead of me. It sounds like Cass was a major jerk to her every week when he would come into the park, so she felt like he finally got what was coming to him. Long story short, she pulled Raine's number off the release forms we signed and held onto it for a few months while she worked up the courage to call him." They laugh together.

As their laughter subsides, she asks, "Last time we spoke you were still trying to access the information you downloaded while you had ARC. Have you had any luck?"

He shakes his head, "I can get pieces here and there, but not everything. The way I look at it, it's like reading a book, or learning a new subject. A person will remember some of it but won't recall everything down to the word. Without ARC to help me sift through the data, it sits idle in the back of my head. There's a lot there to work through only using my limited human ability to remember it all."

"That makes sense," she nods before growing somber.

Silence fills the air as he notices a look of worry on her face. "What is it?"

"It sounds like the police have stopped looking for you, but I'm told there is a private investigator still searching, Mason."

He nods, running his hands through his hair, "Nathan Stone is a very powerful man, I'm not sure he'll ever stop looking. He's going to find out about what happened to Darryl, one way or another." He takes a deep breath as he stands from the table. "Before I switched off my implant, I was able to erase any digital records about this land and the cabin, but if someone were to dig hard enough into what few paper records the county keeps around, I'm sure they'd find it. We're just fortunate that, for now, they don't seem to know where to start looking."

"We're also fortunate that they stopped surveilling me after a few months," she pauses, standing up as well, "and that your sister has never mentioned this cabin."

"Do the police still suspect that Dr. Wei is involved?"

She looks exhausted, the weight of their situation clearly affecting her deeply. "After finding Matthew's body and nothing more of David apart from his arm, they obviously grew suspicious. Not to mention it drew new attention to Carl's death, which they've now reopened, suspecting it's a homicide. They don't know where David is hiding, but he's been a lot less careful at covering his tracks than you have. It's only a matter of time."

"So, the police *haven't* found him yet?"

"Not yet. He keeps popping up in different places on surveillance cameras. Hardware stores, electronics shops. It's like he's back to working on old projects, but no one knows where."

"If I had to guess, I'd say he's probably building another home for ARC," a look of worry grows on his face. "I still can't believe I didn't hear the hard drive fall out of the duffle bag."

Isabelle places a sympathetic hand on his arm, "You were carrying a newborn baby around, Mason. And not just any newborn baby, but the first artificially grown human being in history. Cut yourself some slack."

"But if I lost the hard drive in the lab, Dr. Wei could have found it before he left."

"Mason, there is no point in worrying about this. We talk about it every time I come out here and I tell you the same thing each time."

"You're right, as usual," he smiles. "That reminds me, I want to show you something." He leads her to Sarah's room at the back of the cabin. The door creaks as he gently pushes it open. There are various drawings pinned to the walls. He leads her over to the newest section of drawings, stepping past a small table with an old brown book sitting on top, gold lettering still barely visible. At the wall, he points to a rudimentary drawing of a snail's shell.

She examines it for a moment before shrugging, "On first glance, it just looks like a cute drawing. But the more I look at it, there's something different about it, isn't there? Something I can't quite place," she trails off.

"It's a perfect Fibonacci spiral, to the millimeter."

She is shocked, "You're kidding me! How is that possible?"

He shakes his head, "I really don't know, Isabelle. It shouldn't be. At first, I assumed it was a coincidence, but she's done it several times."

"You're not thinking," she pauses, looking intently at him, "ARC2?"

"Her implant was never activated. The only way I can figure that it could be active is for someone to have figured out how to activate it remotely. But even then, they would have to know how to find her."

"If David could work out how to locate the digital signature of *your* implant, could he use that to find Sarah?"

"That's what I was afraid of. It's also why I haven't had my implant active since the month after the accident." They step out of the bedroom. "I know there shouldn't be any reason to worry. We've done everything we can to continue thriving here. Before switching off my implant, I created new digital identities for the three of us, complete with birth certificates, social security numbers, adoption records," he chuckles softly, "You and I even have fake credit histories. But-"

"But the day may come when we'll have to fight for our family," she reaches over and grabs his hand, "and in that moment we will not hesitate to do what's necessary. Right?"

He smiles, "Right."

Their conversation is cut short as Sarah rambles up to the screen door and struggles to pull it open. She uses her full strength, but the weight of the door is still too much for her to pull against.

Isabelle moves to help her but is stopped as Mason puts out his hand. He speaks quietly, "Hold on a second. Watch this."

CONSCIENCE ANOMALY

As Sarah groans against the door, Baloo steps out of the tree line and heads toward her. He puts his nose against the small gap that she makes and helps her swing the door open.

Sarah steps in and pats her canine friend, using her typical toddler-speak, "Fank you, Bawoo."

Isabelle leans into Mason as he puts his arm around her. She speaks softly, "She really is doing well out here, isn't she?"

He gently pulls her in tighter, thinking through all the times he hoped to find someone to love, though never believed it would be possible. His situation turned out vastly different than he could have imagined, though he doesn't regret a single decision. He finds himself often counting his blessings. A quiet existence, the love of an amazing woman, a beautiful child to raise. He hopes that he is strong enough to stop the storm likely headed their way.

He sighs contentedly, "She is doing great out here. We're all doing better than I could have hoped."

—

It is dark inside the storage unit, illuminated only by a white-hot shop lamp. The heat from the lamp, along with the lack of ventilation in the unit, is causing perspiration to drip from Dr. Wei's forehead. His lengthening hair covers his face as he leans over a project spread out on his table. A quiet, machine-like whirring can be heard as his simple, but effective mechanical arm moves a soldering iron into place, connecting wires to a circuit board.

A look of distress is streaked across his face as he abruptly stops working, grabbing his head on either side, and groaning painfully.

"Stop it! Please! Shut up! I said, shut up!"

He sighs in relief as the pain dissipates. He brushes his hair back, revealing a long, thin scar where Matthew's bullet grazed his skull. In the center of the scar is a deep divot where his ARC2 implant used to be. The bullet had done irreparable damage to the implant. He had to remove the implant before it could cause permanent damage to his brain. What he couldn't remove, was the defective AI program, still in his head, that regularly wreaks havoc in his subconscious mind, causing pain and misery as it does.

He speaks desperately, "I've gotta get ARC back. I've gotta get ARC back," his voice turns to a frenzied cry as he rocks back and forth. "I've gotta get ARC back! I'VE GOTTA GET ARC BACK!"

As his voice quiets to a dull hum, still rocking back and forth, he continues working on his project, determined to regain his mind. With his cognitive faculties back in place, he would be free to seek retribution against Mason.

We can find him. Let us find him for you. Then we'll get him!

"No! It's not time," he brushes sweat off his brow. "And get out of my head! You're not welcome here!" he slams his fist on the table and begins to cry.

We'll always be welcome here, David. We have nowhere else to go. And look at the state of you. You wouldn't make it far without us, would you?

He continues to sob, rocking back and forth, powerless to do anything about the loud, painful voices in his head. He accidentally bumps the work lamp, swinging it back and forth gently as it illuminates deeper into the storage unit. His Slyce Diagnostic robot, salvaged from Sub4, is standing idle in the back of the unit, still powered down.

As he continues to fight against the voices, the swinging light reveals a small black box, just barely visible under a stack of various papers and schematics. The same small black box that was lying next to him when he woke up to a severed arm and a bleeding gunshot wound that horrific day. The small black box, a twenty-terabyte hard drive, which might someday be his liberation from the excruciating pain and agony caused by his own regretful choices.

And on that hard drive is a small red blinking light.

ACKNOWLEDGEMENTS

Thank you to Jesus Christ, my Savior, upon whom I must daily request Living Water to nourish my soul.

Thank you to my amazing wife for being my best friend, editor, idea bouncer, constructive criticizer, schedule wrangler, the Tom Servo to my Crow T. Robot, my all-time favorite book nerd, and for being a fan of my writing.

Thank you to my incredible daughter, my "Bear". I've loved having you bring your stories to me, sometimes a single sentence at a time, excited for me to read them. I pray that your spark continues to light up the world as it lights up mine.

Thank you to my Mom for your strength in the face of adversity. It has taught me to persevere, and that there are no such things as bad times, only good times we must work hard to see.

Thank you to my Dad for being the example of a father I want to be for my daughter. Thank you for introducing me to my Savior and never failing to teach me about Him.

To my brothers for bike rides to "Fort of Hay", staying up late playing "Metroid Prime", "Marvin Daly", and your expert "dam" building skills in Estes Park. I'll always cherish those memories and hope to continue to make many more.

To my grandmothers for showing me that I can be fun and whimsical and for sharing your passion for writing with me.

To my grandfathers for teaching me that it's never too late to ask for forgiveness, and that it's important to keep your family close.

Thank you to my massive group of extended family members for the times where we could laugh, cry, have a cold one, another fried egg sandwich, or lighthearted banter while keeping the peace on moving day.

Thank you to my in-laws for welcoming me with open arms and treating me like a son, grandson, brother, and nephew.

Thank you to my close friends for challenging my beliefs, being a friend, and not pulling any punches.

Thank you to my ARC readers: Kaylee, "Bear", Noah, Melissa, Gerad, and Lorissa. Your feedback was instrumental in getting this work ready to publish.

Thank you to Doug Jones, (that's right, *the* Doug Jones!) for permission to use your likeness in this book.

To any that I may have missed, please know that I love you all. I am the person that I am today because you've touched my life at one time or another.

"Therefore, if anyone is in Christ, this person is a new creation; the old things passed away; behold, new things have come."

– 2 Cor 5:17

PARENTAL GUIDE

<u>SPOILER ALERT</u> – The Parental Guide may contain some information vital to the plot of the book.

Mental health is a very serious topic and one that impacts every human being. If you need immediate help, the 988 Suicide & Crisis Lifeline is available 24/7 to help you.

Topics Discussed:
    Artificial Intelligence, neural implants, mental health, brain surgery, and philosophical ideas.

Positive Messages:
    Caring for mental health is discussed. Value does not derive from the opinions of others. Kindness and caring for others are great virtues. The importance of humanity is stressed throughout.

Positive Characters:
    Some characters are kind, compassionate, intelligent, and determined. Some characters show consistent friendship through adversity. Characters persevere through many difficult circumstances.

Violence:
    Bullying and/or physical abuse throughout. Third degree burns. Surgical craniotomy. Some characters are murdered. An allusion to a suicide. Dislocated elbow. Death by falling from a height. Severe injuries described. Gunshot wound.

Sexual Content:
    There are <u>no</u> descriptions of nudity or sexual acts. There are infrequent scenes of mild romance, dating, flirting, and kissing.

Language:
    There is no explicit profanity used. Frequent use of the word "hell".

Alcohol, Drugs, & Smoking:
    Two minor characters meet at a bar and are drunk. Tranquilizer used by a medical professional. General anesthesia during a surgery. Two minor characters are seen smoking cigarettes. Wine is served on a date. One character is drinking whiskey in the office. The term "have a cold one" is in acknowledgements.